Jennie Dodd was raised in the picturesque market town of Shrewsbury, famous for its medieval castle, steep narrow streets, little alleyways, and timber framed buildings. Situated on the River Severn the town nestles in amongst the ancient Shropshire hills of the Stiperstones, the Long Mynd, Wenlock Edge and the Wrekin. Educated at the Wakeman Grammar School, Jennie developed a keen interest in art, a love of English literature and truly excelled in sport. She considers her appreciation of the natural world to be most important to her. If she isn't reading or writing, you will find her outdoors pursuing activities she considers have enriched her life, horse riding in particular has been a life-long passion.

Jennie Dodd

RIDE THE WIND

AUSTIN MACAULEY PUBLISHERS™

LONDON • CAMBRIDGE • NEW YORK • SHARJAH

This is a work of fiction. Names, characters, businesses, places, events, locales, and incidents are either the products of the author's imagination or used in a fictitious manner. Any resemblance to actual persons, living or dead, or actual events is purely coincidental.

A CIP catalogue record for this title is available from the British Library.

ISBN 9781398474161 (Paperback)
ISBN 9781398474178 (ePub e-book)

www.austinmacauley.com

First Published 2023
Austin Macauley Publishers Ltd®
1 Canada Square
Canary Wharf
London
E14 5AA

Table of contents

Foreword

And God took a handful of South wind and from it formed a horse, saying:
'I create thee, Oh Arabian. To thy forelock, I bind victory in battle.
On thy back, I set a rich spoil, And a treasure in thy loins.
I establish thee as one of the Glories of the Earth…
I give thee flight without wings.'
– from Ancient Bedouin Legend

This novel has been inspired by my family's love of Australia.
and
Is written in memory of the Mighty Simba.
Mileoak Ingwala (18/6/1994–17/8/2005)

Chapter One
Simba to the Rescue

Chaney had been out snorkelling for some time. She loved to observe the myriads of brightly coloured fish which were to be found in abundance in the cool, crystal waters which lined the beautiful coastline of Western Australia. It was a deliciously blue sea that lapped rhythmically and endlessly onto sandy beaches which stretched for mile after glorious mile.

She delighted in watching the shimmering shoals of hundreds of fish, all seemingly moving as one linked and synchronised entity. Chaney also relished the chance to collect unusual shells as well as multi-coloured fans of delicate coral and was not afraid of diving right down to the seabed to reach them.

Simba had been snoozing, lying in the sand alongside his master, Michael, Chaney's father. He sat up and looked far out to sea. His ageing eyes took but seconds to identify Chaney's unmoving body, apparently floating effortlessly in the water some two hundred yards out from the shore. Growling loudly, he instantly stood to his feet.

'What is it, boy?' Michael asked anxiously. 'What is it?'

The old dog barked once, as if in reply and then padded out into the waves. Michael watched him swim out to sea and noted with relief that he was heading in Chaney's direction.

'Rachel,' he said in exasperation, 'have you seen how far out Chaney has gone? When Simba fetches her back, she's going to get a good telling off from me.'

Rachel, his wife, sat up quickly, replaced her sunglasses and gazed in the direction in which he was pointing.

'Where's Dakota?' she asked immediately.

'She's taken Enzo for a walk,' replied Michael, 'and I've given her some money to bring ice creams back.'

They both stood up and looked anxiously out to sea. Chaney was the youngest of their two daughters and always getting up to mischief of one kind or another.

Chaney had been following a small pod of baby dolphins which had taken quite an interest in her. They had been circling around for some time, and one had come so close, she had been able to reach out and gently stroke its nose. Suddenly, as if summoned by the matriarch, the babies had raced away. They swam so fast that they were lost from view in a matter of seconds.

It was then that she had spied an eagle ray slowly cruising along just yards from where she was swimming. Its two wings, which Chaney estimated had a span of about eight feet, were barely moving. It appeared to be almost hovering, as if it were waiting for something to happen, or perhaps waiting to decide, and deep in thought. As she watched it, unmoving and silent in the almost-turquoise water, Chaney could clearly see the distinctive white spots on its inky blue body.

The ray had an ungainly, odd-looking head, on top of which sat two bulbous raised eyes. The eyes were cold, clinical and devoid of expression, except that they seemed to be staring directly at her. Chaney had the uncomfortable feeling that the eagle ray was as interested in her as she was in it.

Then without warning, the huge ray flapped its great wings twice in quick succession. It soared away sharply to its left, and as it did so, Chaney felt the force of its powerful acceleration through the water as the strong current, caused by its sudden departure, lapped fiercely against her relatively tiny frame.

She raised her head briefly up out of the water and was shocked to see just how far out she had swum. Turning towards the shoreline, she began to swim back. Then, to her horror and for the first time in her short life, Chaney was to know real fear when swimming in the sea.

Heading straight for her and less than three feet away, was a large sea snake, its streamlined, boat-shaped body and flattened, paddle-like tail zigzagged toward her at an incredible speed. She froze in the water, unable to move either her arms or her legs. The mouth of the snake was wide open, ready to bite. Chaney prepared for the pain, convinced the snake was going to attack her. She waited to feel the venomous fangs penetrate her unprotected flesh, wishing now she had at least worn her wetsuit and believing she was about to die. She did not know which type of snake it was, but she could see its fawn-coloured skin was marked with a series of alternating black bars and spots. A vivid pattern like that meant only one thing – the snake was poisonous!

It was almost upon her, when a huge disturbance in the water pushed Chaney towards the seabed forcing her several feet down. She took in several mouthfuls of seawater and began to choke, thrashing her arms and kicking her legs wildly to get back to the surface. As she clawed her way upwards, the headless body of the snake floated past her.

Suddenly, she felt Simba take hold of the back of her swimsuit, and within seconds found herself being pulled away from the remains of the snake and dragged back to shore. Chaney breathed a sigh of relief. She gratefully allowed the old dog to tow her back to shore. Although Simba struggled even to walk on land with his elderly bones now riddled with arthritis, he was still a magnificent swimmer. They flew across the waves at such speed that Chaney felt as if a motorboat was pulling her.

'Good boy!' she shouted to her deliverer, realising that she could never have swum so fast by herself, even with her flippers on.

Once on dry land, Chaney dropped to her knees and hugged Simba with a boisterous, unreserved enthusiasm which was so typically her. As she patted and kissed him, she received Michael's impassioned lecture, but not one word in ten reached her ears.

'Who's the best dog in the world?' she whispered to Simba, whilst planting numerous kisses on his wet nose and wrapping her arms lovingly around his neck.

Dakota returned with the ice creams, and Enzo, the younger of the two Newfoundland dogs and by rights still a mere puppy, watched jealously as Chaney fed all of hers to her beloved rescuer. Simba was in his element. He happily drooled gloopy saliva all over his mistress, as he lapped-up every delicious mouthful.

'Well,' said Michael, offering his last piece of wafer cornet to Enzo, 'we need to be packing up and heading for Perth within the next half hour if we are going to make it in time for the girls' show jumping competition.'

Accordingly, the family quickly gathered all their belongings and chatting excitedly headed back towards the car park.

At that moment, someone else too was vacating the beach. However, this someone was not of humankind. She was an elfin creature, a beautiful, dark-haired fairy, on a special mission and, sadly, with a heart as black as her hair. Her eyes narrowed as she noted with concern that her wand was barely glowing. Clearly, her powers were fading, and she was only too aware that if she were to get back to the fairy kingdom safely, she needed to leave now. Hunting down the bar bellied sea snake had taken much longer than she had anticipated. The human child who had gotten in her way and whatever the furry creature was that had been with her at the time had almost cost her dear. In the end, it was more by luck than judgement that her cutting spell had hit its intended mark and the snake's head severed as planned.

Cloaking herself in an invisibility spell, she had landed on the beach to remove the venom glands. That done, the head was left on the sand, blistering in the midday heat, as Alba flew high into the air and, taking her prize with her, began the long flight home.

Sometime later and aware that her magic powers had only just sufficed, she landed on top of one of the fairy castle's turrets. Breathing a sigh of relief at her safe return, she looked down into the courtyard. Below her, she could see Queen Charlotte busily engaged watering the fountain, surrounded by several handmaidens trying to point out that it was the roses which needed attention.

Stupid, silly, senile sovereign, Alba thought to herself. *The sooner I sit on the throne the better.*

As she watched, a small mouse and an albino wallaby approached the queen and gently led her to the rose garden.

'Yes,' snarled Alba, 'and there are my two excellent guinea pigs; who better to test out my potion? Those nasty, vindictive creatures have never had a good word to say about me. How delightful, how interesting. I wonder if there are any horrid side effects other than the intended one, if the spell works? I can't wait to see.'

She took off again, and within minutes her isolated cottage came into view. Situated on the outskirts of the village and almost hidden in an overgrown wilderness once resembling a well-tended woodland copse, the dark dwelling provided Alba with exactly the living quarters she desired.

It was a three-storey building, and each floor very differently designed. The ground floor had only two small windows in total and was very dark. Even at midday, with the sun at its highest point in the sky, anyone looking in would have seen only darkness. This was what Alba had wanted. All prying eyes were kept at bay. The second floor had more windows, though not enormous, and black wooden shutters attached to the outside of every one meant that privacy and seclusion could be achieved at a moment's notice.

Alba considered the third floor her real home and her pièce de résistance. This level contained her kitchen, her bathroom, her main lounge and her master bedroom. The windows were large and wide and afforded a wonderful view of the sky at night. Alba loved to look at the moon and would often lie awake during the hours of darkness admiring its celestial beauty.

She entered her house through an open upstairs window and immediately flew to the kitchen. The snake's venom glands were placed in a saucepan of water over low heat, and Alba stirred the mixture slowly, whilst once again flicking through the pages of her book of ancient spells.

Alba had an inherent weakness in her powers of alchemy and of concentration in that she tended to rush things. She always wanted everything done that second, in an instant, and so she scanned the complex conjuring instructions rather than read through them carefully.

As soon as the saucepan had started to boil, she turned the heat down to simmer and retired to the bathroom to shower and change before going in search of Prince Kyle. He was the only son of Queen Charlotte and King Ariel, and she was convinced she had won his heart. Indeed, as far as Alba was concerned it was only a matter of time before he proposed marriage.

As she showered, she thought about Queen Charlotte. In Alba's eyes, the old queen had become the subject of ridicule. What the royal crown needed now was to regain respect. Strong leadership was required, and Alba genuinely believed she would make the perfect wife for the young prince. She would re-establish the power of royalty and insist upon the subservience of all the elfin kind of the kingdom.

Stepping out of the shower, she wrapped herself in a soft towel and made her way to the bedroom. She lay upon her bed, eyes closed, daydreaming of her life as Queen Alba. An unpleasant thought entered her mind – the mouse and the wallaby were not the only creatures in the kingdom to question her suitability as queen. She was sick of hearing the name of Aislinn mentioned. Aislinn, her rival for Kyle's affections, born a whole three days after Alba and yet treated by all with such reverence and admiration. Prissy, predictable, and ever the "miss perfect" Aislinn, who spent all day and every day making centuries-old herbal potions without using her magical power at all! *What is the point in that?* thought Alba. *She might as well be human.*

Alba stood up and walked to the window. It was a beautiful evening, perfect for a romantic assignation, although Kyle, of course, was not aware of Alba's secret intentions. She would seek him out and flaunt her obvious beauty, display her physical grace, provoke his admiration with her slender, delicate feminine frame. She knew how best to work her womanly wiles, how to flutter her eyelashes, how to flash her brilliant, white smile and amaze him with her intelligent, witty conversation. How could he or indeed any other fairy resist her special charms?

It was then she was reminded of the potion. Aislinn would be no match for Alba, once the latter's black magic had done its work. The venom of a bar bellied snake was the crucial ingredient for a character changing spell. Once combined with the crushed tail of a marbled scorpion and the fried body of a funnel-web spider, the concoction produced dramatic results. Anyone drinking this vile mixture would undergo an instant personality change – they would become the reverse of what they had been previously. Aislinn, renowned for being kind and good, would become cruel and evil. *Who will stick up for her then?* Alba thought wickedly to herself.

She gazed out through the window, watching the sun's red glow as it sank behind the mountain tops far to the west. Suddenly, there was the sound of a loud explosion from the kitchen, and a searing red-hot glow burst in through her bedroom door. Alba raced to the kitchen. Had she read the spell's instructions carefully, she would have known that the mixture required constant stirring, that the water would require constant topping up. Bar bellied snake venom evaporates incredibly quickly, and as it loses its moisture, its temperature rises to extraordinary levels.

Nothing remained of the saucepan, although it appeared as if small pieces of shrapnel had pierced the kitchen walls and ceiling. Anyone walking in at that moment would have thought a machine gun had been unleashed inside the room and fired to its full capacity. Small holes punctured the plaster work on every side.

Alba screamed in frustration, and lifting her wand almost proceeded to destroy anything left in the kitchen that was still standing. Then she caught a glimpse of herself in a cracked mirror.

Well, she thought, *explosion or not, I must say I do look very pretty.*

Temper now well and truly under control, she used her wand to plug up the holes. Repairs done, she stood in front of the mirror admiring her appearance. She smoothed her long black hair, applied a layer of black mascara to her thick, long eyelashes and a vibrant sheen of bright, red ruby lipstick to her full and pouting lips.

'Here I come, Kyle,' she said aloud. 'Here I come, ready or not!'

Chapter Two
Temper Tantrum

'Aislinn, surely you've collected enough wool by now?' enquired the young man in an uncharacteristically impatient voice. 'If we do not leave now, we'll miss the black Arabian jumping altogether. He and his rider are already in the arena!'

'My basket's full to overflowing,' was the reply. 'I've got enough fleece here to knit a winter scarf for every man, woman and child in the kingdom. Would you carry it for me please, Kyle?' she said, sounding more than satisfied. Handing the now-fastened basket to the young man standing beside her, she stood up and made ready to leave.

'Of course,' he replied. Taking the basket from her outstretched hand, he continued, 'Quick, follow me.'

Within seconds they had vacated the large timber barn in which the sheep shearing contest had been held. Moments later, they were perched like two lovebirds on a leafy branch atop one of the many acacia trees which lined the avenue side of the show-jumping arena.

'Look, there he is!' Kyle called out excitedly, directing Aislinn's admiring gaze towards a handsome black Arabian stallion. They both drew breath and waited nervously for his rider to begin her approach to the first fence.

'No wonder you were so anxious to watch him, Kyle. He is beautiful. Just look at the shine on his coat. Why, it's dazzling. I can honestly say I've never in my life seen a more magnificent horse.' As she spoke, Aislinn smiled warmly up at her companion. Kyle's eyes, however, remained fixed on the arena and his precious Arabian.

Just then the hooter sounded, and the young female rider spurred her mount into action. Kyle and Aislinn listened carefully as the announcer introduced the horse and rider to the watching crowd.

'Ladies and gentlemen, the final rider in this year's Royal Perth Show is Chaney Meredith on Black Star. Chaney's sister, Dakota, riding Galaxy Invader, is already through to the jump-off. Let's see if younger sister Chaney can perform as well! She certainly must have a chance riding this super-looking Arabian. I'm sure we would all love her to echo her sister's performance with a clear round.'

Almost before the announcer had finished speaking, the first fence – a spread with parallel bars – was down.

Kyle groaned and watched with increasing disappointment as the black stallion tore around the course at breakneck speed but making mistake after mistake. 'Why on earth is his rider making him go so fast?' Kyle asked in confusion. 'With his Arabian pedigree, that horse should be clearing these fences with ease.'

They watched the horse approach a treble combination with bated breath.

'Oh no,' whispered Kyle as the black stallion accelerated even more into the first of the three fences. 'If only his rider would take her time, and just concentrate on getting a clear round. You see the judges only take time into consideration when the horse and rider compete in the final jump-off. How fast they go in this first round is totally irrelevant. That rider needs to slow the horse down and focus all her efforts just on getting him to make the jump,' Kyle explained to an equally confused Aislinn.

'I agree,' Aislinn replied. 'Whatever is she thinking of?'

The poles of yet another fence clattered to the ground. They watched in absolute dismay as the black stallion completed a disastrous round. At the end of it, the clock showed the fastest time of the competition, and by some margin, but every fence was down. Chaney and Black Star would certainly not be in the jump-off.

Horse and rider returned from the arena to the exercise paddock. A tall blond-haired woman was waiting for them. She calmly took hold of the reins as the young rider dismounted. The woman frowned as the disgruntled rider immediately stormed off. Kyle noted, with some amusement, the rider's angry face as she strode towards a white campervan parked on the far left of the paddock. The rider undid her hat and threw it to the ground. The hat was quickly followed by a riding crop and jacket. Then, in rapid succession, riding boots were kicked off in temper and promptly hurled in opposite directions.

Two large dogs on long chains attached to one side of the campervan watched the sudden approach of the dark-haired girl and made to escape. The dogs attempted to hide behind a nearby horse trailer, stretching their chains to the limit. The angry young rider observed their behaviour with even more annoyance and disappeared into the campervan, slamming the door so hard behind her that it nearly fell off its hinges.

The woman holding Black Star's reins had been joined by a tall, dark-haired man and a young teenage girl. The girl resembled the woman so closely in looks that it was obvious to Kyle and Aislinn that they had to be mother and daughter.

'Well,' she said, 'are you going to speak to our daughter, or am I?'

'I'll see to Star,' they heard the man standing next to her reply, 'and speak to Chaney later when she's had time to calm down. For the time being, let's concentrate on getting Dakota and Galaxy ready for the jump-off.'

'You might want to save Chaney's boots first,' the tall fair-haired girl advised, as she pointed towards the younger and bigger of the two dogs. The dog was in his element, chewing on and salivating copiously over the two black leather riding boots generously donated for his pleasure by his temper-tantrum-prone mistress.

'Enzo, drop!' the man commanded loudly and in his firmest voice.

The dog reluctantly obeyed. Two wet and well-chewed boots dropped to the floor, as the older dog barked his disapproval of the puppy's behaviour. At the same time, the door of the campervan reopened, and a now somewhat red-eyed, contrite and downcast-looking dark-haired girl came into view. Stockinged feet stepped down onto the grass. Trembling hands picked up the boots.

'Bad dog,' she said to Enzo, holding the boots above his head.

For a moment Enzo considered retrieving the boots again for another delicious chew, but a quick glance across at his master convinced him otherwise, and instead, he cowered low and began to whine miserably.

'I'll just stow this stuff away,' the girl said sheepishly to her family, 'and then I'll give Star his cool down whilst you support Dakota in the jump-off. Sorry about before,' she concluded.

'I should think so!' her mother replied sternly. 'It's high time, Chaney, you showed an ability to lose gracefully. You don't see Dakota making a spectacle of herself and behaving like that every time she loses!'

'Sorry,' Chaney repeated through gritted teeth. 'I just lost my temper with myself for being so stupid and riding Star so badly. I wanted to prove to everyone how fast Star is and show off his jumping skills as well. Anyway, good luck in the jump-off,' she said turning to her sister. 'I really hope you win.'

The two girls gave each other an affectionate hug, and then Dakota went to prepare Galaxy for the final jump-off, whilst Chaney unsaddled Star and began to groom him lovingly.

Kyle and Aislinn flew down to land unseen on top of the campervan. Kyle wanted to get a closer look at the Arabian. They listened to Chaney as she began to brush his wonderful shining coat.

'Never mind, boy,' Chaney said as she fed Star some of his favourite titbits.

The pedigree name of Chaney's horse was Black Star, and his Arabian lineage should indeed have made him the clear favourite to win. Star with his distinctive head shape and high tail carriage was a joy to watch. He was a pure black stallion, except for a white star on his forehead. He had a flowing mane and proud head, and Chaney loved him with all her heart.

'I made you go far too fast, didn't I?'

The black stallion nodded his head up and down as if agreeing with her, and the old dog, having joined them, barked again, as if to reaffirm Chaney's words. It seemed that he too had understood her meaning and thoroughly agreed with the reason she had given for their disappointing performance.

Chaney looked down at the ageing dog and said laughingly, 'Alright, Simba, you don't have to rub it in too. I know I was at fault.'

Simba rewarded Chaney's honesty with numerous licks to her young, flushed face. It was a face now covered in slimy dog drool.

'Thanks,' she said affectionately, as she attempted to wipe the bulk of his saliva away with the back of her hand. 'Just what I needed!'

Dakota won the red rosette, missing out on the winning blue by just three seconds. Kyle and Aislinn stayed to watch the presentation, before returning home.

Some hours later the white campervan, pulling a horse trailer behind it, was well on its journey home.

Meanwhile back in Aislinn's village, work had already begun on turning the raw fleece into fine wool. As Kyle and Aislinn worked together, they discussed the events of the day. Kyle loved any opportunity he was afforded to talk about horses. He had been fascinated by the four-legged creatures from an early age.

'I envy those people with their horses,' he admitted to Aislinn.

'What's to envy? After all, we have our own farm ponies,' Aislinn replied.

'Yes, I know,' he agreed, 'and I appreciate they do a grand job pulling their carts and carrying heavy sacks of produce to market. But can you not see the difference in our small, stocky ponies to these fine creatures? Why, I can walk faster than our ponies can run.'

'Oh, Kyle, don't exaggerate,' Aislinn reprimanded laughingly.

Kyle, however, continued undeterred. 'Well, anyway, our farm ponies may be strong; but when you see how these creatures can race and jump, when you watch their speed across the ground, when you see them leap twenty feet in the air, don't you feel your heart stir, your blood pound and a yearning to ride like that yourself? It's as if they can fly without wings.'

Aislinn sensed his great passion and continued to listen.

'When you study human history,' he explained, 'you realise just how important the horse has been in man's development, enabling him to explore his environment, to discover new lands, to cover huge distances and eventually transform vast areas of wilderness into thriving agricultural settlements. They're such wonderful creatures, Aislinn.'

'Do you mean man is wonderful or the horse?' she jokingly teased.

Kyle answered her question by rolling his eyes and awarding her a wry smile.

'Well,' continued Aislinn, 'having seen those two particular horses today, I can at last understand your fascination with them. What were their names again? Galaxy and Black Star, wasn't it?'

'Yes,' answered Kyle enthusiastically, 'Galaxy is a gorgeous white Andalusian, and Black Star an equally magnificent Arabian. Did you know that the Andalusian breed was developed in Southern Spain? It was considered the ideal cavalry horse.'

'Not much use for warhorses these days,' Aislinn replied.

'No, that's true, thank goodness,' agreed Kyle. 'But in these modern times the Andalusian is still an important breed – in Spain, especially. Did you know that they are often used in bullfighting?'

'I'm sorry to hear that,' replied Aislinn. 'Why is it they chose the poor old Andalusian to take part in bullfights?'

'They catch the attention of the audience because of their wonderful presence, and are incredibly brave and fearless,' Kyle replied. He paused for a moment, as if he were gathering his thoughts. Secretly, he wanted to change the subject of conversation. He knew Aislinn well enough to know that, from her turn of phrase, she did not approve of bullfighting.

'Now Arabians, on the other hand, dominate the discipline of endurance riding and have a well-deserved reputation for intelligence, spirit and stamina.

Both breeds have numerous qualities which make them excellent showjumpers. I could have watched those horses all day and, what's more, I think the black could have won; that is of course, if his rider had been more experienced.'

As they continued to work and talk happily together about the horses they had seen that day, they were blissfully unaware that someone was watching them. A very pretty, young woman with long black hair was eyeing their every move and desperately trying to overhear their conversation.

She was slowly hovering towards them and trying to appear as nonchalant as possible. Her facial expression was one of mild disinterest and good humour. Indeed, she was doing an excellent job of pretending to be out for a pleasant early-evening meander and merely passing through the village without any specific aim. In truth, she had been looking for Kyle for some time.

Aislinn looked up from her work and spotted Alba some distance away from them. 'What on earth is Alba doing?' she commented to Kyle. 'She's acting very strangely.'

'Alba is strange,' replied Kyle. 'She gives me the creeps at the best of times.'

'Shush,' Aislinn whispered, 'she'll hear you!'

Just yards from where Kyle and Aislinn were washing wool, the young woman stopped, knelt on the ground and began to adjust the pretty red moccasins she was wearing. She listened with ears straining to catch the drift of what they were saying. The words 'wonderful' and 'gorgeous' were instantly recognised, and the woman immediately drew an unhappy and – for her – very unpleasant conclusion. She straightway believed that Kyle was paying love-struck compliments to the young lady working quietly at his side. Kyle: the man she herself had set her heart on marrying, the man who she had honestly believed would very soon propose marriage to her. It was too much for her to bear.

The pretty face twisted and contorted with rage as the green-eyed monster rose in her bosom. Now she wore an ugly expression, and her thoughts and emotions were as black as her hair. Anger and hatred flared in her dark eyes as jealousy came to ride on her back – a vicious jealousy that pulled her away, took over her thoughts, charged her emotions with red-hot anger and led her blindly out of the village. She flew back to her home, where alone, unwanted and unloved, Alba cried bitter tears into her pillow.

The trailer containing the actual subject of Kyle's conversation – those two wonderful horses – and the campervan pulling them, was still winding its long, lonely journey home.

To Michael, the journey seemed never ending. Mile after mile of highway stretched out ahead of him in the darkness. The two girls, their mother and Enzo slept soundly. Michael, however, remained at the wheel all night, and Simba kept him company. Simba, although old and tired as he was, loyally maintained a constant vigil by the side of his master and refused to go to sleep. Finally, as dawn was breaking, the welcome sight of their homestead came into view. The aged dog barked happily as the campervan pulled onto the familiar drive. His barking woke Chaney.

'Oh, are we home already?' she asked sleepily.

'What?' echoed Dakota. 'Are we home?'

Loud cries from a dozen kookaburras, like the laughter of a madman with hysteria, confirmed that they were, indeed, home. The girls listened to the familiar, if still somewhat unnerving, sound.

'Spooky or what?' said Chaney as she peered through the half-light and early morning mist towards the river, and the kookaburras' nesting grounds.

Chapter Three
Sibling Rivalry

The next morning, the girls awoke late. As they breakfasted, their father, Michael, came to say goodbye. He would be away on business for several days. Chaney noted with concern how tired he looked. There were dark circles under his eyes, and his complexion was unusually pale.

'Dad, you look awful,' she blurted out rather tactlessly. 'Have you slept at all?'

'Don't fret yourself about me. I intend to catch up on some sleep on the plane,' he replied.

'How long are you away?' asked Dakota.

'Oh, five, possibly six days at most, but in the meantime, you two need to switch the emphasis of your training and focus only on getting the horses ready for the endurance event. The National Championship is just a few weeks away, and you ought to start preparing,' he advised.

'I can't wait to take part. You know how much I love trail riding!' Chaney cried out excitedly. 'Just think of it, 160 kilometres of unknown terrain with goodness only knows how many new challenges and obstacles for us to navigate. And riding the two best horses in the world, we're bound to win!'

Dakota laughed at her sister's enthusiastic outburst, but Michael looked concerned.

'Chaney, neither you nor your horses have experienced anything like this event before. It's a demanding competition, and you are all going to have to train hard if you want to succeed. I do agree with your comment about the horses, however. They are both fine thoroughbreds and will be difficult to beat.'

He avoided stating the obvious; that it would be how they were ridden which would be the deciding factor as to who would ultimately win the race. Chaney might well have her wonderful Arabian to ride, but would she, he wondered, be able to mimic Dakota's control and steadiness in tough situations?

Dakota's horse, Galaxy (whose true pedigree name was Galaxy Invader) was a pure white Andalusian horse. Galaxy always caught the eye, with his long head with broad forehead, his muscular arched neck, short body with powerful hindquarters and strong fine legs. Like Star, he was intelligent and clever, quick to learn new skills, and devoted to Dakota. He was bigger than Star, standing over 16 hands high, and was the best jumper Dakota had ever ridden. This ability gave him a distinct advantage in clearing any obstacle that might lie in their way as they navigated through the forest trails. In any case, who would win did not matter; the two girls were intent on racing as a pair and had already decided that if they could, they would cross the finish line first but also together.

'Try and get the horses out of the paddock as much as possible. Do some extended rides; following the river trails would be a good idea or, better still, getting up into the hills. But', warned Michael, 'make sure you take your mobiles with you and let your mother know the route you intend to take, and an approximate time when she is to expect you back home.'

'Okay, Dad, will do,' responded Dakota happily.

'And look after your mother,' Michael continued. 'Help her around the house and with the dogs. I'd be especially grateful if you make sure Enzo doesn't push poor old Simba around too much whilst I'm away. Stick to the routine of feeding them separately, otherwise Enzo will scoff the lot and Simba will be left with nothing.'

'Don't worry, Dad. I'll keep an eye on Simba. If Dakota's in agreement, I'll feed Simba, whilst she sees to Enzo. I love you, don't I, old fella?' said Chaney, as she gently stroked the soft furry head of Michael's shadow. Simba, as always, was at his master's side.

'Yes, I'm happy with that idea,' agreed Dakota.

Michael kissed his daughters goodbye and, as he did, wondered to himself – and not for the first time – how two sisters could be so vastly different. They were like chalk and cheese.

The fact that Dakota and Chaney were sisters could not be denied, but a stranger would never have guessed their relationship merely by looking at them. Dakota was as fair as Chaney was dark and older by just under three years. Dakota was also tall, athletic and elegant. Chaney, in contrast, was relatively short, skinny and ungainly. Both girls had long hair which they normally tied back in a ponytail. Dakota was blond-haired and blue-eyed like her mother.

Chaney, on the other hand, had jet-black hair and large brown eyes, identical to her father.

In temperament and character, they were again hugely different. Dakota was serious, reliable, steady, prudent and practical. It was in her nature to be thoughtful and cautious, taking her time before making any decision. Dakota, or 'Tota' as she was known to her friends and family, had a well-deserved reputation for good behaviour. She was conscientious in every task she undertook, and her head always ruled her heart.

Unlike her sister, Chaney was mischievous, highly imaginative and wilful. She acted instinctively, often rashly, was unreliable, ignored advice, and was inclined to be rather boisterous. Chaney was also renowned for her terrible temper tantrums. She did her best to avoid being given tasks and inevitably allowed her heart to rule her head. Perhaps her one saving grace was that she had a heart of gold and an indisputable love of all animals. Chaney was often referred to as 'Buggy', but no one, it appeared, not even Chaney herself, could explain why.

Dakota often tried to rein in her younger sister's erratic, impetuous behaviour by giving cautionary advice. Chaney resented the unwanted interference, and caustic words would follow, usually ending with these two phrases:

'You're so painfully dull, Dakota!'

'Better dull, Buggy, than to be a silly little girl like you.' This remark would inevitably be Dakota's quick parry to her sister's insult.

Sometimes when Dakota felt Chaney was ignoring or refusing to take her well-meaning advice, she would call either one or both of their parents to add weight to her argument. Chaney hated this more than anything and was very resentful that her parents always seemed to take Dakota's side.

'Just because she's older than me doesn't mean she has to be right!' This was the other phrase Chaney could be heard to repeat at least twice a day.

It was bad enough if just their family was involved in disputes between them, but if they criticised one another in front of friends or family guests, their arguments would become vitriolic in the extreme. Neither sister liked being shown up in front of peers or visitors, and there had even been occasions when physical blows had been thrown. Yet, as the saying goes, 'blood is thicker than water' – and woe betide anyone picking on either sister, when the other one was around. They instinctively rallied to each other's defence at a moment's notice. However many times they might fight like cat and dog, there was still an unbreakable bond between them; eternal and unspoken blood ties which would never be ignored or broken. Their common ground was the love they bore for each other, their animals and their parents.

Alba also breakfasted late that morning after waking with a blinding headache and swollen eyes from all her crying. A few hours' sleep, however, had changed her perspective of the events of last evening. Jealousy and anger had somehow slipped away unnoticed, but her infatuation with Kyle had returned to fill the vacuum. As she crunched through slightly burnt toast, she began to question whether she had been correct in drawing the conclusions she had over Kyle's conversation with Aislinn.

I didn't actually hear him say that Aislinn was gorgeous or wonderful. In hindsight, he could have been talking about the weather, for all I know. It wasn't as if they were holding hands or anything, she thought to herself. Alba suddenly realised that his attention had been more on the wool he'd been washing rather than Aislinn. *I've been such a fool! Will I ever change? Why is it I always jump to conclusions before ever waiting to establish the facts? I put myself through hell, and for what? It's so typically me!*

Alba continued to question why she had tortured herself so over Kyle. Two slices of toast later, she was convinced that it had all been a stupid mistake. Anyway, how could Kyle possibly prefer Aislinn to her?

Aislinn! Weak, weedy Aislinn who spends all day and every day growing silly, soppy herbs! I must be mad getting myself into such a state over her, she thought.

Breakfast over, she washed and dressed herself in her best new dress. She knew Kyle spent most mornings at the library and decided that would be her first port of call. In a matter of minutes Alba landed lightly on the bottom step of that vast medieval sandstone building. Smoothing her hair and straightening her frock, she climbed the nine remaining steps and pushed open the huge outer doors. Stepping inside a small inner porch, her eyes first caught sight of two tall guards, standing like stone statues on either side of the magnificently sculptured wrought iron gates which barred the entrance to the library itself.

Sitting at a reception desk placed just in front of them were two creatures from the kingdom – individuals Alba knew well and with whom she shared a history. They were as displeased to see her, as she was to see them.

'Fossett, Gilpin, how lovely. Doing your bit for the community are we? Library duty again, is it?' she said through gritted teeth. 'Here's my library card, Fossett. And before you ask, no, I don't have any books to return.'

'Just remember the rules,' was the brief, gruff reply. 'No talking and,' the voice emphasised, 'no flying!'

'I know, I know,' Alba replied irritably, 'you don't need to remind me. By the way, I shall probably be some time. I'm working on a project to rid the world of malaria.'

At these unexpected words, similar thoughts and feelings immediately passed through two incredulous, sceptical minds, and inadvertently, two sets of eyebrows rose simultaneously in disbelief to convey them.

Noting their response, Alba was even more irritated. 'My research thus far', she continued, trying to convince them of her good intentions, 'would suggest that finding ways of depleting mosquito numbers by altering their natural habitat, is our best option.' She looked at the stony faces staring up at her and quickly realised from their cold expression that she was flogging a dead horse. Without waiting for a reply, she turned on her heels, and completely ignoring the two sentries on duty – as if they were just there for decoration – she pushed the ornate iron gates apart and strode through, head held high.

'A likely story,' remarked the one called Fossett, as he deposited Alba's card into the 'present' box. 'Knowing Alba as we do, my guess would be she's studying ways of increasing the mosquito population, not reducing it! What a load of codswallop.'

'Shush,' replied his colleague, 'she'll hear you. I do wish you wouldn't deliberately try to aggravate her. Be advised by me, being on the receiving end of one of her infamous paybacks is no fun at all, AND I should know!'

Much to Alba's delight, she had anticipated correctly. Kyle was sitting at a desk near the meteorology section of the library. Narrow slants of sunlight rained in through the tall, Gothic arched windows, affording the visitor, as always, a spectacular sight. Thousands of books lined thousands of shelves, and tall mahogany rolling ladders stretched from floor to ceiling. High above in the buttresses, supporting the mighty timbered beams of the roof, the hideous faces of hundreds of stone gargoyles projected out. Their enormous heads, all depicting strange, mythological creatures, stared down on those daring to enter through the hallowed ancient doors below. They commanded silence.

Alba's eyes slowly adjusted to the strange light. She watched as Kyle was joined by two other young men carrying enormous leather-bound books which looked incredibly old. Alba instantly recognised the two men as Kyle's best friends. One, named Darius, was a tall dark-haired, dark-eyed fairy, and a reputed favourite with the royal family. The other equally tall fairy had long, fair hair and striking blue eyes. His name was Sebastian. Alba knew that he was a student at the same University as Kyle and had a reputation for being quite the academic. Indeed, she had heard Kyle praise Sebastian's knowledge and intellect on several occasions.

Alba felt slightly peeved that their presence would mean it would be more difficult for her to converse with Kyle alone. To make matters worse, Darius and Sebastian had never helped Alba's cause where Kyle was concerned. Whenever she attempted to flirt with him in their company, either one or both would make fun of her remarks, laugh at her expense and inevitably make her feel uncomfortable. No, Alba did not like either of them. However, she had set out her stall that morning on speaking with Kyle and was not going to let them stop her.

The library was surprisingly busy, but much to her satisfaction, there was a free desk only a foot away from where Kyle was working. Walking with an exaggerated tilt and swagger, she made her way to the chosen desk. To her annoyance, Kyle did not even look up from his study. Leaving her bag on top of the desk, she crossed the library floor to a section of books immediately in front of Kyle's desk. She climbed several steps up the ladder, pretending to look at books on the seventeenth tier. Her right foot left the rung of the ladder and swayed backwards and forwards in the air. A bright, shiny red shoe swung from side to side, like the pendulum of a grandfather clock, and still Kyle remained unaware of her presence. He was so engrossed in his studies that even if she had been waving a red flag, he would not have noticed. She stretched up to reach a book on the eighteenth tier, and the skirt of her dress rose well above knee height, exposing an exceptionally fine and slender leg. Kyle was oblivious to it all. Thwarted in her endeavours to attract his attention, Alba returned to her desk empty-handed.

How on earth am I going to get him to notice me? she thought to herself, by now feeling somewhat frustrated. Then she had a brainwave. With hips swaying from side to side, she strutted up to Kyle's desk. Taking hold of a closed book lying to one side, she asked, 'If you've finished with this one, would you mind terribly if I borrow it?'

Without even looking up, Kyle waved his right hand as if to say, *Just go away and get on with it – I'm busy!* Sebastian carried on reading, his mind so fully occupied that he didn't even hear her. Darius, however, had been observing her antics and gave her an amused grin.

'Want any help reading it? There are some terribly, terribly long words in that particular volume,' he said teasingly, deliberately mimicking her choice of vocabulary.

Alba was not amused. She was shortly to be even less amused. Alba remained at her desk, pretending to study the book she had borrowed, and hoped eventually that Kyle would want it back. As time passed, she gradually noticed that the three young men were becoming very animated in their whispered conversation. Kyle was smiling widely and looking rather excited. Once again, Alba strained her ears to listen to what was being said. What she heard left her in no doubt as to where Kyle's affections lay, and once again, jealousy and anger immediately leapt to stand beside her.

The covers of the book she had taken from Kyle's desk were slammed together, and in high dudgeon Alba stormed across the library floor. With every step, Alba's fury mounted, until she was halfway to being strangled by it. Not caring now whether Kyle was watching or not, Alba marched towards a dimly lit alcove in which special books were stored. Enormous, intricately embroidered tapestries – centuries old, decorated with scenes from an ancient past and embellished with cryptic warnings written in a long-forgotten language similar to Sanskrit – barred her entry to that sacred section. Hands shaking with rage hurled the drapes apart, and Alba flew inside like a vulture to a carcass, with fingers open-clawed, desperate to find a book that would quench her thirst for blood.

Chapter Four
Dogs and Brussels Sprouts

Dakota and Chaney's family owned a small homestead called Kookaburra Heights, consisting of thirty hectares of vineyards with plantings of various grape varieties. The grapes were produced as a source fruit for a winery based in the Margaret River area. Despite its relatively small size, the farm produced an excellent annual crop. The land was very fertile and, running adjacent to the Swan River as it did, was always well-irrigated. It was an ideal place for growing vines and the perfect habitat for birds that survive mainly on a diet of fish.

The kookaburra is a large kingfisher-type of bird native to Australia, and hence the reason why a great many of them had colonised the trees which grew in abundance along the riverbank. The river meant there were always rich pickings of fish to be had all year round. The name 'Kookaburra' derives from the loud and unmistakable call that the bird makes. The call seems to echo, and some people say it sounds very much like human beings laughing hysterically. In the evenings, especially after twilight, the sound can seem a little eerie or unnerving. For Dakota and Chaney, however, it was a noise to which they had become accustomed. That said, Chaney in truth still found the sound a little scary at times, especially when she was left alone in the house at night.

The farmhouse in which they lived was a modern build. The ground floor was spacious, with a huge kitchen, dining room and family lounge. Surrounding the house was a large walled garden which boasted its own outdoor swimming pool. Built into the wall at the back of the garden was a wide wrought-iron gate which separated the formal garden and pool area from a large stable block and an adjoining paddock.

Some people envied the girls and thought them spoilt. This was hardly surprising, considering that their lifestyle was the stuff of which other girls' dreams are made. You see, it wasn't just that Dakota and Chaney had a magnificent home; they were also lucky enough to have their own thoroughbred horse each and the company of two affectionate, loving and very large Newfoundland dogs.

This breed of dog excels at water rescue due to their webbed feet and innate swimming abilities. They can take on rough seas, ferocious waves and powerful tides with ease. Living by the coast, the dogs made for great family pets. In fact, it was a daily occurrence for the girls to ride their horses on land and the two dogs on water. Unlike other dogs, their swimming stroke is not an ordinary 'doggy paddle'. They move their limbs in a down and out motion remarkably similar to that of breaststroke – which as a result is much more powerful. Chaney and Dakota would often ride on their backs in the sea or be brought back to shore against their will if either of the dogs decided that the girls had swum out too far! Only last week Chaney, who had been out snorkelling, had been pulled back to the beach by Simba. He had taken a firm hold of her bikini top in his jaw and had refused to release it, no matter how hard she struggled.

Newfoundland dogs have thick brown fur along with heavy droopy lips and a jowl designed to make expansive dog drool. An affectionate greeting from either dog always resulted in being virtually drowned in saliva. Simba was eleven years old and, as such, an elderly gentleman in human years. Enzo, in contrast, at just three years of age was still a virtual puppy, although already he had outgrown his senior partner. Simba stood 22 inches tall at the shoulder, whilst Enzo had already reached 24 inches in height – and was still growing!

Both dogs had undergone intensive obedience training and were unbelievably well-behaved. There was just one slight problem: Enzo dominated Simba. The old dog was sometimes at the mercy of the young energetic pup and had to be protected from Enzo's exuberant behaviour. The family devised several ways to limit the bullying. For one thing, they were fed separately, otherwise Enzo would wolf down all his food and then proceed to steal Simba's meal. Dogs, after all, are pack animals, and there is always a 'leader of the pack.' When the dogs were on their own, it was Enzo who was leader. But when they were with the family, it was Michael who was in charge, and his word was law. The dogs attempted to accompany Michael wherever he went, even on the occasions when he needed to go to the bathroom. The only time they left his side was at mealtimes when they strangely sat either side of Chaney at the table.

Of course, it was taboo to feed the dogs at the table. Dakota and Chaney had been given strict instructions that this was something they must never do.

Rachael, their mother, constantly reminded them how important it was to maintain this rule.

'A dog needs to know his place and how to behave. Never, on any account, do you feed them from the table. Have I made myself clear?' Rachael would demand. She would not be satisfied until both girls had responded positively.

'Yes, yes,' they would assure her, nodding heads so forcefully that they were in danger of dropping off.

At mealtimes, Dakota ate everything that was put in front of her. Chaney was more difficult. She didn't like salad, wasn't too keen on fish and abhorred certain vegetables, most particularly Brussels sprouts. Chaney was never allowed to leave the table until her parents were satisfied she had eaten enough of the right food to keep her well and healthy. Making her stay at the table seemed to do the trick, and it was often surprising how quickly she managed to clear her plate when left to her own devices. The dogs too seemed to know when her plate was clear and would immediately return to Michael's side.

Simba, possibly due to his age, occasionally had an unpleasant digestive problem. He was guilty of farting. It was fortunate that this did not happen all the time, because the smell was truly revolting. It seemed to coincide with days when sprouts were part of the family's evening meal. Luckily for Chaney, her dislike of sprouts and Simba's horrible farts had not yet been connected by the family, not even by Rachael.

Rachael was standing in the hallway at the bottom of the staircase. The front door was wide open, and a warm gentle breeze carried the delicate perfume of sun orchids into the house. Several wooden tubs placed on either side of the front porch were full to bursting with this specimen of plant. The flowers are scented like strawberry jam and attract a great many honeybees. Today, however, Rachael was feeling too irritated to notice the sweet fragrance of her sun orchids, even though they were now in full bloom and at the height of their scent and beauty.

She was waiting for Chaney, and anxiously eyeing her watch for the fifth occasion in as many minutes. Rachael was becoming more and more frustrated as precious time passed by.

'Chaney, will you hurry up, please? The dogs have been in the back of the car this past quarter of an hour. Surely you can hear Enzo whining. They're anxious to be off, especially in all this heat.'

'Coming, Mum!' was the reply.

'At last,' Rachael whispered to herself.

She put the key in the lock and waited, once more glancing at her watch. Had she turned to look at the flower tub on her left, she might have been astonished at three little winged creatures also collecting nectar from her sun orchids. Like hummingbirds, these tiny beings were hovering above the centre of a flower, reaching deep inside for the rich, sweet juice they were now accustomed to gathering. They had visited Kookaburra Heights many times before, but just like today, they remained unseen visitors. They were wearing small wooden barrels over their left shoulder, supported with a narrow strap of leather.

'My barrel's full now, Kyle,' said one of the fairies to another.

'As is mine,' was the reply. 'How about you, Darius?'

'This last flower should do it.' A few moments later the handsome dark-haired fairy fixed the lid to his barrel. 'Yes, I'm done.'

'Let's get back to the kingdom,' said the blond-haired fairy who had spoken first. 'We must have more than enough for the physicians to make their medicine.'

Three sets of wings spirited away in the blink of an eye.

As normal on Saturday mornings, the girls were to help their mother with the weekly shop. Their journey would take them past South Beach, a recognised dog beach, where the dogs could exercise to their hearts' content. Enzo and Simba barked excitedly, knowing what lay afoot. It was a weekly treat they looked forward to with some relish. Chaney finally emerged from the house but minus her hat!

'Hat?' her mother enquired.

'It's early yet. I'll be okay,' was the nonchalant reply.

'Hat!' repeated her mother, but this time as a command.

Chaney, quashed, returned into the house and re-emerged minutes later wearing a bright pink cap.

'That's my cap, Buggy!' Dakota complained. 'Where's your own?'

'Don't know,' replied Chaney. 'I couldn't find it. Well, do you want me to keep you waiting even longer, or can I borrow yours?'

'No, you can't borrow my cap,' replied Dakota angrily. 'You know very well you'll lose it, just like you do everything else of mine you borrow!'

'I don't lose your stuff, you liar. If I borrow anything, I always put it back,' Chaney retorted, equally as angry. Chaney hated to be criticised.

'Oh yes, of course you do; and pigs may fly!' Dakota returned, determined that Chaney was not going to borrow her hat.

'Girls, girls – for goodness' sake, can we stop all this bickering?' Rachael interrupted. 'Your father will be back today, and there is work to be done before he is, not least the shopping. Dakota, please,' she continued, 'just let her borrow your hat for today. If she loses it, you can buy yourself another one out of her pocket money.'

'What!' squawked Chaney, now even more annoyed at the suggestion of losing her pocket money.

'Enough!' Rachael turned to glare at her younger daughter with her piercing blue eyes. She had a look, not used very often, that quelled rebellion in an instant. In that moment Chaney knew she was beaten and remained sensibly silent.

The car reached the main highway. Rachael waited for a gap in the traffic and then pulled on to the offside lane. Dakota kept looking out through the window on her left, anxious to catch her first glimpse of the sea. As always, the girls were feeling excited and elated as they looked forward to a cooling dip in the surf. The dogs, and Enzo in particular, could hardly contain their exuberant enthusiasm.

'Can't you stop him barking, Buggy?' Rachael said, with obvious irritation in her voice.

'Sorry, no. I've even tried giving him one of his doggy treats, but he's just turned his nose up at it!' Chaney replied, half-laughing.

Chapter Five
Supermarket Subterfuge

At last, the car was pulling up in the long car park which ran adjacent to South Beach. Enzo was on his feet with his wet nose pressed up against the window before the car had even drawn to a stop. He jumped down onto the hot tarmac as soon as Dakota had opened the back door. A more-reserved and stately Simba carefully padded down, using the tailgate as a step to aid his descent onto the tarmac below. The ageing dog was slightly arthritic and his movements on land were now slow, painful and laborious. He loved being in the water, however. His bodyweight supported, he felt free and almost youthful again. It was only in the water that he was able to give Enzo a run for his money. The old dog could still swim as fast as the now-dominant puppy. Simba was in his element in the sea and often had to be bribed out of the water with a tasty titbit. Only when Michael was with them would he come out on command.

They had been swimming in the sea with the dogs for almost twenty minutes when Chaney suddenly called out to her big sister. 'Dakota, why don't we have a Newfy race? I'll hold Enzo's tail, and you take Simba's.'

The girls swam out, until they were just able to touch the seabed standing on their tiptoes. Side by side and exactly level, they called the two dogs to them. Then, tails in hand, Chaney shouted, 'Go!' The two dogs set off immediately.

'Get me to the beach, Simba! Quick, boy, quick!' Dakota urged the old dog on with all her might. She laughed with delight as she trailed behind him, bouncing up and down in the surf. It was like being towed by a motorboat and extremely exciting.

Chaney, too, was calling out loudly. 'Come on, Enzo! Swim, boy, swim!'

The girls flew through the waves as the powerful dogs hauled them back to shore. Simba was more than up for the challenge, and a delighted Dakota, who had initially thought she had drawn the short straw in being allocated the senior

– and now sadly arthritic – dog, was the first to reach their towels back on the beach.

'Loser, loser!' she taunted laughingly, as a sullen-faced younger sister flopped down beside her. Just then, as if to add insult to injury, Enzo decided to shake himself off right next to her. A shower of doggy droplets of seawater and drool splattered all over her. The two girls screamed loudly and then burst out laughing simultaneously.

'Can you two dry off now, please? When you're ready, we'll go and get the shopping.'

As she spoke, Rachael picked up a small piece of flotsam which had been lying in the sand and threw it into the sea. Enzo immediately gave chase, bringing it back to her in seconds. This process was repeated several times over with ever-increasing gusto on Enzo's part. Simba watched the proceedings with marked disinterest and continued to swim up and down at a leisurely pace. Had Michael been throwing the stick, Simba too would have been doing his utmost to fetch it.

Simba was used to Michael being with them. All morning his eyes had been scouting the beach, looking for the return of his beloved master. Michael was the centre of the old dog's world, and recognising this devotion, Michael always did his best to try to satisfy Simba's needs. In particular, he had become very clever in attempting to give the ageing dog some success against his younger counterpart. Michael would throw a stone or stick for Enzo to fetch, and as the young dog charged into the surf to collect it, he would throw another for Simba. Unfortunately, the young dog was so quick, he inevitably returned, prize in jowl, in plenty of time to then set off and return with Simba's challenge before the old dog had even had time to move.

'Never mind, my faithful friend,' Michael would say tenderly, stroking Simba's head. 'You'll always be my best boy.' Simba would bark happily, as if he had understood.

Finally, Simba had been persuaded to leave the sea, and the car was on the move again. The supermarket was only minutes from the beach. Rachael found a parking space with ease. It was Dakota's turn to remain in the car with the dogs. Each week the two girls took it in turns to watch over them. All the windows were wound down, and a gentle, cool breeze drifted through the interior of the car.

'Well, come on then, Buggy. We need to get a move on,' Rachael said with a sense of urgency, as mother and daughter walked briskly towards the store.

Chaney selected one of the larger trolleys, checked the wheels were functioning properly, and followed her mother into the air-conditioned hypermarket. Chaney allowed herself a brief, satisfied smile as the trolley behaved itself beautifully, easily manoeuvring through a narrow gap between two giant stacks of boxes of chocolate finger biscuits. The right-hand pile diminished by one box as Chaney's trolley passed through.

Rachael headed immediately for the fruit and vegetable section of the store. It was Chaney herself who selected the first item of produce. She placed a large radicchio lettuce into the trolley, which completely concealed the finger biscuits. Rachael noted only the lettuce.

The shopping gathered pace. A selection of fruit and vegetables were systematically added to the trolley's ever-increasing load. A box of Fruit Loops, another of Coco Pops, and two bars of chocolate were hidden by large bags of root vegetables. A giant tub of bubble-gum ice cream and another of raspberry ripple were buried under a variety of fresh fruit. They progressed to the meat and fish counter.

'Don't forget the burgers and sausages for our camping trip,' Chaney eagerly reminded her mother.

'You're going to need some baps to put them in,' her mother replied. 'Leave the trolley with me and go over to the bread counter and get what you need,' she instructed. 'Not too many, mind. You're only out for one night, so six should be ample.'

In seconds Chaney had returned with a bag of twelve baps, and a freshly baked French stick. Chaney carefully placed the French stick to one side of the trolley, largely hidden by other produce.

Finally, the shop was complete and a now fully loaded and almost-overflowing trolley was wheeled to the checkout.

'Shall I start putting stuff through the till while you buy Dad's lottery ticket and newspaper?' Chaney enquired innocently.

'That's very thoughtful of you, dear,' her mother replied.

A number of items went through the till first, and by the time Rachael had returned, only legitimate purchases were being proffered to the cashier. It was then that Rachel picked up the stowaway French stick! As she lifted the bread out of the trolley, Chaney's expression changed, and her heart turned to stone.

Rachael glared at her youngest daughter and said, 'This, young lady, is coming out of your pocket money – and you can eat the rest for tea!'

Chaney grimaced, as the now French tube – rather than stick – was rung through the till. Chaney had eaten all the bread on the inside and only the outer layer remained. It was an empty tube of brown, dry, crisp crust. The yummy soft white centre had completely gone.

The cashier announced the final total, and much to Chaney's chagrin, she heard her mother gasp and say loudly:

'Goodness, I don't know where the money goes these days. Things seem to get dearer every week!'

Chaney silently wheeled the trolley and bags back to the car, whilst her mother settled the bill. Dakota watched her little sister approach. Chaney's body language spoke volumes. The drooping shoulders, bowed head and trailing, plodding feet were a good indication that all was not well. Chaney was soon overtaken by her mother.

'That child will be the death of me,' Rachael muttered angrily to Dakota as she helped to open the doors in readiness for the shopping bags to be loaded on board.

'Why, what's she done now?' Dakota asked.

'She's only added a French stick to the shopping without my permission, and then proceeded to eat its entire centre before we've even reached the checkout!' was the exasperated reply.

An unknowing Dakota responded with, 'Well, at least it was only a French stick,' trying to help decrease the weight of her sister's offence.

As the last shopping bag was loaded, the remaining crust of the French stick was waved angrily at Chaney. 'I meant what I said – this will be your tea tonight, young lady,' Rachael said sternly.

Looking at the pair of them, Dakota was reminded of a policeman waving his truncheon fiercely at an escaping felon.

If the two girls were quite different in looks, personality and temperament, one could equally say the same about their parents. Their mother, Rachael, could be rather draconian at times. She was a strict disciplinarian, level-headed and down to earth. Rachael was also loyal and very protective. If you were ever in a battle, you wanted Rachael on your side. Michael on the other hand was incredibly sanguine by nature, over-trustful if anything, liberal and charismatic. When Michael walked in a room, it lit up, and his smile could melt even the hardest of hearts.

The two sisters generally behaved well for either parent. They wanted Rachael's approbation to avoid her wrath, whereas with Michael they were always actively seeking his approval and desperate for his attention. It was a good parenting combination, and as children go, Dakota and Chaney were relatively well-behaved.

Thank goodness Dad's back, thought Chaney to herself as the car finally pulled away. *He'll soon talk Mum around – no worries.*

Chaney waited until the car sped past the sign saying 'Kookaburra Heights: next turning left'. As the car slowed to make the turn, Chaney, who had been devising a plan of action throughout the entire journey home, put on her sweetest voice.

'Mum, I'm really sorry about the bread. Would it help if I put the groceries away, feed the dogs and lay the table for tea? I know you must want to get ready for Dad coming home.'

Rachael eyed her daughter in her rear-view mirror. 'Hmm…you must think I was born yesterday. I know you, Chaney Meredith…you wouldn't offer to help unless you had a particularly good reason,' she said suspiciously.

'Not at all,' was the convincing reply. 'I'm simply trying to apologise.' Chaney looked innocently into her mother's hard, blue stare, whilst at the same time trying to appear remorseful and contrite. It was an Oscar-winning performance. Rachael's expression softened somewhat.

'Well, in fact, that would be immensely helpful. Yes, thank you. Make sure you stick to the routine now, with the dogs.'

'Don't worry, Mum. I know what to do. I've fed them loads of times,' Chaney replied confidently.

The car pulled into the garage. Rachael was secretly delighted that Chaney had volunteered to help. She wanted to look her best when Michael walked in through the front door.

'Right,' she said, 'if you're sure you can manage, I'll go and have my bath.'

'Buggy, do you want me to stay and help you with the groceries?' Dakota enquired as she unloaded the first two shopping bags.

'No, I'll be fine,' Chaney replied. 'You better get down to the paddock and check on the horses. I'll join you as soon as I've finished here. Remember, those horses haven't seen us since this morning!'

At last, all the groceries were in the kitchen. Chaney could hear the bathwater running as she stowed the chocolate biscuits and bars into her bedside cabinet.

The multi-coloured Fruit Loops and Coco Pops were hidden in a kitchen cabinet behind boxes of muesli and porridge oats. The bubblegum and raspberry ripple ice creams were placed out of sight in the back of the freezer, and twenty-two inches of bread stick crust were mashed and mingled with two bowls of dog food.

Chaney watched with sublime satisfaction as the dogs devoured all the food in their bowls; every morsel had been eaten. As the bowls were licked clean, Chaney smiled to herself, knowing that as fast as the food had disappeared, so too had all remaining evidence of the bread stick and her heinous crime. It took her less than five minutes to lay the table. That done, she made her way to the bathroom and knocked on the door.

'Dogs have been fed and the table is laid, Mum. I'm going down to the paddock to help Dakota with the horses.'

'Okay. I'll give you two a call as soon as your dad's back,' her mother replied cheerily.

Chapter Six
Equine Exploits

Chaney raced down to the stable block. She grabbed her tack and joined her sister in the paddock. Dakota had already saddled Galaxy and was busy putting him through his paces over some jumps. As paddocks go, this one was quite large and easily accommodated a number of vertical and oxer jumps, as well as two hog's backs and a wall jump. The white Andalusian was showing his class and clearing everything in style.

Star galloped over to Chaney as soon as she entered through the gate. The horse was clearly happy to see her, whinnying noisily but standing perfectly still as she fastened his saddle. She was up and mounted in no time.

If the girls were fond of their dogs, they idolised and adored their horses even more. The horses could not have been more loved or cared for. Both Dakota and Chaney took their responsibility over the welfare of the horses very seriously and attended to time-consuming daily chores with absolute devotion. They never complained even though they had to be up early every morning, normally at 5 am. Before leaving for school, they had groomed, checked, fed and turned the horses out into the paddock. The stables too would have been mucked out diligently, fresh straw put in and ample forage left in the paddock for Galaxy and Star to graze on throughout the day. The water troughs also had to be checked and freshly filled.

Happy that both horses had had sufficient exercise for the day, the girls walked them back to the stable block. Riding gear was safely stowed, and as the horses tucked into their evening feed, they received an even more thorough grooming from their respective mistresses. On extremely hot days, sometimes the horses would be hosed down in the yard before being tethered back in their stable. Tonight, however, everything had to be made ready for the extended training planned for the coming two days.

'Are you done, Buggy?' Dakota asked.

'Yes. I just need to put my riding hat and boots back in the trailer, ready for when we leave,' Chaney replied.

In the tack room, a long wide display board which ran the length of the back wall was pinned with dozens of multi-coloured rosettes. The board was divided into two. On the right was Dakota's area and to the left was Chaney's. Chaney's board had far fewer rosettes, but there were ten blue rosettes, indicating ten victories. Dakota's board was covered with red and white rosettes, but only six were blue. Dakota was by far the more successful of the two sisters in equine competition and had earned a huge number of second and third places, most particularly for dressage and show jumping. All the blue rosettes had been won for dressage. In show-jumping events Dakota had often gained a clear round, but somehow, she always managed to miss out on time. An opponent – just as had happened in the Royal Perth Show – would inevitably beat her, and often by the smallest of margins. The red rosette from that show was the latest addition to her display.

Dakota could also be guaranteed upon to plan how a course should be tackled. She calculated her route between the fences, counted the necessary strides required to each jump, worked out her line of approach and estimated her optimum speed carefully. It was unusual for Galaxy to get a fence down, but he was never quite quick enough to earn the overall victory. Dakota always accepted defeat gracefully.

Chaney, on the other hand, took defeat badly. Indeed, at such times her behaviour left much to be desired. Riding crop, hat, boots and jacket would be thrown in temper in every direction; and the dogs, especially, would take one look at Chaney's angry face and run for cover.

In show-jumping events, Chaney was like a bull in a china shop. She and Star would charge around the course at breakneck speed. Their performance at the Royal Perth Show was nothing if not typical, as was her reaction to losing. Indeed, it was all or nothing where Chaney was concerned. It either went incredibly well and she achieved a clear round and first place with a remarkably fast time, or she finished near the bottom of the field and with almost every fence down. Dressage, an event which requires patience, was not her forte and not a single dressage rosette was displayed on her board. Speed, however, was a recognised strength. Chaney had won a great many flat races, and Star was fabulously quick and brave.

As the girls walked back to the house, they could see a familiar car parked on the driveway.

'Good. Dad is back,' Chaney commented happily. 'I hope he's got tea ready – I'm starving.'

He had, and they all ate hungrily.

'Come on, Buggy, finish up that broccoli,' said Michael at the end of the meal. 'We need to clear the table and go over the maps again. I want to make absolutely sure that the pair of you can work out grid references exactly – we don't want you getting lost.'

Rachael and Dakota began clearing the plates away. Michael went to gather up the maps which were kept in his office, and Simba followed. Chaney quickly slipped Enzo a green vegetable under the table. The broccoli was wolfed down, unseen, in an instant by the young dog. The old dog, Simba, would take forever to chew his food and swallow it down. Consequently, Chaney hardly ever used him to help her empty her plate of unwanted food. She knew if she did, it was only a matter of time before she was caught out. Giving Simba Brussels sprouts was a last resort and done only because it appeared that Enzo hated this vegetable as much as she did. Broccoli, however, was gratefully accepted, and Chaney eagerly carried her now-empty plate to the kitchen sink.

'There you go, Mum,' she said proudly, handing her plate over.

'Good girl,' her mother replied warmly.

Michael returned with all the maps, which were duly laid out on the table. The maps were studied for some considerable time. The two girls were tested on providing accurate grid references and, much to their relief, passed with flying colours. Mobile phones were charged and emergency numbers checked. First aid kits, water bottles and food bags were also filled and checked.

When Michael was happy that his two daughters were as well prepared as possible for their camping trip, they were escorted to the campervan.

'Are you sure everything you need is in the trailer, ready to go?' he asked.

'Yes!' was the unanimous reply.

'Chaney are you sure?' he repeated.

'Yes, I'm sure,' she answered, sounding slightly vexed. 'Why is it you're asking me for a second time? I notice you didn't ask Dakota!'

'Oh, perhaps I was remembering the Fremantle show last month,' he replied sarcastically, 'when a certain person found she hadn't got her riding hat or boots five minutes before the dressage event in which she was supposed to be competing!'

Chaney remained silent, gritting her teeth again.

Michael approached his daughters and kissed them both on their foreheads. 'I love you guys,' he said tenderly.

'Love you too,' was the simultaneous reply, as Chaney's hand reached out for his to show that everything had been forgiven.

'Straight to sleep now,' he instructed, closing the campervan door. 'We all have an exceedingly early start and a long day ahead of us tomorrow. Your mother and I will set off as soon as we are ready.'

He returned to his wife, trying to conceal his tiredness. He stifled a yawn as he re-entered the lounge. In truth, he was dreading the long drive which lay ahead of him.

'Are you sure they'll be alright on this camping trip?' Rachael asked in a worried tone.

'We can't wrap them up in cotton wool all their lives. And think about it; in less than two weeks they will be taking part in an endurance event and out at night on their own. What happens if one of the horses goes lame? They need to know how to cope should they be forced to bed down for the night,' Michael replied, with absolute conviction.

'But I can't help worrying. What about snakes or scorpions? What if there are poisonous spiders in the grass, or what if wild dogs invade their camp?' Rachael continued anxiously.

Michael laughed. 'Believe me,' he said jokingly, 'with Star and Galaxy stomping around all over the place, any and every bush creature in the vicinity of their campsite will have moved at least half a mile away within minutes. And if a pack of hungry, starving dingoes were to attack or try to steal Chaney's sausages or worse still – heaven forbid – her marshmallows, she will have frightened them off before you can say 'Ned Kelly'! She's as formidable as her mother when challenged…and eventually, I think, will be equally as beautiful.'

'Flatterer,' Rachael replied, half-smiling, half-frowning.

'Come on,' said Michael, 'we need to get to bed ourselves. It's going to be a monumental night and an equally demanding day tomorrow, and I for one need at least a couple of hours sleep before I begin the drive.'

Chapter Seven
Strange Meeting in the Bush

The two riders and their horses galloped neck and neck across the open grassland. Their destination was a rocky outcrop on the horizon, which was crowned with a small but distinctive cluster of boab trees.

'Come on, Star, go boy!' cried Chaney, desperate to beat her older sister. The black Arabian rose to the challenge, and with every stride pulled further and further away. As Chaney reined Star in beneath the swollen trunks of the boab trees, Galaxy, her sister's horse, was a good two lengths behind.

'Okay, you win.' Dakota laughed.

It was early morning, and the air was crisp, cool and almost silent. As they rested their horses, they could hear mole crickets calling from the ground as the bush showed signs of waking. Just then, a chorus of kookaburras broke the morning stillness. The familiar sound made them both relax despite their new and foreign surroundings. Looking up into the strangely twisted branches of the boab trees, Chaney was suddenly startled by a flock of budgerigars taking flight; an array of bright green, yellow and blue feathers soared upwards and away.

'Walk on,' said Dakota to Galaxy, and the two horses moved off again with the girls talking happily together. For the rest of the morning, they worked the horses minimally, except when natural obstacles occurred which they could use for jumping practice.

Dakota and Chaney, with their horses Galaxy and Black Star, were now right in the middle of training. For the very first time, the two girls had decided to enter Australia's legendary Endurance Riding Championship. This prestigious event, covering over 160 kilometres of wild bushland, drew riders from all over the world, many of whom had international standing.

It was an exciting prospect, and the girls' and their family were aware of the importance of the race. After all, endurance riding is a very Australian sport, reflecting the history of the nation; in particular, that of the bushmen and stockmen who had ridden their tough horses over huge distances in those early days when Australia was first discovered. Many had perished in the attempt to harness vast areas of barren wilderness to agriculture. The girls, of course, would not have to endure such hardships as faced by those early pioneers. Indeed, they would have the luxury of following carefully marked trails and would be well-supplied and equipped.

Nevertheless, to win, Star and Galaxy would have to travel at speed over difficult terrain. Now that the school holidays had arrived, they had been able to come to one of the largest National parks of Western Australia. They had journeyed to the famous and beautiful Karijini Park, where they could test their riding skills on unknown trails and their navigational skills in unfamiliar territory. The two horses had taken to this new discipline like ducks to water.

'No wonder they call this the sunburnt country,' said Dakota looking out across the vast plains which stretched for mile upon mile in every direction. She noticed a troop of kangaroos hiding in the dappled shade of a copse of eucalyptus trees and then, just beyond, another group of trees growing in the shape of a perfect circle. She pointed the trees out to Chaney.

'If you look,' she said, 'you'll see the grass following the tree-line is very green. I wouldn't be surprised if there wasn't a secret watering hole there or maybe even an underground stream. Time for another race, I think, and then we'll stop for lunch.'

The horses galloped at full pelt, but this time it was Galaxy who reached the circle of trees and the natural water-jump first. An unexpected and altogether welcome narrow band of water encircled a wonderful oasis: a babbling brook just a couple of feet wide but providing delicious, cool, clear drinking water. Dakota saw the stream well in time and cleared it with ease. Chaney and Star galloped through causing great clouds of spray to shoot up into the air, soaking them both.

'That was refreshing,' said Chaney licking the drips from her face.

They now found themselves in the middle of a clearing which was exactly circular in shape, and around its boundary, tall full-grown jacaranda trees displayed their brilliant purple blossoms. Somehow the air seemed cooler, even though the sun remained directly overhead. The sky above was bright blue, and a soft breeze caressed the lush grasses of the forest floor, making Chaney think of the sea. Waves of green swayed to and fro in the sunlight.

'How beautiful,' Chaney whispered to Star, who nodded his head in agreement. She pulled gently at his reins, bringing him to a stop, and dismounted. Dakota and Galaxy followed suit.

'Time for lunch, I think,' Dakota said to Galaxy. Reaching into her saddlebag, she pulled out a large red juicy apple for him and another for herself. The horses were left untethered and began to graze on the tender sweet grasses of the forest floor, whilst the two girls sat down on a fallen tree stump to eat the remainder of their lunch.

Suddenly, a strangely high-pitched voice said to them, 'Oh please, can you help us?'

The two girls jumped with surprise; they had thought they were quite alone and miles from civilisation. Dakota looked around but could see no one.

'Did you hear someone speak?' she asked Chaney.

'I did,' Chaney replied, 'and so did Star, by the look of him.' She had noticed that he, too, had his ears pricked. Star neighed in response and tossed his head back and forth excitedly.

'Please can you help?' said the squeaky voice again and looking at her feet Chaney was surprised to see a small brown mouse.

I must be seeing things, thought Chaney to herself. *Mice can't speak.*

Star, however, had also seen the little mouse and had lowered his head right down to the ground to say hello. Chaney smiled as she watched Star neighing softly to his new friend, as if afraid he might frighten the tiny creature away.

The mouse looked up at Chaney and said, 'Yes, it is me speaking, and I really do need your help.' Then he called out, much louder, 'Alright, everyone, it's safe to come out!'

To Dakota's and Chaney's surprise a whole host of woodland creatures began to assemble at their feet, including a very elderly looking albino wallaby, with silver ears and long white whiskers.

'Hello,' said the wallaby in a voice quite different to the high-pitched squeak of the mouse. Chaney listened carefully to his words as he began to address the girls in a deep, well-spoken, husky tone, which to her sounded incredibly old and wise. 'My name is Fossett, and we really do need help.' Fossett assured the two girls that he and his friends meant them no harm, and as they both slowly regained their composure and sat back down on the fallen tree stump, he began to tell them an amazing tale about an evil, jealous fairy called Alba who had misused her magic powers to try to destroy another fairy called Aislinn. Alba had conjured one of the deadliest and powerful of spells known to fairy kind. She had almost succeeded in her wicked endeavour, and Aislinn's very life was now hanging by a thread.

Chapter Eight
A Race Against Time

'You must understand,' the wallaby continued, 'we are short on time. Aislinn has been poisoned, and we know of only one person who can cure her. She needs the medicine of the Koori Shaman. He is the most powerful of the Dreamers, the chosen one,' Fossett explained. 'He has met with the Sky God, who has favoured him with magical powers beyond belief. The Shaman lives in a cave just below the summit of a mountain called Bluff Knoll. It will be a race against time to bring Aislinn to him. She gets weaker by the minute, and the royal physicians have estimated she has less than forty-eight hours to live.'

'What Fossett has said is true.' Chaney and Dakota were suddenly aware of a fairy hovering at eye level just between them and looking and speaking first to one and then the other.

'My name is Ariel, and I am king of this kingdom. Sadly, even my magic cannot help Aislinn, and all our hopes therefore lie with you. Can you help us?' he repeated.

The two sisters could see how sad the old man looked. He was dressed all in green, had an amazingly long white beard, a hook nose, and grey hair spilling from under a golden crown which sparkled in the sunlight. His face, however, looked pale and wan, and his eyes conveyed an expression of worry and grief. The girls could hear the whirring sound of his bright silver wings as he hovered in front of them.

'Fossett, tell Prince Kyle that help has miraculously come to hand. Go straight to the infirmary and have him bring Aislinn here immediately. Quick now, time is of the essence,' commanded the king.

The old wallaby bounded away at top speed to carry out King Ariel's bidding. Dakota frowned as she watched the wallaby disappear into the bush. They had not yet agreed to help, although the old king appeared to take it for granted.

We cannot do this, she thought to herself. *It is far too dangerous. What's even worse is that Mum and Dad will be expecting us at the rendezvous point tomorrow.*

She looked across at her younger sister. Chaney was on her knees on the ground, making friends with all the woodland creatures, and from the happy expression on her face, it was clear to Dakota that she was oblivious to the peril of their situation.

As she watched her sister, another fairy joined them, only this time it was a much younger man, dressed in a blue jacket with matching knee-length leggings. His wings were also silver, but they appeared to glow stronger still in the afternoon sunshine and looked more powerful than those of the old king. The wings created a much louder whirring sound, causing Chaney to look up immediately. She stood to greet him.

Chaney was fascinated with the wings of the fairies, which were very distinctive. Each fairy had a double pair of wings that were almost transparent, apart from the unusual yet beautiful tracery which gave them their colour. They looked nothing like the fairy wings Chaney had seen illustrated in her storybooks at home. She tried to think what the wings reminded her of. An idea almost formed in her mind and then was lost as the young man spoke.

'I cannot believe my own eyes, that it is really you,' he said, in a voice filled with emotion. 'This is more, much more than I could have hoped for. That you and your wonderful horses should be here to help us at this dreadful time is beyond my wildest dream. Now at last, I have some hope. I have watched you train your horses and ride in many competitions, as has Aislinn. I believe you have the ability and skill to complete the difficult journey which must lie ahead. If we work together, I am sure we can succeed in this mission. With such horses as these, how could we possibly fail?' he said, looking with unadulterated admiration at both Star and Galaxy.

Dakota remained thoughtfully silent, whilst Chaney waited for her sister to speak. As the awkward silence continued, Prince Kyle flew to kneel at the feet of the two girls, and looking up into their faces, he was suddenly aware of their unease. He was also struck by the steel in the blue eyes – for written in Dakota's expression was a clear reluctance to help.

'I beg you…please, please will you help us? You are Aislinn's only hope, and we really must get going soon. She is so terribly ill and much weakened. I've watched her condition deteriorate with every passing day. Please help us, for even at this very minute, I fear for her life.'

Kyle spoke with such urgency in his voice that Chaney could not help but be moved by his impassioned plea. She noticed how distraught and upset he sounded, and she looked across at her sister with her brown eyes appealing for mercy and, by now, welling with tears. Dakota, however, avoided Chaney's gaze and maintained her own silence.

Kyle continued to plead, 'We must leave now, I beg you, or it will be too late to help my beautiful Aislinn. It will take many hours to reach the Shaman and that is assuming we can locate him quickly. They say the cave is well hidden. Please can we leave now?'

'But why do you need our help?' asked Chaney, finally finding her voice. 'Why don't you fly there yourselves and take the sick fairy with you?'

'If only we could,' replied King Ariel, with more than a tinge of sadness in his voice. 'But what you must understand is that our magical powers begin to fade immediately if we leave the sanctuary of the fairy kingdom. Once outside its borders, our fairy powers diminish rapidly, even our ability to fly. Any fairy that is brave enough to even attempt this task alone could not and would not be able to fly even half the distance needed to reach Bluff Knoll. Two have already tried and are now recovering in our infirmary. This is my son, Prince Kyle,' he said, gesturing towards the fairy dressed in blue, 'and both those fairies would have perished, had not Prince Kyle managed to bring them back.'

'But Bluff Knoll is part of the Stirling Mountain Range and is such a long way away,' said Dakota. 'Why, it would take us all of two days to reach it, unless we ride through the night.'

'Let us hope you will be in time,' said King Ariel, 'for without the help of the Koori Shaman, Aislinn will soon be lost to us forever. You have also anticipated correctly and will undoubtedly need to ride through the night as well as in the day, which is why my son Prince Kyle will accompany you. He will use his magic to light your way through the darkness and his powers to protect you when he can. Be warned; his powers will fade, and when they do, he will need time to recover. With rest, his powers can be replenished, but as he regains his strength, he will be relying on you to protect him. At such times he will be powerless to defend either himself or you. Now, if you are prepared to help, you must leave at once. Gilpin will also come to help in the search to find the Shaman. He has visited his cave once before.'

As he spoke these words, the little mouse who had spoken to Chaney right at the beginning of this strange meeting in the forest crept forward.

'Once we reach the summit, we must look for a path of blue wreath flowers. The cave is well hidden, but the flowers will guide us to the entrance. Aborigines call these flowers the floor of the sky. You'll understand why when you see them,' Gilpin said with feeling.

'We'd love to help you and help Aislinn, of course,' said Dakota, 'but it's our parents, you see. If we should fail to make the rendezvous with them at the arranged time, they'll be worried sick.'

'Don't forget they're not expecting us back until tomorrow,' Chaney reminded her.

'That's all very well,' Dakota continued, 'but it would take a miracle to get us to Bluff Knoll and back in time, even assuming we can find the Shaman and that he has sufficient time to work his healing magic. It's impossible, Chaney…we'd never do it.'

'We've got the mobiles,' insisted Chaney, who was determined to help the fairies if she could. 'If we find we can't make the deadline, we can text them and delay it.'

'Mum would be furious. You know how long it has taken Dad to persuade her to let us come in the first place!' Dakota spoke with real trepidation in her voice.

'I know,' replied Chaney, 'but this is a matter of life and death. We must help them, Dakota. We just must. Could you ever forgive yourself if the fairy died and we hadn't even tried to save her?'

'Please help,' King Ariel pleaded. 'We know how much we are asking of you, but you do need to decide, and quickly. Time is fast running out for Aislinn!'

Dakota hesitated before announcing reluctantly, 'Okay, we'll do it. We need to jettison anything we don't need, mind. The less weight the horses have to carry, the better.'

Grooming and cooking utensils and all the foodstuffs which required cooking were left on the ground, as were both their swags (a type of waterproof bedroll). Water bottles, however, were refilled to the full.

'What about these?' asked Chaney, holding up a first-aid bag and a long piece of rope which had been attached to the pommel of her saddle.

Dakota thought for a moment, and then replied, 'Better keep those with us. We might need them.'

The two girls nodded at each other, and taking hold of their horses' reins, they immediately mounted up. Star and Galaxy had clearly understood what had been said, for they were each champing at the bit and eager to be off.

King Ariel signalled to two fairies hovering in the air a little way off. They flew towards Chaney, bearing a stretcher shaped almost like a four-poster bed on which a tiny golden-haired fairy lay. The fairy looked deathly pale. Prince Kyle alighted upon Star's dark mane and helped Chaney to gently lower the stretcher bed into her saddle bag.

'Kyle are you sure you do not want us to come with you?' said one of the fairies bearing the stretcher.

'No, Darius. You and Sebastian have risked your lives once already, trying to help Aislinn. And if truth be known, neither of you are yet fully recovered! I was surprised when the nurses agreed to let you carry Aislinn's stretcher here, never mind joining me on a journey going way beyond the safety of the kingdom; a journey, I may add, which is bound to be fraught with all kinds of dangers.'

'But Kyle, Gilpin has no magic powers,' said the other fairy. 'He cannot help you as we can.'

'Sebastian,' replied Kyle, 'Gilpin has the sharpest ears in the kingdom and is the bravest creature I know.'

Kyle reached out and took the hands of the two fairies that had carried Aislinn's stretcher to Chaney. He spoke quietly to them. 'Darius, look after my mother; you know how anxious she will be. And Sebastian, stay close to my father. He listens to your advice and will appreciate your counsel. He may not show it, but he will be just as worried as my mother.'

The two fairies nodded and watched sadly as Kyle prepared to depart.

Dakota held out her hand for Gilpin to jump onto. He sprang into the air and landed nimbly in her palm. She gently stowed the little mouse into the breast pocket of her jacket. 'You'll be safe in there, but hold on tight,' she said kindly. Now they were ready to go.

'Good luck, and may God be with you, I pray,' said King Ariel, noticing with affection that Gilpin's head was peering out of Dakota's top pocket and that his bright eyes, sparkling in the sunlight, had a look of real determination about them.

Small you may be, he thought to himself, *and of lowly birth, a mere woodland creature – but with the courage of a gladiator. Kyle has chosen his companion wisely.*

The two horses reared up on their hind legs, pawing at the air with their forefeet as if waving goodbye to the gathered throng of fairies. Then just as suddenly, spurred on by their riders, they were off. As Star and Galaxy galloped across the clearing, Dakota and Chaney turned and bade a hasty farewell to the anxious and forlorn party standing watching their departure and hoping for their safe and speedy return.

For mile after relentless mile, the horses galloped on across the dry, arid bushland. A startled pack of dingoes barked noisily at their passing. A family of emus, woken from their brief slumber, were scattered, long-legged and feathers fluttering, back into the bush. The joey of a koala scrambled back into his pouch for safety, as pounding hooves thundered underneath the branches of the eucalyptus tree in which his mother had been feeding. The white Andalusian, the black Arabian and their riders continued on regardless, for there was but one thought in all their minds – to save Aislinn. Nothing else mattered.

On and on the horses raced across the wild outback. Hour after hour they galloped at full pace, stopping only briefly to take on water. As the afternoon drew to a close, Star was leading, with Galaxy just a few feet behind. Chaney could see the mountain range a long way off in the distance and strained her eyes ahead to ensure a safe path as they journeyed ever nearer to their target. It was important to make sure the horses had safe footing; one bad fall now and their mission might fail. As evening began to close in, the two sisters exchanged positions. Dakota now had the responsibility of finding their route, and her vivid blue eyes scouted ahead anxiously. As they rode on, Kyle and Gilpin explained in full to their riders how Aislinn had been poisoned, and as each sister listened to the tale, they became more and more convinced that they had done the right thing in agreeing to help, regardless of what dangers lay ahead.

Chapter Nine
The Black Moon Fairy

Gilpin began by telling Dakota that Alba and Aislinn had had only one thing in common: they had been born around the same time. Alba was the elder by just three days and had been born under unfortunate circumstances. She had, in fact, been born during a lunar eclipse, and at the time the Ancients (the oldest of the fairy folk) had been genuinely concerned and alarmed. Superstition and folklore would have it that any fairy child born under a black moon would be more likely to follow the dark way, and not the way of light. Black moon fairies often used their powers for wicked and selfish purposes, and almost all came to a bad end. The Ancients said prayers at the time of Alba's birth, hoping to prevent this superstition from becoming true. In addition, by royal command, garlands of red and green kangaroo paw and orange flowering banksias were hung on every house to ward off evil spirits.

Three days later and under a beautiful blue sky with the sun shining high in the heavens, Aislinn was born. Just as she entered the world, the King Jacaranda tree in the Fairy Glen had undergone its transformation: the blackened twisted boughs had straightened and turned gold, pointing like church spires up into the heavens. The Ancients had been overjoyed, and in contrast to Alba's birth, they had forecast that Aislinn would be a special fairy, indeed, and full of goodness.

Superstition and myth proved to be true, and by the time Alba and Aislinn had reached their sixth birthdays, their characters were clear. Alba was as saturnine as Aislinn was scintillating. She was also mean, spiteful and ill-tempered. She loved to tease and could not be trusted to be left with younger children, whom she would inevitably bully. Worst of all, Alba had indeed developed a liking for the Black Arts. She would study old recipes and spells which harmed rather than helped people. If you needed a spell to make someone stammer, grow a wart or become sick, Alba would have all the answers.

But the fairy folk themselves were reluctant to reprimand her, and anyone brave enough to criticise her soon found they were experiencing some ill fate or another. Perhaps their cow would go dry for weeks and produce no milk, or their hens would cease to lay, or they might develop a painful itchy rash – or at worst, go deaf or blind for months. The older Alba got, the more awful her retribution became, and by the time she reached her eighteenth birthday, she was a law unto herself and out of control. Poor Alba could probably number her friends on one finger.

In contrast, Aislinn was all a fairy should be: kind, considerate, caring and unbelievably beautiful. She used her magic in good ways, helping to heal ailments, and she studied hard to learn all the spells that might benefit others. She was an expert on the healing properties of herbs. She was also one of the few fairies who would even talk to Alba, and constantly tried to make Alba see the error of her ways whenever she behaved badly and most especially when she acted out of malice. She never suspected that because of her action, Alba had often cast a wicked spell on her – even though whenever she reprimanded Alba, it usually resulted in Aislinn feeling under the weather for days on end or finding a treasured possession broken or missing.

Only one fairy was safe from Alba's evildoings, and that fairy was Prince Kyle. Prince Kyle was three years older than Alba and Aislinn; and that very year, at the age of twenty-one, he was to announce whom he would choose to become his new bride. This would be done on midsummer night's eve at the fairy banquet, held every year in the beautiful circle of jacaranda trees which was known as the Glen.

On this special night, the jacaranda trees that encircled the Glen would come to life. Their dark and twisted boughs would straighten, turn gold in colour and point to the stars in the universe, transforming the Glen into a giant cathedral. Their purple blooms would double in size and shed a wonderful lavender glow for miles around, lighting the darkness. All the fairy folk would gather in honour of the King and Queen. The royal couple would sit on their golden thrones, surrounded by their royal household. There would be feasting, dancing and music, with celebrations lasting long into the night.

'The trouble was', said Gilpin, 'that Alba was determined to be Prince Kyle's choice. In her own way, I actually think she genuinely loved him.' Dakota listened intently as he went on with his tale. 'But whatever her true feelings were, she would never have been able to control her malicious nature. In fact, she could be rather frightening. I've never met a person who could take offence so easily. The slightest thing could upset her and spark a terrible outburst of temper. At such times she was like a ship without captain or rudder and would take revenge on anyone or anything which crossed her path. She cast her spiteful spells on me on more than one occasion, and for no good reason.'

'Really?' said Dakota with real concern for Gilpin's welfare. 'Why, what happened?'

'There are too many incidents to go into all the details,' Gilpin replied, 'but perhaps her last effort was the most painful. I made the mistake of interfering, of rebuking her when she was chastising Fossett for accidentally bumping into her. She told me off for sticking my nose in where it wasn't wanted. I was petrified when she took out her wand and held it above me. I wanted to run away, but somehow my legs just wouldn't work. I grew a large boil – right here,' he said in a shaky voice, whilst at the same time rubbing his nose. 'The boil was so big that I could hardly see over the top of it. My nose is especially sensitive, you know. I was in such agony! Aislinn got me through the worst days with some of her strongest analgesic potions and did her best to help, even to the point of summoning Alba to my home and begging her to undo the spell. When Alba finally came, I remember looking at her mouth. She had the darkest, cruellest lips, and I was convinced that they almost curved in a smile when she looked upon my suffering. Of course, she told Aislinn she would try to end the enchantment as soon as possible, but for days after her visit the pain grew worse, and the boil got even bigger. I've always suspected she did the exact opposite and prolonged the spell instead.'

'Oh, Gilpin, you poor thing! How horrible!' Dakota exclaimed, in a stunned tone of voice.

Gilpin was quiet for a moment, and then continued with his story.

'What Alba really wanted was the inevitable royal power she would receive as Kyle's bride. It does not bear thinking about. Goodness only knows what wicked acts she might have carried out. Fossett is convinced she had already determined how she would inflict her revenge on fairies that had avoided or ignored her. She would have been the new Queen and mistress of all.'

Gilpin's account of events revealed to Dakota that Alba had attempted to flirt with Prince Kyle for years. She had sought his attention at every opportunity. She had curtsied and smiled at him every time she caught his eye, pretended to be as nice as pie whenever she was in his presence, and had complimented him at every opportunity. Alba had also not been averse to using the odd love potion or two. Unfortunately, on each occasion when she had tried to slip a potion into his drink, it had backfired. On one occasion, when the potion had been intended to make him fall in love with the next object that he set his eyes on – with Alba, of course, standing right in front of him – he had taken a sip from his goblet. But he then sneezed…and as he brought his hand to his mouth, it was his own hand that he saw first! He had then spent weeks telling everyone how lovely his right hand was and had sat for hours gazing admiringly at it.

'Why, I even saw him kissing it!' Gilpin exclaimed, pulling an odd face. 'No wonder Alba was more pleased than anyone when the spell finally wore off!'

Gilpin then centred his tale of events on Aislinn. He wanted Dakota to realise just how important Aislinn was to all of them – not least, Prince Kyle. Dakota soon understood that Aislinn, however, had genuinely caught Prince Kyle's eye; not just because she was so beautiful but also because of her character. Kyle had seen how much she helped others, how clever she was with her healing potions, and that she was always ready to lend a helping hand even to the smallest creature.

Kyle also knew that Aislinn was one of the very few brave enough to correct Alba when she most needed it. Prince Kyle felt a real admiration based on a true friendship with Aislinn. He always felt happy in her company and found that he could talk easily to her. He was often surprised at just how much they shared similar beliefs and ideals. Aislinn always seemed to know what he was thinking, even before he had spoken. He respected and trusted her judgement and sensed that her feelings towards him were a mirror of his own for her. Theirs would indeed be a match made in heaven. They were deeply in love and, in time, would make a wonderful king and queen.

Chapter Ten
Green Eyed Monster

As it began to get dark, both Star and Galaxy had to slow down. It was becoming increasingly difficult to choose a safe path in the fading light. Chaney moved Star forward to take the lead once more, with Kyle – who had left Aislinn's side for the first time that day – holding his fairy wand high in the air to light their way.

As he did so, Kyle began to tell Chaney that he had made a terrible mistake in relating to his best friends that he was going to ask Aislinn to be his bride, but stupidly, within earshot of Alba. Kyle explained that he and his friends had been in the library of the Royal Palace looking at spells to help prevent bushfires from spreading, and Alba had also been reading a book at a desk quite close to where they had been working. As Kyle had confessed his intention of asking Aislinn for her hand in marriage, he remembered hearing Alba slam together the covers of the book she had been reading. Alarmed he had watched her storm across the library floor towards the forbidden Gemini section. He had been about to admonish her on selecting a book which the Ancients had preserved for use, but which they had insisted needed a special permit to be read.

'Gemini books contain spells that have two uses,' explained Kyle. 'These spells were all made up by ancient alchemists who designed them with only good intentions in mind; but it was later discovered that each spell had a second, and sometimes very sinister, usage. This was why they were called Gemini spells. All had a twin use, and all required a special permit to be read. I knew Alba couldn't possibly have had a permit to read any of those books because the reading is always supervised by one of the elders and you have to have a bona fide, crystal clear and proven-beyond-doubt reason to look at them,' Kyle said, in a serious tone.

'I was going to tell her to put the book back, but then I noticed how angry she looked and thought better of it. There was sheer, unadulterated hatred in Alba's eyes, and I was very aware that she kept glancing across at me with an evil glare that could have killed me on the spot. Can you blame me for deciding to leave her to her own devices? What a mistake that was!' Kyle said, without waiting for Chaney's reply. 'And if that isn't the understatement of the decade, I don't know what is!'

It had been in that Gemini book that Alba had found the spell she needed. It was the answer to her prayers; a most wicked spell which would get rid of Aislinn forever. It had taken Alba almost four weeks to collect all the ingredients she had needed, and with the potion made, she had awaited Aislinn's return home, ready to pounce and cast her wicked spell on her innocent victim. Alba had really believed that with Aislinn gone, she might once again stand a chance at winning Kyle's heart.

Since that day in the library, however, Prince Kyle had been afraid for Aislinn's safety. Alba had left the prohibited Gemini book open on the desk at which she had been sitting. Kyle had watched her reading the book intently and observed her making careful notes from its pages. After she had left, he had gone over to close the book and return it to its proper place. He had been horrified to see the evil spell which lay before him.

'It was the Pestilence spell, you see,' he said. 'Probably the most dangerous spell in the entire Gemini group to make and use.'

Chaney listened intently as Kyle's account of events explained how the spell had first come about. It had been made originally to prevent destructive plagues from attacking the agricultural land on which humankind depended. One of its main ingredients was the venom of funnel-web spiders. Chaney was made to understand that many spiders depend on insects for their food, which is why humans also use the venom in their insecticides. But it wasn't just the funnel-web spider venom that Alba needed. Much to Chaney's horror, Kyle then described the page that Alba had been reading.

GEMINI BOOK VOLUME 13
PESTILENCE/VANISHING SPELL

Ingredients:
20 ml of Crocodile blood (must be taken under a full moon)

3 drops of Taipan snake venom (must be milked at midnight)
3 drops each of funnel-web, red-back and white-tail spiders' venom
(taken from live specimens)
2 crushed bulldog ants
The head of a female March fly
A scorpion tail
A water leech (must be fully swollen from a blood feed)
The left eye of a Cane toad
2 centimetres of Box jellyfish tentacle
6 bristles from a gum-leaf skeletoniser caterpillar
7 fairy tears

Advice and Utensils
Solid silver mixing bowl (imperative airtight lid)
Alchemist's own wand for mixing, waxed with platypus oil (optional,
but aids protection)
Glass suction tube
Regulated environment during conjuring elements due to extreme danger
Qualified alchemists only!

'Fossett and I have been doing some considerable research about the pestilence spell since this whole sorry affair began. We discovered that it was first used to destroy a plague of locusts in ancient Egypt,' Kyle went on. 'Once it has been conjured, the spell produces a poisonous sphere. On that occasion the sphere was taken up into the air, some 1,000 feet above the locust plague. No one knows how, but somehow the sphere was able to lock into the movement of the locusts. It's been proven that once locked-in, the sphere will follow the movement of its target below. Then suddenly, as the spell triggers, the sphere hurtles down to earth towards its prey – and at exactly the right height to maximise its effect and cover the whole swarm, it explodes, sending its lethal poison over the entire locust population. Not one locust will survive. The spell has one distinct bonus: it leaves no debris,' Kyle explained. 'Nothing remains except a clean and virgin landscape. Can you imagine the mess if you were left with the dead bodies of millions of locusts to clear up?'

Chaney shook her head. 'I don't know much about locusts,' she replied innocently.

Kyle rose to the challenge, pleased to be able to show off his superior knowledge. 'Well,' he continued, 'did you know that a plague of locusts can consume vast areas of vegetation in a matter of days? They devour everything in their path, including any crops that farmers have been growing. You can understand how devastating this can be for humans living in those areas affected. The locusts cause widespread famine and starvation. Some Aboriginal tribes would have been wiped out in several regions over time, without our help. The spell has been most used in Egypt and was originally developed by the Nile fairies hundreds and hundreds of years ago,' Kyle concluded.

Chaney found herself shaking with fear at the thought of the spell, not least at its horrid ingredients. 'Alba must really have been eaten up with jealousy and hatred of Aislinn to have attempted such a dangerous piece of black magic.'

Kyle nodded, adding, 'And she was also wicked enough to stop at nothing to be rid of her rival, and clever enough to carry it out.' Kyle could not have known how close he was to the truth, and yet how far he was from grasping the dangers and trials that Alba had faced in her efforts to destroy Aislinn.

Chapter Eleven
Alba the Huntress

Once Alba had decided on her scheme, she had been meticulous in her planning and preparation. She couldn't risk gathering any of her ingredients inside the fairy kingdom for fear of being discovered. Her hunting would have to be done outside its boundaries. She rested throughout the day to keep her magic powers at maximum, but each night, as darkness fell, she would leave the relative safety of the kingdom and begin the hunt. Slowly but surely, she began ticking off her list, as one by one she managed to assemble each specific ingredient in the right order, the right amount and – equally important – the right manner.

She waited for the next full moon to get her crocodile blood. It was surprisingly easy. She found a large freshwater crocodile which had just devoured most of a full-grown water buffalo.

You haven't left much hidden for later in that underwater secret store of yours, she thought to herself, as she noted with disinterest the distended, bloated belly. The crocodile was so fat and full that it did not even flinch as she punctured its thick, scaly skin with her hypodermic needle and extracted the exact amount of blood she needed.

Alba found a taipan snake with equal ease, as if the fates were with her; she certainly saw it as a good omen. She had used a 'seeking' spell to illuminate her wand; and seconds after leaving the fairy kingdom, her wand had lit up, its light growing in intensity as she flew towards her precious snake. The wand was placed handle down in the ground immediately in front of the snake, its magical light radiating on and off with a hypnotic pulse. The taipan snake was mesmerised in minutes, and Alba easily milked it of its three drops of venom as the midnight hour arrived.

Funnel-web, red-back and white-tailed spider venom were taken on the same night, and Alba was elated by her success thus far. Everything was going to plan, and Alba's only concern were the seven fairy tears that she needed. *I shall have to choose an unloved child*, she thought, *with little parental protection.*

Over the next few nights, she found her bulldog ants, her female March fly and her scorpion, amputating the required parts, as necessary. The water leech was more difficult. Timing was of the essence – she had to catch one immediately after it dropped off its meal, fully bloated with its victim's blood. At last, after several nights of searching, she spotted a lone kangaroo drinking from a watering hole. Her sharp eyes noticed a large leech attached to its back, sucking its blood. Alba hovered above the kangaroo's head, closely watching the leech's progress. The leech, fully bloated, dropped to the ground, and Alba instantly pounced to capture it. She flew back to the fairy kingdom with her prize, excited and elated.

Alba's house was somewhat isolated, much to her liking, but nonetheless she had taken no chances regarding her wicked scheme. The ingredients of the pestilence spell were secretly kept and well-hidden in an invisible trunk stowed under her bed, and she always checked for prying eyes on her return from her hunting trips. Then, just as she was celebrating the ease at which she had gathered her ingredients thus far, the fates seemed to change sides and Alba began to experience one problem after another.

Firstly, she underweighted her 'stun' spell as she attempted to remove the cane toad's left eye, and as the toad fought back, she suddenly felt its toxic poison hit her face. Alba retreated from her prey in agonising pain and flew to the nearest waterhole to wash the poison off. It took some time for her to recover her nerve and for the pain to ease. Once she was able, she returned to get her eye – and her retribution on the toad at that time was terrible indeed.

Alba rested for two nights after her cane toad experience, before setting out to collect her box jellyfish tentacle. Once again, she used the 'stun' spell to paralyse the jellyfish, but as she was cutting the chosen tentacle free, underwater currents caused the other tentacles to swirl around her, trapping her in their midst. Alba had to wrestle herself free. If the cane toad experience had been painful, this was a hundred times worse. Alba returned home with yet another crucial ingredient for her spell but was not seen again for several days.

Her bad luck worried her, and so with just two ingredients to go to complete her spell, she altered her hunting rules. If fairy tears had to be taken from inside the kingdom, she might as well get the caterpillar bristles from inside its boundaries as well. Another simple 'seeking' spell saw her find her gum-leaf skeletoniser with ease. She used the 'stun' spell to immobilise it and then a simple levitation spell to transport it back to her home.

Alba was being as careful as she could be and used a pair of silver tweezers to remove the six poisonous bristles required from its body. But just as she was about to place the last bristle into the silver mixing bowl, a sudden gust of wind through her open window blew the bristle up into the air. Instinctively, Alba reached for it with her free hand.

The pain was instantaneous and unbearable – a searing spasm of unspeakable agony shot from her fingertips to her jaw. She squeezed her watering eyes tight shut and clamped her right hand over her mouth so hard that the knuckles turned white. Her teeth grated against each other as she locked her jaws together, but a high-pitched, jagged moan still issued from her mouth.

The spasm slowly passed, but the whole of her left side felt on fire. Her hand was numb, and her fingers clicked with every movement, sending vicious little stings the length of her arm. Nevertheless, holding her nerve, Alba managed to retrieve the bristle and, using her tweezers, placed it carefully back in the bowl. Within minutes, the fingers which had been stung had trebled in size. Blood began to ooze from under her fingernails and the skin on the palm of her hand started to split and peel away. The pain was excruciating, and Alba began to cry.

'Stop crying!' she kept telling herself. 'I still have a baby to pinch!' Just then, the penny dropped. A sensible, simplistic idea dawned; Alba collected seven of her own tears and added that last vital ingredient to the mix.

Minutes later she secured the lid of the silver mixing bowl firmly. Now fully prepared, she returned the bowl to the safety of the invisible trunk. The trunk was then pushed under her bed for the last and final time. She staggered over to her bedroom window to look outside, afraid that someone had heard her cries. To her relief, the street was dark, quiet and empty. Alba, by habit, kept herself to herself, and in any case, it was rare for anyone to come near her house; no one wished to be involved in any of her nefarious schemes. She had a well-deserved reputation for always being up to no good, and so people instinctively gave her a wide berth.

But Alba was now in a bad way. Her body had taken in several very unpleasant toxins from the cane toad, box jellyfish and skeletoniser caterpillar. She had a blinding headache, felt incredibly nauseous and could not stop her entire body from shaking. Only a mad person would attempt to conjure the pestilence spell in her condition.

Two nights later she was no better and almost succumbed to summoning Aislinn for help. But her hatred and wickedness steeled her resolve, and in the end, she was able to grit her teeth and bear her discomfort and suffering alone. Indeed, the mere thought of Kyle and Aislinn together as king and queen was enough to make her tear her own hair out. She had come this far and was not going to stop now!

Alba could not put the happy couple out of her mind. It should have been her with Kyle, not Aislinn. It was too much for Alba to bear, and she resolved that, despite her pain, she would act within the week. Aislinn was living on borrowed time. Alba – with her thoughts festering and her hatred growing – remained at home in self-imposed isolation, licking her wounds, determined more than ever to manifest her spell and destroy her rival.

Chapter Twelve
Conjuring the Spell

Three days passed, but still Alba refrained from conjuring the spell. Her body needed more recovery time from the toxins she had absorbed. To her annoyance and frustration, she knew she continued to be affected by the poison. For one thing, she was experiencing bouts of nausea, making it impossible to eat normally and leaving her much weakened as a result. For another, when she held her hands out in front of her, she was shocked to see how unsteady they were. The left hand, still damaged by the caterpillar bristle, trembled uncontrollably. Driven by jealousy Alba may well have been, but suicidal and stupid, she was not.

Then, on the morning of the fourth day, Alba was tucking into a hearty breakfast when she suddenly realised her appetite had returned and the nausea had gone. She held her hands out in front of her, and although there was still a slight tremble in the left hand, the right hand was perfectly steady. Finishing her breakfast, she took the glass suction tube from its hiding place and began to practice the necessary technique using a beaker half filled with water taken from the kitchen tap. Much to her satisfaction, she found not only could she hold the tube steady, but she could also control her breath, and time and again the water was drawn smoothly inside.

As darkness fell that night, Alba attempted to conjure the pestilence spell. The silver mixing bowl was taken from its hiding place, and Alba began to combine the contents with her own wand but minus the platypus oil. Such was her desire and impatience to be rid of Aislinn that she ignored the safety advice set out clearly in the Gemini transcript; hence the vial of platypus oil, which would have protected her wand and maintained its magical powers, remained unopened. Nevertheless, she demonstrated clear skill as a chemist as the ingredients were systematically crushed, ground and stirred, until a vile-smelling green liquid evolved. The liquid bubbled and thickened and then turned black. This was what Alba had been waiting for. Once the colour of the liquid had changed from green to black, the potion was ready.

Alba put the glass suction tube in her mouth and began to draw the contents up. It was a frightening task. Practising with water was one thing, using the actual lethal ingredients quite another. Alba knew that if she ingested any of the poison, she would not survive. It was a critical process. One's breath had to be controlled so that the degree of suction remained the same. As the final dregs of the liquid were drawn into the tube, Alba held her nerve and waited. Slowly the liquid changed from black back to a vivid green in colour. Alba recognised immediately that it was time she attempted the final and most difficult part of the spell.

She now had to create a bubble at the end of the tube by blowing the contents out very, very slowly. Blowing the bubble too quickly and causing it to burst would mean certain death. She stuck to the task, and the bubble began to form exactly as she wanted. As the last drops of the liquid joined the bubble attached to the end of the glass tube, the name of the target had to be spoken down into the last breath required. She had meant to say 'Aislinn' into her last breath – but at that vital moment, weakened by the toxins which had attacked her body, her strength failed her. She lost control of her breathing and was only able to utter 'A' into the waiting – and now revolving – sphere. As she did so, the bubble immediately detached itself from the blow tube and hovered menacingly in the air.

She tried to order it back into the invisible trunk, but the sphere seemed oblivious to her demands. It remained where it was. Now suspended in the air and emanating a dull pulsating sound, which seemed to Alba almost like that of a heartbeat, the sphere also lit the room with an eerie green glow. The strange, unearthly light made Alba feel quite uncomfortable.

As Alba repeated a fifth demand for the sphere to return to the trunk, it suddenly dropped down to hover right in front of her eyes. It was now making a low buzzing sound, and as Alba looked into it, she could see a whirling green mist, circling and swirling around inside its perimeter. In the centre, there appeared to be a vacuum and in that vacuum, as if in the eye of a hurricane, Alba could clearly see the letter 'A'. Then just as abruptly, the sphere suddenly rose into the air again. Alba watched nervously as the 'A' disappeared and the green whirling vapours seemed to fill its entire globe once more. The sphere was beginning to make Alba feel more than a little uncomfortable. It clearly had a mind of its own, and it wasn't long before Alba realised it was following her every move. Wherever she went, it went too, always remaining immediately above her; and when she stopped, it stopped.

Alba was still feeling weak from the effects of the toxins and was desperate for sleep. She lay on her bed and tried to close her eyes, but she could feel the bright glow of the sphere above her penetrating her eyelids. To make matters worse, its low buzzing sound had now become painful to her ears. The noise seemed to reverberate in her head. Sleep was impossible.

Then she had an idea. It occurred to her that a lovely hot bath might be a pleasant alternative. However, she would first need to escape to the bathroom. Once there, she could run herself a delicious bath and enjoy a long relaxing soak away from the sphere. A plan of action formed in her mind. She walked slowly towards the bedroom door and then suddenly made a dash. She bolted through it like greased lightning and then slammed it shut. Alba literally hurtled across the landing and into the bathroom. Closing the door behind her, she leant back against it and heaved a sigh of relief. She looked about her, and much to her satisfaction, there was no sign of the sphere. Her plan of escape had worked.

She ran the hot tap until the water was right up to the rim and then added in an extravagant amount of her favourite lavender oil. The scent was heavenly. Alba dropped her robe onto the floor and climbed into her luxurious bath. Closing her eyes, she slid down into the warm, soothing water and heaved yet another long, low, comfortable sigh. She felt relaxed for the first time in days and stretched out her aching legs and rested her aching back under the water. Only her head and hands remained above the rim of the bath.

After a minute or two of pure pleasure, she opened her eyes and, looking up, found herself staring directly at the sphere. The shock caused her entire body to jolt so fast that a deluge of water splashed out of the bath on all sides. A startled Alba was barely able to suppress the scream which rose to her lips. Her hands grasped the rim of the bathtub so tightly that her knuckles turned white.

Alba froze. A face materialised inside the sphere. At first it appeared as the face of a demon, almost – twisted, evil and warped. It was then she was gripped by a wild panic as she realised the face was none other than her own! To her horror, she found herself looking at a familiar image. It was her face right enough – there could be no doubt about that – as if reflected in a mirror. But it was a frightened face with a white, drained complexion, death-like, drawn and haggard. Eyes full of terror, wide open, peered out at her from the very centre of the sphere. An angry buzzing sound filled her ears as the sphere hovered ominously just inches from her nose. She watched its predatory movement as it swayed backwards and forwards, as if deciding whether to strike. For several minutes she lay perfectly still in water which continued to lap over the sides of the bath. She was transfixed by the sphere's frightening sound and its horrific nearness. Worse still was the sight of that awful face suspended in front of her. She wanted to look away but could not. Like Alba herself, even her own eyes seemed paralysed and unable to move.

It was with a beating heart and some considerable relief that she observed her reflection slowly fade and the letter 'A' reappear instead at its centre. Alba leaned away from the sphere, which seemed to be buzzing more loudly than ever. Keeping her face as far from it as possible, she twisted her body around and somehow managed to extricate herself from the bath. Alba was now completely unnerved. The sphere could clearly move through solid walls, so there was no escape from it. *Still,* she thought, *that might not be a bad thing. At least I know there will be no escape for Aislinn when the time comes.*

By this time, even Alba was feeling threatened by the sphere. She kept reminding herself that it was she who had conjured the spell, therefore how could she possibly be its target or in any danger? That said, she was beginning to wonder why it was following her so closely. 'Must be my tears in the spell's mix, that's what it'll be,' she told herself reassuringly, 'or the fact that I didn't bother to use the platypus oil.'

She made her way back to the bedroom and, opening the wardrobe door, selected a black, long-sleeved top and matching black leggings. Aislinn's house was in the middle of the village, and Alba wanted to make herself as invisible as possible so as not to be seen. She would wait until nightfall and for the cover of darkness, and then in the blackness, she would cast her wicked spell and obliterate Aislinn once and for all. She sat on the edge of the bed staring out of the window, waiting for the sun to set, and the sphere waited with her.

Kyle continued his account of events. 'I was afraid what Alba might do, and so I had been shadowing her movements, hoping to protect Aislinn from any danger.' He told Chaney that as Aislinn arrived home one night, he had seen Alba lurking in the shadows at the edge of the bright lamplight outside Aislinn's door, clearly waiting to strike. As he crept up behind her, he could see she was holding a green glowing spherical object in her right hand. It was about the size of a small tangerine, and Kyle had recognised it at once from the picture he had seen in the Gemini book. It was none other than the pestilence spell! Before Kyle could stop her, she stepped out from the darkness and blocked Aislinn's path. Aislinn had been too shocked to move, and as she stood rooted to the spot, Alba had thrown the sphere high into the air above her.

Alba had expected the sphere to recognise its target within seconds, but it did not. It spun in the air, whirring around and around immediately above them. Kyle had raced to Aislinn's side and, throwing his arms around her, had pulled her gently to the ground. His body folded around hers, protecting and shielding her from any harm. The sphere stopped in its tracks and then hurtled like a heat-seeking missile towards Alba. It struck in a blinding flash of light, and Alba was blown to pieces.

For some moments, Kyle could hardly breathe. The air felt thick, and thousands of darkly coloured particles like dirty snowflakes, swirled around him until at last a black cloud of smoke rose into the heavens. The air was suddenly clear, and Kyle could breathe again.

'Thank God for that,' Kyle said with relief. Then looking down at his precious Aislinn, he could see a small speck of green liquid had landed on her face. Before he could help or speak, the liquid had been absorbed into her skin, leaving behind it an ominous dark, pulsating circle. Aislinn had lost consciousness in his arms and Kyle had carried her back to the palace and to the King's physician to seek help.

The Ancients had looked up every possible antidote for the spell but could find none. Her only hope was the magical healing power of the Koori Shaman.

'Is the Koori Shaman very special? Does he have stronger magic than you?' asked Chaney.

'What I am about to tell you now, I do not want you to worry over. But if you are to understand why he has great magic, I must tell you something of Aboriginal beliefs and the mythological stories behind the power of the Shaman.'

Chaney felt slightly anxious as Kyle began his explanation.

'Do you know what an extra-terrestrial is?' Kyle asked in a rather cautious tone of voice.

'Oh yes,' replied Chaney, 'a being from outer space. I loved the film ET.'

'Well,' Kyle continued, 'the Aborigines believe that the Koori Shaman is a descendant of other world travellers. In Wandjina state, legend has it that sky gods came down to earth to impart their superior knowledge to the primitive people who inhabited the land at that time. It is said that some members of the tribe were taken up into the clouds in a giant egg. I suspect that you and I might have referred to that particular mode of transport as a spaceship.'

'Or a flying saucer,' Chaney ventured eagerly.

Pleased that his student was listening so ardently, Kyle continued. 'When the chosen tribesmen returned to Earth, they discovered they had been given great powers: magical powers which subsequently set them apart from the rest of their people. Over time and as a result, they were worshipped like gods. That is how the Shaman came into existence.'

'Gosh,' Chaney said, interrupting again and sounding a little frightened. 'I read in a magazine the other day about a man who claimed to have been abducted by alien beings. He had been taken up in a UFO and was missing for days. The worst thing was that he remains convinced the aliens had carried out all sorts of experiments on him. Ugh, it makes me shudder to think!'

'Exactly! And it doesn't necessarily follow that if other life forms exist, they will all be magnanimous and friendly,' continued Kyle. 'Anyway, backing up; these age-old legends are the 5,000-year-old cave paintings at Kimberley. They depict strange-looking creatures, very human-like in appearance, dressed in weird garments that make them look like ancient astronauts. There's one painting in particular, Chaney, which shows something so similar to a flying saucer, that it is hard to believe it could be anything else. You could go and see them for yourself. Sadly, I've only been able to see copies of the paintings in library books. But Kimberly is not that far from your neck of the woods, being in North-western Australia, and visitors go all the time to see them. You ought to get your father to take you.

It's such fascinating stuff, and as my history professor pointed out, Aboriginal traditions, their rituals and initiation ceremonies all bear the hallmarks of people being challenged, taken away and returning somehow changed – made greater. Can you see what I mean? The elements bear such amazing similarity to the UFO abduction you were referring to. All I know is that the Koori Shaman have been given wonderful, magical powers which mankind and fairy kind can only guess at. That is why we must find him in time to save my precious Aislinn.'

This was their mission, and they must not fail.

'I cannot live without her. My life would be meaningless…I could never love another,' said Kyle. 'Aislinn must be my queen.'

Chapter Thirteen
The Raging River

It was the middle of the night and pitch dark. The moon lay hidden behind a thick mass of cloud, and without the light from Kyle's wand, neither Chaney nor Dakota could have considered pushing their horses on. Even so, it was mighty dangerous, and both horses often stumbled as they trod the difficult and dangerous path underfoot. The snow-capped peaks of Bluff Knoll appeared ever nearer, but all were now feeling miserable, forlorn, tired and hungry.

As they neared the dizzy heights of that great mountain, the task ahead of them seemed more insurmountable. They knew only too well that the long, treacherous and arduous climb to reach the summit would test their endurance to the limit. The girls worried that they would not be able to meet the demands soon to be placed upon them. Would their riding skills be sufficient? Even more worrying was the fact that both Galaxy and Star were nearing exhaustion.

Unexpectedly, there was a break in the clouds, and the two sisters were able to see the landscape ahead. They were suddenly transfixed by a translucent horizon which seemed to shimmer in the moonlight, silver lights moving and swaying in one direction. Then they heard it – the sound of water, moving fast and furiously. In an instance, it lay before them – a mighty river, swollen and angry. Eyes full of dread looked across a vast expanse of foaming white water, hissing in temper and fringed by jagged banks of black rock, thorn bushes and ancient trees groaning to prevent their age-old roots being torn out of the ground. Heavy rains had fallen in recent weeks, flood waters had breached the normal riverbanks, and a torrent, a mile wide, lay before them. The girls reined their horses to a halt, staring hopelessly at the obstacle which barred their way. Prince Kyle was the first to speak.

'We cannot give up now,' he said. 'We must cross. I will fly ahead and use my wand to light your way. We have no time to look for another, safer crossing. Aislinn will die if we are delayed. We must try.'

Kyle led the way, with Star and Chaney close behind. Galaxy and Dakota followed nose to tail, and all were frozen to the bone within seconds. The water swirled about them waist-deep, and Chaney was surprised by the strength of the current. Twice, Star had nearly lost his footing, and Chaney found herself stroking his neck and telling him not to worry.

'We'll be okay,' she told him. 'We simply have to keep going.'

Suddenly, she heard Dakota scream: 'Look out!'

Chaney looked upriver to see a huge, fallen tree trunk hurtling downstream and heading straight for them. Her heart sank. The tree was massive. They had no hope; it would sweep them away, and they would all be drowned!

'Chaney, get Star to the other side,' shouted Kyle, as he soared into the air and pointed his wand at the rapidly approaching tree. Dakota and Chaney heard him cry out again, but this time in a tongue they did not understand. If the water had been cold before, suddenly it felt like ice. Within seconds Chaney's legs convulsed with pain and then went numb. She couldn't feel her feet in the stirrups. She couldn't feel her legs at all. She had no control over Star, and she sank onto his proud neck, letting go of the reins in her distress and whispered, 'Forgive me,' into his pricked ears. Chaney did not see the water turn to ice around her, and she did not see the tree trunk grind to a halt as the river froze around it.

Star bravely used all his strength to force his way through the icy waters and carry her to safety. Kyle was using his wand to direct a path for Star to follow and was calling out loudly to the horse encouraging him on. A thin, yet radiant ray of light from Kyle's wand shone like a laser beam down onto the surface of the ice, melting a narrow track through which the horse could move. Galaxy followed Star's lead, staying close behind. Dakota, too, had been overcome by cold and exhaustion. She lay slumped across Galaxy's withers. Poor Gilpin found himself crushed by the weight of her body, trapped as he was in her jacket pocket. It was all he could do to breathe.

The two courageous horses battled on through icy waters, carrying their precious cargo to safety. At long last, and almost on the point of complete collapse, Kyle was able to lower his wand and, much to his relief, watch Star slowly escape from the grasp of the frozen river. Step by step, and with enormous physical exertion, the tired Arabian was able to climb the steep muddy bank. Slipping and sliding as he did so, the black stallion finally managed to reach safe, relatively flat ground, some fifteen feet above the now fast-melting river.

Galaxy, however, was not so fortunate. Halfway up the steep and slippery slope, he lost his footing and fell heavily. Losing his balance altogether, Galaxy slithered uncontrollably back down into the freezing, swirling water below. There was an almighty crash as his body hit the icy surface. Jets of arctic spray rose into the air as Galaxy tried to regain his footing, desperately struggling to keep his precious mistress from being totally submerged under the dark torrents which once again swept about him.

Star watched with growing concern as the white stallion, time and time again, tried unsuccessfully to clamber up a bank which was no longer solid. Indeed, the ground under Galaxy's feet was the constituency of treacle. It clung to his legs, like a drowning man clings to his rescuer. It was a thick, hungry mud which sucked him down as if wanting to devour his feet, sapping all his strength. Finally, after many minutes, it was as if Galaxy had given up and accepted defeat. The exhausted Andalusian could move no more. He stood motionless, with head bowed and his muzzle held so low that it was almost under the water. It was all he could to do to stay upright. He needed every ounce of energy he had left merely to stand still and resist the power of the current. The river, no longer frozen, was now flowing at full force once more. Relentlessly and cruelly, it tried its best to sweep him away. Galaxy began to close his eyes. He was so very tired that all he wanted to do was to sleep.

Star saw the danger and whinnied noisily to Kyle. The fairy prince understood immediately what Star had told him to do and raised his wand. With the little power the wand had left, the rope on Chaney's saddle was made to unravel at one end. In a split-second the loose end sped through the air, straight out like an arrow from a bow, across to Galaxy. A lasso formed and secured itself around Galaxy's neck. As it did so, Star snorted loudly at his friend. Galaxy, however, did not respond, and seemed to sink even lower into the icy water. Giant whirlpools surged around him, tearing Dakota's feet from their stirrups. She was in dire danger of being swept away. Star called out again, neighing even more vehemently.

The despairing Andalusian heard his friend's entreaty. His eyelids flickered, his ears pricked, and he listened to Star's call. Star was urging him to be brave, to try to climb out of the river and to carry Dakota to safety. Finding his courage and strength once more and aware of Star's determination to save him, the brave white stallion attempted to move his legs. As he did so, he felt the lasso around his neck tighten and a strong pull from the rope, which had become his lifeline, helping to drag him out of the water.

Moving backwards, degree by degree and hoof by hoof, with the rope securely attached to the pommel of Chaney's saddle, Star hauled his friend up onto the safety of the bank. Galaxy would have slipped back several times, had it not been for the tension on the rope maintaining his position on the bank as he struggled to reach the top. Like Star, every muscle and sinew in Galaxy's body strained to the task – a body no longer pure white, but dark brown and stinking of rancid, thick, congealing mud.

By now, Chaney had recovered sufficiently to watch the whole process. She too began to call out to Galaxy, encouraging him on. His desperate attempt to pull himself up out of the thick quagmire reminded her of a pelican she had once seen which had been covered in crude oil. It had happened after an oil tanker had run aground and then leaked much of its cargo into the sea. The poor pelican had been trapped in a thick slick which had drifted inshore, polluting a long stretch of the coastline. She had helped to rescue the bird which had been in a pitiful state, its feathers tarred, black and stuck together. She remembered it had been unable to move even its wings. Poor Galaxy looked little better than that bird as he frantically tried to climb the bank and escape from the mud which had sought to keep him captive. Little by little, he inched closer and closer, until he finally managed to pull himself clear of the mud's spiteful grasp. At last, Chaney could touch Galaxy's soft but panting muzzle and hear for herself, even above the roar of the torrent below, the sound of nostrils flaring as he tried to regain his breath.

Much to the relief of their rescuers, and not before time, Galaxy and Dakota were clear of the water and once again on dry land. Just at that moment, the tree trunk which had threatened them earlier swept past at devastating speed. Released from its icy prison and carried by the raging waters, it hurtled past, taking everything in its path with it. Galaxy and Dakota would not have been spared. Even out of the water, had Dakota been sitting upright, she would not have survived. A lofty branch projecting out from the main trunk of the tree and overhanging the bank would have knocked her clean out of her saddle. The fact that she remained slumped over Galaxy's withers had saved her life. The branch flew through the air just inches above her head, making a loud whooshing sound.

Chaney was shocked to the core. She watched the tree hurtle downstream and the branch cruelly smiting everything on the bank with which it made contact. If Chaney had not realised before what dangers they might encounter on their mission to save Aislinn, she was under no illusion now. Dakota had almost lost her life, and Chaney was horrified by what had happened. Until that moment, she had viewed their journey merely as an adventure, little more than a glorified Sunday School outing. The river crossing, a crossing which might well have resulted in watery graves for them all, had been nothing if not a wake-up call. Dakota lay unconscious across Galaxy's trembling withers, and Chaney, shivering with cold herself, understood for the first time the peril of their situation.

Kyle saw instantly what a close call it had been. Galaxy and Dakota had escaped certain death by the narrowest of margins. 'Thank God,' he whispered, as the light from his wand went out. His eyes slowly closed, and he fluttered and fell like an autumn leaf in a November gale to the ground.

Back at the campsite, the two dogs were also in cold water, but nothing like the icy waters that Dakota and Chaney had had to endure. Michael was throwing a stick into the lake, and Enzo was chasing after it with enthusiasm. The old dog, however, showed no interest. Simba seemed preoccupied to Michael and full of tension. In addition, – and much to Michael's concern – not only had Simba not eaten any of his meal that night, but he had also been whining and howling for hours. Simba stood by his master's side in the shallows, and no amount of tempting could make him take his usual, and normally much-cherished, swim. Michael looked up at a cold full moon suspended in a vast dark blue sky. It was a moon which tonight seemed to be casting long melancholy rays of silver across the water.

'Light their way and keep them safe,' he whispered, pressing the palms of his hands together as if in prayer. He kissed his own index fingers, imagining as he did so that they were the foreheads of his own sweet girls. On the walk back to the campervan, Simba kept licking Michael's hand as if in sympathy, and throughout the long evening, the old dog kept a loyal and faithful vigil at his master's side.

As Dakota recovered consciousness, she tried to take a proper breath but choked and coughed up water and spat out mud. Chaney went to her aid and offered her a drinking bottle. Dakota looked as if she were about to cry. It took several minutes, but gradually both sisters began to recover from their hazardous crossing. Finally, when Dakota's eyesight and breathing had returned to normal, they found Gilpin anxiously waiting to speak to them. He was wringing his paws, and his face wore a worried, almost frantic expression.

'I can't find Kyle,' he said in a trembling voice. 'I've been looking for ages, and I'm really concerned for his safety. He's been missing since Galaxy managed to climb up the bank!'

The entire party was cold, wet and close to exhaustion, but they set about organising a careful search. The girls dismounted, and Chaney, using a number of nearby stones, marked a line on the bank which was to be the starting point of the search. Yard by yard, working slowly further and further away from the river, they would cover every inch of ground. Chaney and Star would search in an easterly direction, whilst Dakota and Galaxy would venture west. Gilpin would try and use his keen sense of smell to locate Kyle and watch for signs of the wand coming back to life. They had all almost given up hope when Gilpin's sharp eyes saved the day. Kyle was indeed lying on the riverbank – unconscious, close to death and half-buried in mud.

He was still clutching his wand in his hand, when suddenly it sputtered briefly and then went dead. No light shone from it, but Gilpin, by the best of fortunes, had seen its brief spark. He raced to Kyle's side, and in the nick of time prevented Kyle's head from being engulfed by the mud. Gilpin shouted to the others to help him. Star and Galaxy heard his high-pitched cries, and both pulled their mistresses towards the sound.

'Help me, quick!' Gilpin said as they approached. 'Kyle's sinking in the mud. I can't hold him much longer!'

Not a minute too soon, Chaney lifted Kyle's seemingly lifeless body from the quagmire in which it lay.

'He's still alive,' she exclaimed joyously, 'but covered in mud. More worrying', she added, 'is that he feels chilled to the bone.' Chaney used her handkerchief to wipe at least some of the foul-smelling mud off him. 'He needs warmth. Good job we brought the first-aid kit with us.'

Dakota, however, made no reply. Having been so much longer in the icy water than her sister, Dakota too was feeling the effect of her long exposure to cold and wet. She was showing signs of hypothermia, shivering uncontrollably, and finding it difficult to speak.

Chaney pulled the emergency blanket from the first-aid bag. Taking out a small pair of scissors, she cut a strip just wide enough to wrap around Kyle and, securing it about him, gently laid him to sleep in her saddle bag next to his beloved Aislinn. She turned to smile at her sister and was immediately horrified at Dakota's appearance. She was as pale as death and shivering so badly that she could barely stand, let alone ride. Chaney acted in seconds. The emergency blanket was wrapped carefully around Dakota's shoulders. Helping her sister to mount, Chaney proceeded to fold the blanket around Dakota's legs as well, giving her as much protection from the elements as she possibly could.

Two chocolate bars also found in the first-aid kit were fed to the horses, and one small segment from each bar was given to Dakota to eat. Chaney unselfishly went without. Meanwhile, Gilpin had retrieved Kyle's wand from the mud. He called up loudly to Chaney above the noise of the river to help lift him back up, and Chaney lovingly obliged.

'Dakota's not well,' she said. 'You better ride with me for a while.'

Chaney placed Gilpin in her breast pocket and then mounted Star. She drew him alongside Galaxy and checked the emergency blanket was securely tied around Dakota before the party set off once again to reach Bluff Knoll. After the risks they had taken in crossing the river, their task of finding the healing Shaman in time to save Aislinn seemed of even greater importance.

By now, the clouds that had hidden the moon for almost all their night's journey had parted. They could see the great circle of mountain peaks in the distance, and they resolved to go on and reach the summit if they could. Gilpin began using his sharp eyes to seek out their route, giving valuable assistance to Chaney and Star as they led the team on the final leg of the journey. Their destination lay ahead and, although Chaney was tired and hungry, she was determined that their mission would be a success. Nothing was going to stop her.

The hours passed, and Dakota began to recover. 'I'll take the lead now,' she called out to her sister.

Chaney was more than happy for her to do so. She was struggling to maintain concentration. Her eyes felt sore and seemed to keep shutting of their own volition. It was a relief not to be responsible for finding a safe path. They rode on silently, making good ground. After a while, however, Chaney began to complain.

'Can't we stop just for a minute or two? We can see the mountain now, and I'm so, so hungry.'

There was no reply.

'Dakota, did you hear me? I'm so hungry I could eat a dead rat!'

'No! We cannot stop!' Dakota exclaimed in exasperation. 'We have to keep going. For goodness' sake, Chaney, think about something else other than your stomach.'

'And remember…I'm just a mouse,' Gilpin added, rather nervously, from inside Chaney's pocket.

Chaney felt cross. Dakota's reply had annoyed her. *She's always the same,* Chaney thought to herself. *Completely ignores anything I say and never appreciates anything I do. I almost wish I hadn't given her anything to eat. It's alright for her; at least she has had something, even if it was only two small pieces of chocolate. I, on the other hand, have had nothing at all!*

She glared down at Gilpin, and catching his eye, rolled hers, as if to say, *I'm hardly likely to eat you! I said dead rat…not silly mouse.* Gilpin smiled weakly.

They rode on, with Chaney becoming hungrier and crosser by the minute.

Chapter Fourteen
The Mighty Ravine

After another hour or two of riding, they finally reached the lower slopes. As they began the ascent, progress now became even more difficult. The mountain was shrouded in a thick mist which seemed to curl around the peaks and float eerily into gullies, like vanishing will-o'-the-wisps trying to hide. Tired eyes strained in the poor light, but no matter how hard they tried, they could not find a clear path to follow. To make matters worse, the climb was steep and treacherous and both horses were even closer to exhaustion. Dakota noted with concern how low Galaxy was holding his head and that every ten steps or so, he would stumble, his hooves slipping on loose rock. She knew he was struggling, but as always giving his all for her. She released the reins with her right hand and patted his neck.

'Good, brave boy, Galaxy,' she said comfortingly.

At last, the end was in sight. They had just the final peak to climb, but in that moment of triumph came dismay. Disappointment darkened their faces as they beheld a mighty ravine separating them from the summit. A two-hundred-foot drop lay between them and the pastures they needed. To make matters worse, the ground on which they were standing was at least ten feet below the level on the opposite side of the gorge. Not only would they need to clear the twenty-foot gap between the sides of the ravine, they would also have to jump ten feet up. It seemed an impossible task.

'Let's ride on a bit further,' suggested Dakota, looking at the terrifying gulf which lay between them and the ridge opposite. They trotted on for some time, following the cliff edge cautiously, desperately hoping to find a narrower gap or an alternative crossing. But it was to no avail. The enormous cleft remained the same, and even more worrying was the fact that the weather was closing in. Dark, black clouds were gathering and writhing above them, and a bitingly cold easterly wind had begun to blow and was bullying them along.

As they rode on, the temperature began to plummet. An angry, brutal wind now whipped their hands and faces, causing fingers and noses to freeze. Chaney cried out in fear as a particularly strong gust of ice-cold wind hit against them like a blow from an invisible sledgehammer. Once or twice, they felt themselves almost blown over the edge of the cliff, and sensibly, they reined the horses further away from the steep sides of the ravine and the sheer drop which awaited any horse or rider making a mistake!

Then, as if things were not bad enough already, came the snow! Light flurries at first, but as the wind increased, so did the snowfall. Within minutes it was the thickest, densest snow Dakota had ever seen – a complete white-out. She strained her eyes to see across the ravine, but it was impossible. By now, the blizzard was raging with such ferocity that visibility was down to a matter of metres.

Dakota knew she had to decide, and quickly. Conditions were worsening, and the longer she put off making the jump across that terrifying abyss, the more difficult and dangerous the jump would become.

She reined Galaxy to a halt. A fierce, violent wind and blinding, driving snow was now battering against them unmercifully. Turning to her sister, she called out above the noise of the tumult, 'Galaxy and I can do this. I'm going to make the jump from here.'

'No,' said Chaney, 'you'll be killed! I couldn't bear that!'

'Please, Chaney…just wait for us here.'

'No, Dakota. No. I can't allow you, especially in these blizzard conditions!' Chaney cried out in terror. 'It would be suicide. You'll never make it.'

'Chaney, we have come this far against all odds. We cannot give up now,' Dakota replied, trying to sound calm, whilst in truth her heart was pounding.

Chaney fell silent. Gilpin knew what he had to do and leapt across from Star's withers onto Dakota's lap. Dakota carefully stowed him in her breast pocket.

'When I make the jump, you'll need to hold on extra tight,' she warned him.

Dakota turned to face Chaney once more and held out her hand for the saddlebag containing Aislinn and Kyle. Securing it about her, she wheeled Galaxy around and moved away from the edge of the ravine. Chaney felt sick and could barely watch her sister prepare to make the jump.

By now the wind was howling with frightening ferocity and the snow falling so thickly that it was difficult even to see the edge of the cliff in front of her, let alone the ridge on the far side. Taking a deep breath and buttoning her breast pocket to keep Gilpin safe from harm, Dakota spurred Galaxy into action. They galloped headlong towards the huge chasm. Galaxy jumped with all his might, and Chaney watched in wonder as the great Andalusian horse vanished from her sight, disappearing into a cloud of pure white swirling snow.

Miraculously, Galaxy cleared the ravine with ease, landing comfortably on the other side. Chaney breathed a great sigh of relief as she heard hooves clattering on rock from across the void, quickly followed by a loud victory whoop from her sister.

Dakota skilfully brought Galaxy to a stop and slowly walked him back to the cliff edge. The wind seemed to make one last final howl, and then little by little began to subside. Dakota waved to Chaney across the black chasm and then pointed to the sky. Dark clouds remained overhead, and the snow flurries too were continuing.

In light that was fast fading, Dakota shouted instructions across to her sister. 'Try and find some shelter and wait there for us. We'll find the Shaman and come back for you.'

It was the middle of the night back at Moingup Springs. The campsite was silent, and everyone except for Simba was asleep. The old dog had been pacing up and down for several hours. He had been ordered by his master to be quiet, but as the brave Galaxy prepared to make his heroic leap of faith across the ravine, it all became too much for Simba. He began howling and barking as loudly as he could, desperate to wake his master and let him know that he sensed the girls and their horses were in danger. Michael hurtled through the door of the campervan and tripped over Simba who was standing right outside. Recovering his feet, Michael gently pulled the old dog to him by his collar.

'Simba, quiet, boy, quiet – you're going to wake the whole camp up, barking at this rate.'

Simba looked appealingly into his master's eyes, whining gently as he did so.

'You're worried too, aren't you, old fella? Come on, there's a good boy. You can sleep inside tonight, as a special treat.' Michael led the way back into the campervan, and silence ruled the campsite once again.

It was well after midnight before Chaney finally dismounted and was able to tend to Star's needs. Taking Dakota's advice, Chaney had searched in vain for shelter. None was to be found, and accepting defeat, they returned miserably through the constant snowfall to the place where Dakota and Galaxy had made their courageous and monumental leap across the ravine. Horse and rider were chilled to the bone, hungry and anxious. The once-proud Arabian was bent with exhaustion and, despite the cold, soaked in sweat from his exertions. Chaney used her own blanket to wipe him dry, and then covered him with what warm clothes she had.

The cold was bitter and intense. Frost glittered and twinkled on snow-laden, steep and inhospitable mountain slopes. Chaney felt dismayed at how little food or comfort she could offer him. The ground, covered in a thick layer of snow, afforded little vegetation and no grazing at all. But if Chaney had a bad night, it was no better and possibly even worse for Gilpin and Dakota.

Hardly surprisingly, the summit too was covered in a thick layer of unseasonal snow, and no matter how hard Gilpin tried, he could not unearth a path of blue wreath flowers. A black cloud hung over the summit, cutting out all moonlight, and in the total darkness which surrounded them, finding the Shaman's cave was impossible. Dakota kept checking the saddle bag to see if Kyle was awake and could light the search with his wand, but Kyle remained unconscious. Hour after hour, Gilpin buried his little nose in the snow trying to sniff out the rare plant and the path for which they searched, but to no avail.

As light dawned on the second day, Dakota began to give up hope. Worse still, Gilpin was feeling the effects of his fruitless endeavours – his nose was frostbitten. As his body succumbed to the effects of hypothermia, he began to forget what he was doing or why he was there.

It was Kyle who, at long last, came to the rescue. Having had a good night's sleep, Kyle left the warmth of Chaney's saddle bag fully recovered. Dakota quickly explained the events of their long night and expressed concern that her sister had been left alone for several hours. Kyle immediately flew back across the ravine to Chaney and told her that the Shaman had still not been found.

'Do not feel you need to risk that jump – it is far too dangerous,' he warned. 'Now that I have some of my powers back, I am sure we will find him soon. Just stay put.'

Kyle returned to Dakota. 'She's okay, and I've told her to wait for us. Where has this snow come from, and in the middle of summer?' he said, looking around in amazement. Taking out his wand, he cast a melting spell.

Within seconds the snow had vanished, and the blue wreath flowers were unveiled in all their glory. They stretched across the ground as far as the eye could see. It was an expanse of radiant blue, and Dakota immediately understood why the Aborigines had named them 'the floor of the sky.' She reached down to collect a very tired Gilpin from the ground and put his shivering body into the inside pocket of her riding jacket. She stroked his head and told him to sleep.

'Kyle and I will find the cave,' she assured him. 'You've done your bit. Get some rest.'

She climbed into the saddle once more, and with Kyle sitting on Galaxy's withers, they began to follow the path of flowers along a wide plateau which ran around the base of the summit. Kyle held his wand aloft to light their way. It was still very dark. The black cloud which seemed to be hovering and unmoving above the mountain was now blotting out the early morning sun, as it had done the moon throughout the previous night. Worse still, it was snowing heavily again, and the blue flowers were fast disappearing under a carpet of white flakes.

Then they saw him. Through a flurry of swirling snow, the outline of an Aboriginal man slowly appeared.

Chapter Fifteen
The Mystical Shaman

Dakota felt her heart leap with delight. *At long last, we have found him! Now perhaps, we do have a chance to save Aislinn and get back home without too much delay,* she thought to herself, with an enormous sense of relief. Her hand instinctively dropped to gently touch the saddle bag in which the stricken fairy was sleeping.

They could see a tall, gaunt figure standing on one leg, silhouetted against the backdrop of a cold grey sky. Kyle immediately shouted a greeting, but in a tongue Dakota did not understand. The old Shaman looked at them and, un-answering, pointed his spear at the rock face below his feet.

Dakota strained her eyes to see through the thick veil of snow which was falling and could just make out the narrow entrance of a cave in the rock wall ahead of them. She dismounted and walked Galaxy towards the small fissure she had spotted. Dakota had intended on leaving Galaxy outside, but as the old man joined them, he caught hold of Galaxy's rein and led him inside. The entrance was just wide enough for the horse to pass through. Dakota and Kyle followed behind. Once inside, Dakota was amazed not only by the Shaman's appearance but also by the cave itself.

She was standing in a huge cavern with enormous tunnels branching off from the main chamber in all directions. Giant stalactites hung from the high rock ceiling above, and even more monstrous stalagmites jutted out from the floor below, pointing upwards like troll's fingers at their ethereal brothers and sisters. She could hear dripping water and, glancing around, noticed rock pools on every side of the cavern, each with its own reflected colour. The pools seemed to emanate their own light, and green, red and turquoise hues radiated off the smooth shiny rock which lined the interior of the cave. More beautiful still were the thousands of gossamer threads draped across the cavern walls and bedecking the entire roof high above them. They appeared as bright, dazzling necklaces of sparkling silver reflecting the light from the water below, and on which appeared to be strung millions upon millions of miniature tear-shaped pearls.

'Spider webs', said Kyle, 'and their eggs.' A fact which immediately burst Dakota's bubble and broke the illusion altogether.

The Shaman would have appeared frightening to Dakota had she not been with Kyle. For one thing, his emaciated Aboriginal body was smeared all over in weird-looking grey clay. His arms and legs were painted with thin black stripes and his body and face dotted with double lines of small white circles. He wore only a loincloth made of animal skin and a red headband which did little to control the wild locks of curly grey hair draped around his shoulders. The Shaman had the longest white beard Dakota had ever seen, and carried a long, flint-tipped wooden spear decorated with snake carvings.

Dakota watched and listened with interest as Kyle hovered at head height in front of the Shaman. She recognised the foreign tongue which Kyle had spoken once before and a name. Alba was mentioned several times.

Finally, when Kyle had finished speaking, he called to Dakota and asked her to bring Aislinn's stretcher. The stretcher was duly laid at the old man's feet. Dakota noted with considerable concern that Aislinn's complexion was now a ghastly white colour and that she seemed to be struggling to breathe. Kyle too looked more concerned than ever, and as he spoke to the Shaman, Dakota could hear the sense of urgency in his voice.

The old man picked up a long piece of rope which had been lying to one side of the cave. He spoke very briefly to Kyle in the same tongue, and then left the cave.

'Where's he going?' asked Dakota, anxious that Aislinn's treatment should begin.

'He says he cannot do his work when we are surrounded by evil,' replied Kyle.

'Evil?' repeated Dakota, looking puzzled.

'Yes. He says he senses a dark force – a malicious presence above us. That's why he's taken his bullroarer. Listen,' Kyle continued. 'You'll probably be able to hear it.'

Dakota listened intently at first, and then within minutes the sound could be heard clearly. She went outside to see what was happening and spotted the Shaman standing on the very summit of Mount Bluff. He was whirling the rope around in the air, high above his head, and as he did so, it made the most enormous roaring sound.

As Dakota watched, she saw to her surprise that the black cloud which had been suspended above the mountain since their arrival seemed to be dispersing, breaking up – and then suddenly it was gone. Only blue sky remained, and at long last she could feel the warmth of the sun's welcome rays. It was then that she remembered her parents. She felt a tug at her heartstrings, knowing how worried they would be. Taking out her mobile, she switched it back on and texted:

'Delayed, unable to make rendezvous today. Camping out second night, all fine. Will ring tomorrow. Please don't worry.'

That done, she returned to the cave.

A blue sky adorned with a golden sun greeted Michael's eyes as he left the campervan and headed to the shower block. As he walked along with Simba following behind, he checked his mobile for messages. Disappointingly, there was still nothing from the girls. By the time he returned, Rachael had prepared a full English breakfast, and the two sat down together in the warm sunshine to enjoy their meal.

'How did you sleep?' Rachael enquired, noting the dark circles under her husband's eyes.

'Hardly at all,' was the reply. 'Simba kept me awake most of the night. He was howling and whining till about 3 am. I'm surprised he didn't wake you. I had to go out to him to shut him up. I was so afraid he would disturb the entire campsite that I let him come in with us; and then, no doubt to thank me in his own inimitable way, he proceeded to snore loudly for the rest of the night. I think we ought to have a relatively easy day today.'

Rachael nodded, happy also to have a restful day. She too had hardly slept for worrying about her daughters' safety. Michael checked his mobile again. There was still no message.

'I don't really want to decide on what we do today until I get a grid reference from the girls. When I know where they are, I can plan the rendezvous point more accurately. We've got three options. Either we stay here until we hear from them, or we assume they have stuck to the route we planned, and we make our way up to Dales Gorge.'

'What's the third option?' Rachael asked.

'We pack up now and drive to Tom Price via Mount Bruce.'

'What's at Dales Gorge?' Rachael asked with interest.

'A very well-recommended campsite and some super scenery. There's a walk, not too taxing, which even Simba can manage. The footpath follows an easy route from the so-called circular pool to the spectacular Fortescue Falls. The dogs would love it and could enjoy a refreshing afternoon swim in a really beautiful setting.'

'Sounds good to me,' Rachael replied happily.

At that moment, Michael's mobile went off. He read the text from Dakota. Rachael watched his expression change from one of relief to one of concern. After reading the short text, he immediately tried to ring Dakota back. Her phone was switched off. He tried Chaney's number, but like her sister's phone, that too was switched off.

They remained at the campsite at Moingup Springs. The police were contacted and given as much information as possible. Michael knew that if a search was to be set up, it would start from the exact place where the girls had last been seen. Michael was sick with worry, and he could hardly bear to look Rachael in the eye. He knew she had been against the girls camping out in the first place. She had thought him foolhardy.

Why have the girls disobeyed me? he asked himself. *I expressly told them to keep their mobiles switched on at all times. They are going to have some explaining to do when they get back!* He gritted his teeth so tightly together they felt like they might crack apart. Returning to Rachael, he assumed an air of confidence and – unsuccessfully – attempted to hide his fears from the woman who knew him better than he knew himself.

They stood together, staring out into the bush in silence for a moment, whilst a cold wind blew up from the valley. They both looked worried now, and Michael felt his shoulders slump. He was helpless. It was incredible the power Rachael had over him. The difference between misery and happiness was the right word from her.

'You cannot anticipate everything,' she said. 'You must not blame yourself. You've taught them all you know, and as you rightly said, when they ride out on the endurance event, we will not be there to protect them. They'll come through. They're your daughters, after all.'

'Our daughters,' he corrected. 'And with such an amazing mother, why should we fear for their safety?'

'Then don't fear,' she replied. 'Stop blaming yourself. Come on…we still have dogs needing to be walked.'

Chapter Sixteen
A Ring of Spiders

The Shaman gestured for Kyle and Dakota to sit well back from Aislinn. They obliged, and as they did so, the Shaman lifted Aislinn from her bed and laid her on a carpet of ferns which he had placed on the floor in the centre of the cavern. He walked to a rock pool at the back of the cavern and lifted out the most beautiful abalone shell Dakota had ever seen. Its centre had a mother of pearl lining, into which he now placed sweet grass, cedar and sage. The shell was laid on the floor at Aislinn's side. Then picking up a didgeridoo which had been propped up against the cave wall, he moved to sit cross-legged on a rock ledge on the opposite side of the cavern. From their vantage point Kyle and Dakota watched him with interest and listened intently as he began to play. A strange mystical sound reverberated from the ancient wooden instrument, which Dakota noticed had been decorated with strange carvings of scorpions and spiders. It was more ornate even than his spear.

She watched fascinated as the Shaman continued to play. She could see his lips vibrating as he blew air into the mouthpiece. The air seemed to echo down the tube, producing a droning sound with an eerie, mystical quality. Then the Shaman began using his long figures to tap on the side of the didgeridoo, and a repetitive rhythm was now added to the already unique sound. Dakota felt as if she wanted to close her eyes and sleep. Her eyelids felt incredibly heavy, and her entire body yearned for rest. Slowly, slowly, her eyes closed as the hypnotic rhythm lulled her to sleep. Had Dakota remained awake, she would have seen narrow slits opening in the rock face. She would have witnessed the gossamer threads all around her begin to jangle, as if they were attached to bell-pulleys in the servant's quarters of a stately home and an angry master were summoning his butler.

Then from deep inside those cavernous walls, the call was answered. An army of wolf spiders began to emerge. Hundreds and hundreds of tyrannical-eyed and hissing spiders poured out through the open cracks, their colours mirroring exactly those of the Shaman himself.

Suddenly, it seemed as if the level of sound had increased, and Dakota was brought back to full consciousness. She looked at the floor with trepidation. It appeared as if the ground all around her was moving; for a moment, as her eyes struggled to focus, she thought they were in the midst of an Earth tremor. Then she saw them: a circular wave of spiders gushing like a tsunami, revolving as one great swathe around the cave.

The tapping of the Shaman's fingers was drowned by the noise of bony, bristly legs clattering across the stone floor. Hideous heads of white and black were mounted like death masks on their grey-legged bodies. Dakota felt like an uninvited guest at some grotesque Halloween ball, as the spiders clambered skeleton-like down the walls and gathered in vast numbers on the cavern floor. As each spider joined the throng, it appeared to start dancing. Eight feet tapping the stony ground with jerky, bent-legged and chaotic movements, whirling, hopping and jumping over one another, as if in haste to reach their prey first.

A wave of hungry, monstrous and threatening spiders moved as one giant maniacal circle around the perimeter of the cave. The ring of spiders grew bigger and bigger, and as she watched in horror, the circle seemed to be closing in on Aislinn. A ripple effect had begun, which moved not out but in towards the centre. A frightening horde of awful, macabre, ghost-like spiders revolved like a fairground Waltzer around the stricken fairy, their continuous ring now clattering more and more loudly. As the tide of terror moved along the ground towards Aislinn, Dakota could stand it no longer. She made to jump up to run to Aislinn's rescue, but Kyle quickly shouted above the loud drone of the didgeridoo and told her to stay put.

'Watch,' he said. 'This is where he will begin his magic.'

The spiders suddenly stopped dead in their tracks. Aislinn's limp and seemingly lifeless body was surrounded by the evil-looking arachnids. The dark circle of eight-legged bodies stood perfectly still. They were now only a foot away from the tiny bed of ferns on which she was lying. Their heads, equipped with eight eyes, were raised – as if they were intent on seeing Aislinn for themselves.

As Dakota watched, she noticed that the spiders' eyes were beginning to reflect a red glow. The glow gathered in intensity until the entire cavern was illuminated, as if by the fires of hell itself. In every direction, an unearthly, dazzling ruby light seemed to radiate out from the mass of dark bodies which covered the floor. So strong was the eye-shine of the spiders that it hurt Dakota's eyes to look at them.

Then without warning, the Shaman stopped playing his ancient wind instrument. The resulting silence, however, was immediately filled with the sound of hissing. The noise seemed to echo around the vast cavern, bouncing off every wall. Dakota could feel her body trembling, so threatening was the sound. Every spider had begun to hiss, exposing venomous fangs; and drop after drop of poison now dripped from hairy jaws, either falling to the floor or onto the spider in front. The red light intensified still more as millions of eyes were reflected on a toxic liquid floor.

The Shaman began to take slow steps towards Aislinn, and as he did so, the spiders' bodies began to sink little by little, feet first, into the ground, until only their raised fangs and the horrible eight-eyed heads remained. There was a sudden flash of light and the hissing noise stopped – the spiders had miraculously disappeared altogether. At first, Dakota thought they had left their glowing eyes behind. Then she realised that, in their place, burning coals now surrounded Aislinn's still body.

The Shaman began his medicine. Picking up the abalone shell, he stepped onto the hot coals which encircled Aislinn, chanting and singing as he danced around and around. Every so often he would pick up a glowing coal with his bare hands and place it in the centre of the shell. Then he would waft the smoke which arose from its burning contents onto Aislinn's sleeping frame. It appeared to Dakota that the smoke had a life of its own and that it would wrap itself around Aislinn's body like bandages around an Egyptian mummy. He danced all day. The sun rose and fell, until a full moon governed the heavens once more.

After Kyle had flown back to Chaney to tell her that the Shaman had still not been found, she and Star had waited for some time on the lower slope of the ravine, hoping upon hope for the others to re-join them. Hour after hour passed by, and still there was no sign.

The sun began to peep above the mountain top as morning slowly arrived. Chaney kept looking at a sky now rosy with the colours of dawn and abandoning the dark blue of the previous, bitterly cold night. Long hours had passed in which she and Star had endured freezing temperatures, gnawing hunger and little if any sleep. Moving sluggishly as she began to thaw out, she saddled Star and began to walk him around. They were both chilled to the bone. She guided him to the cliff edge and prayed for the sight of Kyle's tiny frame returning to greet her with good news. But it was an empty, depressing horizon which met her eyes, with neither sight nor sound of the others. Once again disappointment and dismay clutched at her heart. Too anxious to appreciate the view, she did not see the grey curve of spectacular mountain peaks which surrounded her on all sides and the endless sky, stretching out for mile after infinite mile, as if she were standing on top of the world.

She looked down into the ravine. The enormous drop filled her with fear. Momentarily, low sunlight stained the drifts of deep snow clinging to rock ledges on both sides of the gorge bright orange. The rays quickly vanished as dappled clouds moved across the morning sky. Chaney shivered in the cold air, as she watched a whistling wind cause spirals of pure white snow to spin back and forth across the terrifying abyss.

'What's happened to them?' she whispered to Star. 'Have they found the Shaman, and if so, could his ancient magic really heal Aislinn?' It was the not knowing which was worst of all. Suddenly, it was all too much for Chaney to bear. 'It's no good, Star,' Chaney said, at length. 'We're just going to have to make that jump.'

Star nodded his approval. She mounted up and they trotted some distance away from the edge of the ravine. Star would need all his speed to make the jump successfully. Chaney made sure they had a good long run-up. Once satisfied they had sufficient ground to reach a full gallop, she spurred him into action. Star was fearless. He reached the edge of the precipice and leaped with all his might. Chaney could not believe the speed at which they crossed that giant chasm or indeed the distance that Star had travelled.

She was horrified, however, at the sound of the impact as they landed. Star hit the ground with such force that the earth literally shuddered beneath him. His strong legs buckled under the strain, and before Chaney had time to think, horse and rider were falling and rolling over and over again. Grey rock, dark green brush and patches of white snow flashed past, all tumbling around her until their wild and uncontrollable movement came to an abrupt and painful stop. Star crashed to a halt when he hit the solid rock face. Chaney, thrown from her saddle, came to a sudden stop as she hit a clump of brush, the main trunk of which hit her midsection like a hammer. Chaney felt her breath plucked from her mouth and tried to think past her pain.

She scraped the dirt out of her nose, her eyes and her ears. She pulled up her wet shirt to inspect the damage. Blue and purple stains were already forming above tender ribs. The left side of her chest looked oddly swollen, and as she tried to breathe, a sharp, shooting pain beneath the swelling caused her to gasp and cry out. Instantly, she was struck by the most frightening of thoughts: if she was suffering, injured…what of Star?

'Please, God, please, do not let Star be hurt!' she said to herself, as eyes whipped by the wind struggled to see through the darkness. She was badly winded for some minutes and unable to get to her feet. Twisting her torso to escape from the mangled branches which held her prisoner, another almost unbearable stab of pain seared across her ribcage. When at last Chaney was able to free herself and to stand, she rushed to Star's side.

She was shocked to see him lying lifeless on the ground. She knelt beside him and placed her hand upon his breast. She could feel his heart racing and hear his laboured breathing. As she tried to comfort him, she was shocked at the volume of sweat which poured from his tired body. Then to her dismay, Chaney noticed a long deep gash which yawned open, and a sickening tide of red which ran the length of his right hindquarter. A river of blood gushed in pulses from his wound. She took off her jacket and pressed it against the deep cut, hoping to stem the flow of blood.

'You'll be okay, Star,' she said, with a quavering voice. 'We've done it – we made the jump. Rest now, boy. You're okay; we've done it.'

Star opened his eyes for one last time to look at his beloved mistress but was too weak to neigh. Chaney felt his heartbeat once more, his body shudder, and then – stillness.

'No, Star, no! You can't die!' she screamed. 'Please don't die!' She clasped the once-proud head in her arms and held him close. The sudden emptiness that gripped her was overwhelming.

'Oh Star,' she sobbed, 'my life will be nothing without you. Please come back to me!'

From sunrise to sunset, Chaney's tears flowed un-stemmed. The black Arabian was no more. Chaney's heart was broken, and her grief knew no bounds. It was as if her life, too, was over. All joy, all hope and all happiness had gone forever; only desolation and despair remained.

Chapter Seventeen
Heartbreak and Hot Coals

At the campsite, Michael and Rachael's worries were multiplying. Simba had been howling inconsolably for some time. They had tried everything to distract the old dog, but he could not be comforted. He refused to eat and showed no interest in going for a walk or a swim. Michael had even put his leash on in a vain attempt to get him to join Enzo. Eventually, Rachael was forced to take the younger dog for his evening exercise without the company of either Michael or Simba.

'It's no use, Rachael. He doesn't want to go, and I really don't want to pull him along. It's not fair on him at his age,' Michael explained, anxious about the old dog's constitution.

'Don't worry,' Rachael replied. 'I'll take Enzo for his walk. You stay here with Simba. We won't be long.'

As Rachael left, Michael undid Simba's leash. The old dog immediately padded over to the horse trailer. He slowly climbed the ramp and lay down on the side where Star was normally tethered.

'What's the matter, boy? Are you missing Star?' Michael asked him gently. The old dog whined pitifully, as if his heart was breaking, and laid his head on the floor between his outstretched paws. Simba remained in the trailer all night. Michael, aware of the old dog's despair, brought a spare swag out of the campervan and stayed with him.

For hour upon long hour the Shaman had danced on the hot coals surrounding Aislinn's bed of ferns – then without warning, the chanting stopped. He stepped out of the circle of fire, to reveal Aislinn sitting up and looking around. Kyle immediately flew to her side and embraced her.

The Shaman was smiling and gestured for Dakota to join them. He took Dakota's hand and placed a small-beaded necklace into it. It had a circular centre made of four different coloured beads. The quadrants were like those of a compass: a section of white beads at the top, north, then a red east, a black south and a yellow west.

'It's a medicine wheel,' said Kyle, 'for good luck.'

The Shaman began to speak to Dakota, but in a tongue she did not understand.

'What did the Shaman say?' Dakota asked Kyle.

It was Aislinn who replied. In a trembling voice which denoted how weak she still was, even if healed, Aislinn proudly told Dakota what had been said.

'He pays you a great compliment. He says this journey – to save my life – has been your walkabout and that you have shown great bravery and great love. The spirits acknowledge that you are no longer a child. He says that courage and goodness will always walk with you and that your ancestors watch over you with pride. He wants to tell you not to worry about your parents; he knows you honour them, and he wants to assure you that your reunion with them will be soon and that they know you are safe.'

The Shaman nodded, and taking Dakota's hands in his, he spoke again in his foreign tongue. When he had finished speaking, Dakota looked once more to Aislinn for explanation. Aislinn, however, seemed strangely puzzled.

'I don't quite understand his words,' she explained, 'but this is what he said. You must wear his gift – the medicine wheel – whenever you ride out on Galaxy. You must trust in the wheel's judgement. The necklace carries with it the spirits of your ancestors, and they will protect you from forces of evil. The Shaman kept repeating the phrase, "Let the wheel guide you, let the wheel guide." I'm sorry, Dakota. I don't quite know what he means by that. But he clearly believes his gift will bring you more than simply good luck.'

Aislinn looked at Kyle to see if he could explain the Shaman's words with more clarity, but Kyle too looked confused. 'I can only say you need to listen to Aislinn's words, Dakota. No one speaks the ancient tongue better than she.'

Dakota listened with eyes filled with tears, and then she turned to the Shaman to thank him.

'Come, Dakota,' said Kyle. 'We know how anxious you are about your parents.'

Dakota gathered Galaxy's reins, and Kyle and Aislinn made ready to leave too.

Chaney did not remember how long she had lain holding Star in her arms. She had not left his side and had eventually fallen asleep with her head resting on his soft muzzle. She had dreamt the strangest of dreams. She had been dancing barefooted on hot coals around Star's lifeless body. She had been chanting and calling to the spirits of the earth and sky, asking them to return him to her. An ancient Aborigine had joined with her in the dance, carrying a burning shell, the smoke from which had seemed to entwine itself around Star's injured body. She remembered the scent of sage and cedar had hung heavily in the air as she had watched, incredulously, the blood from Star's gaping wound seeming to evaporate.

The old Aborigine had picked up a burning coal in his bare hands. He had blown on it, causing a long yellow flame to rise out if its centre. The flame had seemed to detach itself from the burning ember which had given it birth and, like a shimmering, flowing beam of light, had snaked its way through the air towards her. She had instinctively put up her hand to protect herself from being burnt. As the flame reached her, she felt a warm glow penetrate the palm of her outstretched hand and then travel the length of her arm. A soothing sensation of heat had filled her entire upper body, and suddenly, the searing pain in her ribcage had gone and she could breathe without discomfort once more.

She did not remember whether she was still crying when Dakota had returned. She did remember how difficult it was to take in what her sister was trying to tell her: that Aislinn had been saved and would recover. Nothing mattered any more. Star was dead, and she felt responsible. She had asked too much of him; she had pushed him too hard. How could she ever forgive herself?

'Whatever is the matter?' asked Dakota, unable to understand why Chaney was so distressed.

'It's Star,' Chaney sobbed. 'I didn't do as I was told. I never do, do I? And now Star's dead, and it's my fault. I made him jump the ravine, but he couldn't do it. He's dead, he's dead! Don't you see, Dakota, I killed him! I killed him!' She cried inconsolably.

'Then why is he eating his supper over there with Galaxy?' Dakota said, almost laughing. 'You've been asleep, I can tell, and had the most horrid of dreams. Look there, Buggy, see for yourself,' she continued, pointing at the two horses tethered a little way off who were eating some fresh grass and herbs which the Shaman had given them. 'Star is perfectly fine!'

Chaney could not believe her eyes. She sprang to her feet and raced over to her precious Arabian, throwing her arms around his neck. She stroked and patted him as he continued munching at his supper. He was clearly as pleased to see her; his nostrils flared and he whinnied with joyful recognition to see his mistress once more at his side. He moved his head to nuzzle her face. Chaney stroked his neck and kissed his muzzle and felt as if her heart would burst with happiness. Chaney could see he was fully recovered and noticed how fantastic he looked. His jet-black coat was gleaming in the gentle rays of the full moon, his eyes sparkled with health, and he was pawing at the ground, as if anxious to be on the move.

'He wants to begin the journey back,' Kyle announced happily.

'I think you must be right,' replied Chaney – and then she looked back at the ravine, and her heart sank once more.

As if reading her thoughts, the Shaman came to stand beside her and gently placed his hand on her shoulder. He tapped the ground three times with his spear, and miraculously, blue wreath flowers in their thousands seemed to spring up from the earth at their feet. He lifted his spear and pointed at the ravine, and to Chaney's amazement, a bridge of blue formed across its breadth. The Shaman then spoke in his ancient tongue to Kyle once more.

'We need to move,' said Kyle to the others. 'He has given us the floor of the sky to cross the ravine safely.'

The girls mounted quickly, and after shaking hands with the Shaman, the party made its way towards the bridge of flowers. Chaney reached the edge of the precipice first. Her heart was racing, her mouth was dry, and pure terror flowed through her veins. She felt as if her chest was being compressed by a tight iron band, making it impossible for her ribs to move. The mere mechanism of breathing was an effort. In her mind, there were awful visions of Star falling and rolling and crashing into a rock face, dying in her arms.

Dakota pulled Galaxy to a halt beside Star and somehow seemed instinctively to understand Chaney's grave misgivings. An atmosphere of tension and fear hung so thickly in the air, Dakota felt she could have cut through it with a knife. Sensing Chaney's reluctance to cross the narrow bridge which spanned the now dark and silent ravine, Dakota decided she would go first.

She spoke tenderly to her sister. 'It's alright, Chaney. Galaxy and I will lead. Just stay close behind. Put your faith in the Shaman. He will not let us down.'

Dakota edged Galaxy forward, and the horse took his first step onto the bridge. The bridge was barely a metre wide, a narrow band of blue across a vast expanse of black, with a sheer drop into nothingness on either side. Even in the moonlight, it was impossible to see the valley floor below. Well trained as he was, Star needed no direction from Chaney to follow Galaxy's softly swishing alabaster tail across the sky-blue platform. Chaney found herself on the bridge before she knew it.

She looked back at the Shaman in the pale moonlight. As their eyes met, he beamed a broad smile. To Chaney, the sudden exposure of slightly off-white, decaying and now somewhat chipped teeth was like the flash of a camera in the darkness. It made her jump slightly, and its effect was not exactly what the Shaman had intended. Instead of reassuring her, she allowed her imagination to play tricks, and the benevolent Shaman was transformed into a malevolent buccaneer. In her mind she saw the image of a pirate, a wicked captain forcing his prisoners to walk the plank, and in whose hand the Shaman's magical, mystical lifesaving spear had been replaced by a weapon of death. The pirate was brandishing a bloodstained cutlass with an evil-looking blade. She shivered and closed her eyes. She put her faith in Star, trusting that he would carry them across to safety. All Chaney could do was to try to breathe normally.

Her heart continued to pound as she lay forward onto Star's withers and clasped her arms about his neck. Her hands pressed tenderly against his soft ebony coat, quickly picking up the rhythm of his heartbeat. It was a strong, steady, slow beat that she could clearly feel as she held on tightly to him. Suddenly, she realised that her heartbeat too had slowed. It was as if they were one being, hearts beating together in unison.

'I love you, Star,' she whispered to him.

Immediately, Star nickered quietly back to her. Chaney knew that he was telling her that he loved her too. What she failed to realise was that he was also trying to reassure her. He wanted her to know that if there was need, he would carry her to the ends of the earth to bring her to safety.

The strangest thing about that crossing was the sound, or rather the lack of it. The horses' hooves made no noise as they crossed the magic bed of flowers. So quiet was their movement that they might have been naughty children tiptoeing up behind a sleeping grandmother's rocking chair, to surprise her. The only sound that Chaney could hear was that of two hearts beating strongly. Surely and steadfastly, Star followed Galaxy across to the other side. Chaney felt as if she were floating in the air. It really was the oddest sensation, not like riding at all – more like gliding. At last, the silence was broken, and Chaney opened her eyes to the clink of Galaxy's metal horseshoes on stony ground.

And – it was over. Star's hooves trod noisily on solid rock. The magic bridge and the mighty ravine lay behind them. Once safely on the other side, they turned to wave goodbye. To Chaney's disappointment however the Shaman was nowhere to be seen.

'I hope the Shaman can't read minds,' she said quietly to herself. 'If he suspected for one second that I'd pictured him as a pirate, he would think me totally ungrateful!'

'He would understand,' Aislinn called up comfortingly, having heard what Chaney had said. 'You were afraid, that's all. Don't worry about it, and be assured that he will be watching over us on our journey home. And yes,' she concluded, 'it is said that the Shaman does have telepathic powers – especially when he makes eye contact with a person.'

Chaney swallowed hard and, still feeling rather guilty, looked down at Aislinn's smiling face peering up at her from the open saddlebag. Guilt, however, was quickly replaced with awe and wonder, as she watched the bridge disintegrate before her eyes and a shower of millions upon millions of blue petals, like azure-coloured raindrops, slowly drift down to the valley floor below.

As the petals disappeared, the two sisters simultaneously spurred their horses into action. The sound of hooves hitting the ground filled the air. It was an uncomfortable ride for Kyle, Aislinn and poor Gilpin especially. The little mouse's nose was sore, and though he was safely stowed in Dakota's top breast pocket, the juddering motion of Galaxy galloping down the hillside at speed was almost more than Gilpin could bear. Every stride was agony for him.

Michael woke to dog drool. A now clearly happy and excited dog was licking his face and barking loudly.

'I hope this change of behaviour means we are about to get some good news,' he said, patting Simba's head. Carrying the swag, Michael walked Simba back to the campervan. He felt strangely less anxious about the girls, believing as he did that animals have a kind of sixth sense which humans do not. He was hoping, therefore, that whatever the old dog had been sensing – the bad vibes – had clearly now turned to good.

He checked his mobile, but there was still no new message. The police were due to arrive at midday and a decision would be taken then as to whether a search needed to be organised. *Come on, Dakota, come on, Chaney!* he thought to himself. *One of you please ring and put us out of our misery.*

Once again, as if reading his thoughts, the old dog barked loudly at him and wagged his tail back and forth in happy anticipation. Michael knelt at Simba's side, accepting the inevitable dog drool bath which would follow.

'You know they're okay, don't you, boy?' he said, looking into the affectionate brown eyes which were fixed on his face. 'Trouble is, if I tell the chief of police not to set up a search party because you've stopped whining and now have a very waggy tail, he'll think I've gone mad!'

'Woof, woof,' replied Simba as if in total agreement.

Chapter Eighteen
Fossett Shines in the Dark

Anxious to be home, they rode through the night. Both Chaney and Dakota were sick with worry for their parents. 'They must be frantic by now,' Dakota had said to her sister. 'The trouble is, we dare not contact them until we have returned Aislinn, Kyle and Gilpin safely back to the fairy kingdom. If we ring now, they're going to want to have answers, and will expect us to meet up with them straightaway. Oh gosh – this is so difficult, Buggy. I don't know what to do for the best.'

'There's only one thing we can do,' Chaney had replied. 'Send another text saying we are okay and will be home as soon as possible.'

Time was passing and they hardly dared stop, even for food or water. They were desperate to be back by morning if they could, and so they pushed the horses on as fast as they were able. Chaney was becoming increasingly anxious about Star. His body was soaked in sweat again, his heart was pumping loudly, and she could hear his breathing becoming more and more laboured.

As the night drew on, Prince Kyle did his best to light the way, but even he was feeling the effects of the demands of the task. Although he was desperate to return Aislinn to the safety of the fairy kingdom, he was finding it harder and harder to stay awake, and his wand, too, was losing power. Chaney and Dakota could barely see the path ahead in the wand's fading light – and then suddenly, there was complete darkness. Kyle was unconscious, and the wand sputtered twice and went out. They gently laid him in Chaney's saddle bag, where Aislinn was already sleeping peacefully on her little stretcher bed.

Chaney and Dakota pulled on their reins and brought the two horses to a halt. They peered into the darkness, praying for some sign to show them the way. They estimated it was now well past midnight, and both wanted the journey to be over by daylight. They tried to wake Gilpin, but the poor mouse was exhausted, and with his frostbitten nose requiring a powerful painkiller, he could not be roused from his sleep. Hidden behind a dense blanket of cloud, not one star could be seen in the night sky, and the moon had completely deserted them. It was pitch black.

From an early age, Chaney had always been afraid of the dark, and it now enveloped her like the thick velvet cape of a vampire. She felt as if she might have been in a coffin with its lid firmly nailed down, blotting out all hope of life and light. Chaney looked to her left, straining her eyes to catch sight of her sister, but all she could see was total blackness.

'I'm really trying to be brave, Tota. But I can't help feeling frightened,' Chaney called out to her sister in a trembling voice. 'It's so dark, I feel like I've gone blind. I can't even see you.'

Dakota instantly recognised the fear in Chaney's voice. 'I know. Give me your hand, Buggy,' she replied reassuringly. 'I can't see a thing either. It's as if someone has blindfolded me.'

Two sets of wriggling fingers sought each other in the darkness. After several seconds of searching, a connection was made, and two hands gripped tightly. As they held on to one another, other sounds in an otherwise silent void reached their ears. The chink, chafe and champ of bridle and bit as Galaxy and Star nuzzled heads, as if they too were trying to take courage from each other.

Unexpectedly, the distant, solitary howl of a lone dingo shivered through the oppressive night air, locking the strange unearthly gloom even tighter upon the land. Unseen in the total blackness surrounding them, Chaney's young, round face was drawn into a frown, whilst at the same time, her complexion drained of what little colour it had.

A second howl followed, quickly echoed by a third and then a fourth, each one sounding more ominous and closer to them than the one before.

'Dakota, Dad told me that dingoes mainly hunt at night and in packs,' whispered Chaney, her voice full of fear and trepidation.

'They sound a long way off, so no need to,' continued Dakota, trying to allay her sister's obvious alarm. However, she was stopped mid-sentence as the entire pack suddenly began to bay. A cacophony of long howls, deep growls and high-pitched barks quickly jarring against their ears as if the dingoes had sensed the nearness of helpless, vulnerable prey. Even Dakota felt anxious now. The wild dogs were moving in their direction and fast.

'They've been known to attack full-grown cattle and horses,' continued Chaney, refusing to be comforted. Just then, aware that a marauding pack of hungry dingoes was close on their heels, Dakota despaired of their situation.

'Chaney, we have no choice but to carry on. If we stay here, we'll be dingo food within minutes!'

'But Dakota, it would be pure madness to continue the night ride. We'll never keep the horses safe. How on earth can we cross unknown and dangerous terrain, in total darkness and without any guidance,' replied Chaney. 'One of them is sure to break a leg! Star's been injured once because of me already. I won't do that to him again.'

Then they saw it – a white shape in the distance. It was hopping up and down and coming towards them at speed. The shape loomed larger and larger, until it was almost upon them.

'Follow me and quick,' shouted a deep, husky voice they recognised immediately. 'Those dingoes I can hear sound mad with hunger! Best not hang about!' It was Fossett, and not before time, coming to their rescue.

Originating from an enchanted kingdom, the old wallaby possessed several magical qualities, one of which was luminosity. His beautiful white fur coat radiated light in darkness. You might have compared him to how a pair of reactor sunglasses adapts to the strength of the sun rays, only in reverse. The darker it got, the brighter Fossett would glow.

Galaxy and Star were spurred into action once more and galloped after the wallaby, which was clearly visible in the darkness. The albino's heavy hops thudded away, the sound and sight of him making an easy trail for them to follow. They had chased after him for some time, when suddenly the two sisters became aware of the changing light. It was as if they had been riding on a vast stage, in blackout, and suddenly the curtains had been drawn apart to reveal an audience bathed in moonlight.

Dakota looked out across an almost desert landscape, now revealed in an odd grey light. It was a landscape without pity, barren, devoid of trees and plants. Rough boulders, sharp stones and hidden potholes gave it its only definition. A full moon glittered eerily in the sky directly above her head, and sinister moonbeams seemed to track her every move, like a spotlight from a prison tower aimed purposely at an escaping prisoner.

As her eyes became accustomed to the half-light, she saw them – at first like moving shadows, elusive, distinguishable one minute and gone the next. Phantom shapes dotted dark on the ground looming in and out, and then down the wind came the sound of their snarling and baying. On either side, a wild, menacing pack of dingoes were gathering, running parallel to them and slowly, inch by inch closing in. 'Chaney, ride faster, ride for your life,' she shouted in terror.

Chaney could not answer. Blind panic had taken over her mind, and fear had gripped her very innards. She clung to Star's body, her arms wrapped tightly around his neck, reins dangling loosely in hands no longer able to guide him. The brave horse thundered on regardless, determined no harm should come to his mistress.

Galaxy too needed no urging from Dakota as stride for stride he matched Star's speed and pace across that harsh, unyielding terrain, desperate to outrun the savage dogs which threatened to attack them.

In all her life, Chaney had never been so afraid. Her imagination ran riot; she could see horse flesh being ripped from bones, her face and that of Dakota being torn to shreds and their bodies dragged across the ground as vicious teeth bit deep and held on fast, allowing no escape and incapable of mercy. She could barely breathe; her chest felt as if it might explode. Her heart pumped and pumped, faster and faster and her mouth so dry, she could scarcely swallow. Sweat poured from her brow, dripping into wild, dilated eyes, making them burn and smart painfully.

Watching from above, a strange, deep blue moon with odd shadowing at its centre seemed to track their movement. The girls and their horses were in no position to stargaze, but had they been able to lift their attention above ground level, the sight of the astral body above them would have turned the blood in their veins to ice. For drawn on its surface were the marks of deep craters, visible to the naked eye and depicting a definite shape: the image of a dog's head, broad with a long-pointed muzzle, erect ears and a gaping jaw exposing long, razor-sharp canine teeth. Most striking of all, situated on the front of the face and pointing forwards, were two evil-looking, malevolent, snake-like eyes. Black as coal and slit vertically, they stared down at the girls with a look of pure malice mixed with excitement – something in their pernicious, cruel expression, suggesting a feeling of delight and eager anticipation at the sisters' desperate situation.

Without warning, Dakota felt something grip her foot. She looked down to see a pair of slanting eyes, shining green and orange in the moonlight and sharp, pointed yellow teeth grinding into the heel of her riding boot. Instinctively, she lashed out with her riding crop, hitting the beast a mighty blow across its snout. The vicious jaws, dripping saliva opened instantly, and to Dakota's relief, the animal dropped to the ground, rolled away noisily in the dirt, before leaping back up onto its feet. It growled angrily as it returned to join the rest of the pack.

As if in sympathy with the first failed attack, every dog began to howl. Dakota could see the dingoes had now formed a perfect semi-circle around and behind them. Vicious jaws were getting dangerously close to hind quarters, so close that she could hear the gnashing of teeth as the leaders of the pack readied themselves to launch yet another attack. Above the sound of frenzied snarls and the clattering of hooves pounding on earth baked solid, Dakota suddenly heard Galaxy snorting loudly. Star instantly responded with a piercing scream.

The scream rent through the air like a terrible warning. Dakota watched in horror as two dogs jumped simultaneously at the Arabian's back legs. Misery, wretchedness and despair engulfed her, as sharp teeth attached to Star's right and left hock. Just at that moment she heard Fossett cry out:

'Thank God! I thought we were done for!'

There was a blinding flash of light, quickly followed by the sound of yelping. Dakota opened her eyes to see Star galloping on unhindered. The dingoes biting into his hind legs had miraculously disappeared. In their place and flying in the air between her and her sister, there were two fairies, both with wands raised high. The wands were emanating bright, crackling sparks of light which fizzed and whizzed in all directions.

'You're safe now,' said the fairy nearest to her. 'Just follow Fossett; the kingdom's not far.'

'Yes, just follow me,' Fossett called out loudly, 'and we can afford to slow our pace a little now. Darius and Sebastian will take care of those dingoes. That hunting pack won't trouble us again.'

Within minutes both riders began to recover from their ordeal. Chaney had charge of Star's reins once more and carefully followed Fossett's path to the letter. They had not been riding long, when, much to their relief, a hazy purple light could be seen just a little way ahead – and before they knew it, they had entered the Glen. Galaxy and Star were reined to a halt, and jumping down, both girls quickly removed their saddles. They were horrified by the amount of sweat dripping from the horses' bodies, could clearly see how tired they were and noted too how badly both were shivering.

At that moment, the jacaranda trees began glowing even more brightly in the semi-darkness, and suddenly, King Ariel was approaching with his courtiers. He took the precious saddle bag and its contents from them.

'Rest now,' he said. 'I will be back soon. My courtiers have food and water to meet all your needs.'

Dakota and Chaney tended to Galaxy's and Star's needs. 'We cannot take the horses back like this,' Dakota warned her sister. 'Better let them recover a little first before we contact Dad on our mobiles.'

'Have you texted Dad, though?' Chaney asked anxiously. 'Just to let him know that we are okay?'

'Yes,' Dakota replied, 'but it won't stop them worrying. You realise we'll never be allowed to do anything ever again?'

Gilpin, too, was much the worse for wear and feeling just as rotten. His nose had thawed, but with half of it missing, he was in so much agony he could not speak. He also had a deep cut above his left eye. He had accidentally crossed swords with a nasty thorn bush whilst seeking the blue wreath flower. It was fortunate that the thorn had gone in above his eye and not in it!

An excited reception committee was soon assembled. Aislinn – now restored to full health – together with a royal handmaiden called Giselle, tended to the returning parties' needs. Galaxy and Star were treated like heroes. Aislinn, who had prepared a special herbal remedy for tired muscles, applied the ointment thickly onto their legs and bodies. Dakota and Chaney were bathed, fed and fussed over by Giselle, as was Gilpin, and the two sisters watched with admiration and satisfaction at how skilled fairy folk were in the arts of healing and medicine.

By six o'clock in the morning, both horses were also restored to full health and were quietly grazing on the sweet grasses of the clearing. Two hammocks swayed gently in the breeze, attached to three of the jacaranda trees. Dakota and a little mouse with a bandaged nose and patched eye, lying on her chest, lay in one; and Chaney, looking more peaceful and content than she had ever done before, lay in the other. They were all fast asleep, but on the floor beneath them sat an old albino wallaby.

It was Fossett on nursemaid duty. He was keeping a watchful eye on his precious charges and quietly humming the tune of an ancient fairy lullaby. The lyrics of the lullaby, however, had been adapted slightly to suit his needs. As he sang, he moved the large feet of his hind legs backwards and forwards in time to his tune. In his right hand, he held a delicious bunch of sweet clover, and in his left, a goblet of juniper berry juice. Every so often he would stop in his musical duties to take advantage of his favourite food and drink. He could feel the warm rays of the sun penetrating his thick fur, and a soft breeze caressing him and keeping him cool.

Fossett had an unusual singing voice, which due to the deepness of his speaking voice always surprised first-time listeners. He sang falsetto and could reach incredibly high notes with ease. The entire song would be sung in this way, and Fossett's performance would always be equal to that of any professional opera singer. The sound of his voice had a strange, haunting quality that seemed to echo in the air around him. It was mesmerising, intoxicating and, like the Shaman's music, had an almost hypnotic effect on anyone listening. Eyelids became heavy, minds became still and quiet, as if every trouble in the world had somehow vanished leaving behind only peace and tranquillity. Tired, tense bodies quickly relaxed and sweet dreams beckoned, as his dulcet tones drew the listener into a deep, restful and rejuvenating sleep. He sipped his juice and sang on:

'Slow horses slow,
As through the woods we go,
We would count the stars in heaven,
And hear the grasses grow.
Though shadows now are dark
Safe on your bed of bark
No need to fear.
For Fossett's here. Oh – oh – oh.
Watch the cloudlets few,
Dapple the deep blue,
With our open palms outstretched
We'll catch the blessed dew.'

He stopped singing for a moment and, eating the last of his clover, snuggled down in the long, soft green grass making himself even more comfortable. *What bliss!* he thought. His best friend was back safe and sound, even if his nose was rather the worse for wear again, and miraculously, the girls and their horses, too, were unharmed. It was then he noticed a single black cloud in an otherwise clear blue sky. It seemed to be stationary, as if suspended by an invisible thread and unable to move.

Fossett suddenly shivered. The blackness of the cloud had reminded him of Alba, and for a moment he felt as if the cloud was watching him. The uncomfortable feeling lasted for a second or two only, before Fossett's eyes alighted on an altogether more pleasing sight.

Dozens of beautiful blue hummingbirds were darting to and fro between the jacaranda trees, stopping now and then to drink the delicious nectar of the flower. They would hover in front of the chosen blossom, their wings beating so fast that they were almost blurred from sight. Then they would reach deep inside the flower with their long narrow beaks, to reach the rich nectar contained within. Fossett watched, fascinated.

Chapter Nineteen
A Yo-Yo with Hiccups

It was close to midnight when, finally, Dakota and Chaney awoke, and both were horrified that they had slept through an entire day. As they wiped the sleep from their eyes, they could hardly believe the transformation which had taken place within the Glen. Once again, the jacaranda trees had come to life. Their branches had straightened and turned to gold, and their purple blooms had doubled in size and glowed magnificently in the darkness, lighting the whole of the forest floor beneath them.

'Look, Tota, look. Isn't it beautiful?' said Chaney, as she pointed up at the magnificent blossoms and through them to the night sky.

Dakota gazed up at a vast canopy of the deepest blue, littered with thousands of tiny white pinpoints of light and dominated by the celestial body of the moon. It was a splendid, full and radiant moon, which tonight seemed almost close enough to be able to reach out and touch.

Rachael, too, was contemplating the beauty of the night sky. She was standing outside the campervan, looking up at hills bathed in dappled, silver moonlight. The moon appeared to be trying to play a game of hide and seek behind fluffy black clouds. Rachael, however, was in no mood for games. She was worried sick about her daughters and, unable to sleep, had wandered outside for a breath of fresh air. Simba, who had been howling on and off for the past three days and nights, came and sat at her feet. He seemed strangely quiet and settled, and not at all agitated as he had been before.

Rachael suddenly caught sight of an outline, a silhouette on the horizon. As her eyes strained to make the figure out more clearly, she was also aware that she could hear singing. The clouds of the night sky parted, and the rays of a radiant moon lit the hills in an unexpected blaze of silver light. Now she could see the thin Aboriginal man and his painted body easily and hear his singing. He appeared to be dancing and was holding what looked like a spear in one hand, pointing out into the distance with the other.

As Rachael listened to his song and its strange, haunting melody, she felt her body relax. All the tension and anxiety she had been feeling seemed inexplicably to drain away. She turned to look at Simba momentarily, and when her gaze returned to the faraway hills, the horizon was empty. The gaunt, tall figure of the Aboriginal man had vanished. Instead, in her mind's eye, she had a vision of her two precious girls. They were riding their horses, they were smiling, and they were heading home. Simba barked and began wagging his tail.

'You know too, don't you, boy? They're safe, and they're coming back.'

At that moment, the girls were climbing out of their hammocks and surveying the wondrous sights all around them. Dakota could not believe how beautiful the Fairy Glen looked, but her heart turned to stone as she thought about her parents.

'What must they be feeling?' she thought to herself. 'They will be out of their minds with worry.' She took her mobile phone out of her pocket and switched it on. There were dozens of missed messages and calls, and all were from her parents. Afraid they would be too upsetting to read or listen to, she simply texted:

'Back tomorrow. We are all fine. Moingup Springs best rendezvous for us. See you about midday. Sorry so late. Xxx'

As the two girls continued to survey their surroundings in awe and wonder, they were joined by Aislinn and Kyle.

'My father, King Ariel, wishes to speak with you. We've come to take you to him,' said Kyle. The two fairies flew ahead, leading the way. Dakota and Chaney found themselves walking through a tunnel of hovering fairies, all clapping and cheering as the two sisters made their way forwards to meet with the King. When they reached the centre of the Glen, King Ariel immediately flew to greet them.

'Dakota and Chaney…this is in honour of you,' he announced, pointing to a newly formed flowerbed right at their feet. 'These flowers will bloom perpetually here in exactly this spot,' he continued, 'they will serve as a reminder to all fairy folk of your brave deeds. Your courage will never be forgotten.'

The two sisters looked down and saw a large circle of pure-black tulips surrounded by an outer circle of stargazer lilies. It seemed to Chaney that it was almost in the shape of an eye.

'The flowers are more than they presently seem,' said King Ariel. 'They are a window for us to see how you are faring, and for your protection. If you are ever in danger, this will happen…'

As he waved his wand above the flowers, Dakota and Chaney watched in amazement as the flowers seemed to melt into the ground. In their place was an outer ring of white marble shaped like the iris of an eye, framing the perfect black circle of its pupil. As they watched, a tiny beam of light appeared at the exact centre of the pupil, and bands of light began to radiate out like ripples across water. The pupil gradually transformed into an inner mirror of black glass in which they could see themselves with wonderful clarity. They were standing in the Glen beside Kyle and Aislinn with King Ariel hovering above them, smiling and nodding and looking incredibly pleased.

'I give you my solemn vow that you are now, and always will be, under our protection. But', he continued, 'I must ask that you also make a vow. You must promise never to speak of us to anyone – not even your parents. There are some humans who would seek to capture us for their own financial gain. The fairy kingdom would be inundated with fortune hunters, and our habitat and way of life would slowly be destroyed.'

Dakota and Chaney realised that what King Ariel had said was true. Speaking out loud for all to hear, they made a solemn vow that the existence of the fairy kingdom would remain a secret forever. After the girls had given their oath, there was an odd silence. A hush had fallen over the gathered throng of fairies, as grateful and relieved ears listened to the promise being made. An atmosphere of tranquillity and serenity seemed to fill the Glen, and hundreds of fairy eyes looked with admiration and affection at the two brave sisters.

'I'm hungry,' said Chaney, breaking the silence.

'Then let us feast!' said King Ariel loudly.

'And I declare the new fairy hospital open,' said Queen Charlotte. Queen Charlotte, the King's wife, had been hovering in the air a little distance away from her husband. She flew forward as she spoke, to meet him.

The girls immediately noticed her strange appearance. She was wearing a long, flowing ball gown made of what looked like pink silk. The dress was incredibly creased, however, and hardly seemed to fit her. It had clearly slipped, and she was in danger of exposing more than just her left shoulder! She had masses of wild, grey untamed hair fashioned into giant curls which seemed to spiral out in all directions. Looking at her quite remarkable head of hair, Chaney was instantly reminded of a lion's mane. On the top of the mane, she wore a golden crown encrusted with diamonds and sapphires. Unfortunately, the crown was set at an odd angle, and the girls were convinced it was about to fall off at any moment. At first her striking blue eyes had seemed enormous, but as she drew closer, Dakota and Chaney could see she was wearing spectacles. The lenses of the spectacles were the thickest the two girls had ever seen and magnified the size of the old Queen's eyes at least twenty-fold.

'No, dear,' said King Ariel, turning to look at his wife. 'That was last week. You remember, I'm sure? Tonight, we are celebrating the safe return of Aislinn.'

'Of course, we are, my dear husband – how remiss of me to forget!' And then the ageing Queen, Prince Kyle and Aislinn all clapped in agreement. As they did so, they were joined by a number of the Queen's royal handmaidens. It seemed to Dakota that they very quickly whisked the old Queen away.

If you had been called upon to describe Queen Charlotte's appearance in just one word, perhaps the adjective 'dishevelled' would spring to mind. Even the old Queen's wings looked as if they had seen better days. They were lopsided to begin with, and the top corner of the left wing was bent over backwards, making an odd cracking sound as the Queen struggled to remain airborne.

Chaney also noted, to her amusement, that the wings of all the other fairies beat simultaneously and smoothly. In contrast, Queen Charlotte's wings flapped separately, one after the other, and the damaged left wing seemed to stutter every time it was its turn to beat. Consequently, the ageing Queen was unable to maintain a hover on the same level. Instead, she moved up and down like a yo-yo with hiccups!

Chapter Twenty
River Dance and the Red Arrows

Now it was the King's turn to clap his hands, and magically, tables and soft cushioned chairs appeared from nowhere, as well as all manner of good things to eat and drink. The fairy banquet was a magnificent sight to behold, with hundreds of burning candles floating above the tables. The beautiful flickering light was reflected in the many silver plates and goblets which had been laid out before them. Chaney noticed immediately how the candle flames created a wonderful glow, illuminating each exquisite dish on offer. Dakota suddenly remembered ordering a delicious dish of red snapper at her favourite restaurant overlooking Cottesloe Beach, and a plate serving that very fish immediately arrived in front of her.

'How did you do that?' Chaney queried in some admiration.

'I honestly don't know,' replied Dakota, laughing. 'I just thought about it!'

Ten minutes later you could not see Chaney for the huge mountain of food piled in front of her. Dish upon dish of burgers and chips, bubblegum ice cream, Fruit Loops, popcorn, chocolate gateaux, Danish pastries and croissants lay before her.

The banquet highlighted yet another trait which made the two girls so different. Dakota ate healthily, always following her mother's advice on the importance of a well-balanced diet. Consequently, she ate fresh fruit and vegetables, loved fish dishes and avoided junk food at all costs. Chaney, on the other hand, had an overly sweet tooth – ice cream and chocolate were by far her favourite foods. Chaney was obsessed with junk food. She had to be pulled past the door to McDonald's or JFK's on virtually every shopping trip. Her mouth would begin to water just at the thought of a burger and chips – and all, of course, liberally covered in ketchup. Her parents were aware of her eating habits and did their best to curtail her excesses. But Chaney was nothing if not clever, and often found ways to undo their good intentions.

'It's a good job Mum's not here to see what you've put on your plate,' said Dakota pointedly. 'You would be getting the scolding of your life!'

'I know,' said Chaney, and they both began to giggle.

Midway through the feast, Queen Charlotte paid the girls a flying visit.

'Are you having plenty to eat and drink?' she enquired, with genuine interest.

'Oh yes,' Chaney replied with enthusiasm. 'This is the best meal I've had in my entire life!'

'Good, good – I'm glad to hear it,' continued the old Queen. 'And what is that you are eating?' she asked, pointing her wand at Chaney's bubble-gum ice cream.

'Ice cream, your Majesty,' Chaney courteously replied.

'May I try some?' Queen Charlotte enquired.

'Of course, please do,' responded Chaney.

Immediately, the old Queen stuck her wand deep into Chaney's ice cream. She pulled it out with a scooping motion, and then began to lick the wand clean.

'This is scrumptious, really scrumptious,' she called out loudly to the two handmaidens who had followed behind her. 'May I send one of my courtiers to fill a small bowl for me? I've never tasted anything quite so delicious!' And with that she returned to her throne, ice cream trickling down her chin. The two girls giggled with amusement.

'She looks a bit better now…not quite so untidy,' Dakota remarked to Chaney, once the old Queen had gone. The royal handmaidens had clearly been hard at work. For one thing, her dress had been fastened properly and no longer looked as if it was about to fall off. Her hair, too, had been combed and brushed down, and the diamond and sapphire crown was now sitting squarely and securely on top of her head. The old Queen looked much more presentable and not as she had done earlier, when you might have been forgiven for thinking that she had just been dragged through a hedge backwards. Only the overfull goblet of wine, which she carried in her right hand and from which she was spilling red wine willy-nilly everywhere, gave a clue as to the fact that poor Queen Charlotte was not altogether in control of her faculties.

Like Chaney, however, Queen Charlotte was also making the most of the feast. One royal handmaiden after another approached Chaney on behalf of the Queen to ask if she could sample something else that Chaney was eating. She clearly shared Chaney's sweet tooth. The old Queen's favourite dish remained the bubble-gum ice cream, however. So much so, that by the end of the evening she had had six enormous helpings!

Dakota noted Prince Kyle's love and devotion towards his mother. Every few minutes he would fly back to her side and place her right arm affectionately on his to support her. Even sitting on her royal throne, Queen Charlotte distinctly leant to her left, and at times looked precariously in danger of toppling over altogether. King Ariel too, was clearly very fond of his ailing wife. He remained at her weaker side constantly, and when airborne, his right arm stayed firmly around her waist.

The two sisters thought the fairies entirely charming. One could not fail to see the love which bound them all together. Theirs was a special society, rich in tenderness and full of caring. Dakota and Chaney felt honoured and privileged to be a part of it.

Whilst they ate, strange but beautiful music played all around them and filled the air with melodic sounds and tunes, the like of which the two sisters had never heard before. Dakota and Chaney could see musicians sitting in the branches of the trees and playing on a variety of instruments. They saw what appeared to be giant golden harps which made the most amazing and beautifully haunting sound. When the feast was over, the tables simply vanished, and the chairs withdrew of their own accord to form a seating area just inside the circle of trees. It was time for the Dance!

Both Dakota and Chaney loved to dance, but what they were to witness that special night thrilled them more than anything they had ever seen before. It was an airborne display of sheer brilliance; thousands of fairies moving as one great cloud of colour, like myriads of shooting stars all in unison with one another; perfect synchronisation, fast, daring, and extraordinarily beautiful. Not a 'Strip the Willow' in sight, but hundreds of loop-the-loops, diving, swirling, spinning, and soaring, with the small winged bodies moving now in canon and now as one great body of colour and light. Dakota and Chaney watched, mesmerised at the spectacle of flying which was presented to them. It was the most beautiful thing they had ever seen. Years later, Chaney referred to it as 'Irish River Dance meets the Red Arrows!'

Hours later, a lone voice broke the stillness of the night. 'Dakota, Dakota,' groaned Chaney in an uncomfortable tone, 'I feel sick!'

'I'm not surprised,' Dakota replied unsympathetically, and with that she fell straight back to sleep.

Chaney heard fairy wings hovering above her. It was the ageing queen, Queen Charlotte, who had come back to check on the girls. Admittedly, she was getting slightly senile in her old age, but she had a truly kind heart and could be relied upon to at least try to help others whenever she could. She heard Chaney's discomfort and waved her wand above her. Chaney immediately fell asleep. The old Queen looked at Chaney's now sleeping frame and smiled happily at her own handiwork. *That's what she needs,* she thought to herself. *A good night's sleep and she'll be right as rain.*

Unfortunately, Queen Charlotte was also feeling the effects of an over-indulgent evening, and without giving a second thought to the consequences, she proceeded to wave her wand above her own head. Instantly, she dropped like a stone and crash-landed unannounced into the lap of a sleeping albino wallaby. Fossett awoke with so sudden a jolt that he thought he'd been having a nightmare.

King Ariel arrived and apologised to Fossett for the disruption. As he carried his now-comatose wife back to the palace, King Ariel thought to himself, *The sooner Kyle and Aislinn take over the royal throne, the better.*

It had been a difficult year. Queen Charlotte had made a number of embarrassing errors in recent public engagements. Indeed, there had been two weddings when, instead of blessing the happy couple with long life and progeny, Queen Charlotte had waved her wand – and the bride and groom had suddenly found themselves stripped of their finery and standing only in their underwear!

Early the next day, Chaney and Star and Dakota and Galaxy left the Fairy Glen. They were anxious to be reunited with their parents as soon as possible. Fossett looked sad to see them go. The old wallaby remained under one of the jacaranda trees for some time, watching the horses and their riders disappear into the distance. When at last they were just a speck on the horizon, he turned and hopped back into the centre of the Glen. He lay back in the long, soft grass and closed his eyes. He must have dozed off for an hour or two. When he awoke, the first thing he saw were Darius and Sebastian standing over the spot where the circle of lilies and tulips should have been. As Fossett approached, he could see that the magic eye had formed.

'I don't understand it,' Darius said to his friend.

'Neither do I,' replied Sebastian.

'What? What don't you understand?' Fossett asked with curiosity.

'Why has the eye formed? It should only happen if the girls are at risk of harm. There's something not right, and we need to get to the bottom of it.' Sebastian spoke with obvious anxiety in his voice. 'Ever since the night of the dingo attack, I've had grave concerns.'

'What do you mean?' said Fossett, now feeling even more worried for the girls' safety.

'A hunting pack like that! Darius and I said at the time, we'd never ever known dingoes to gather in such numbers, behave quite so aggressively or to hunt down a kill over that distance. They must have chased the girls for several miles.'

'Oh, they did, and would have caught them had it not been for your timely arrival,' Fossett replied gratefully.

'Well, you have the Shaman to thank for that,' said Sebastian. 'He'd picked up your thoughts, your desperate cries for help and directed them to us. We knew straightaway of the danger you were in and what had to be done.'

'The Shaman,' Fossett repeated. 'I'd wondered as much.' And looking down at the magic eye he added, 'I've got a hunch we'll need his help again and soon! I can feel it in these old bones of mine, something is very wrong,' he concluded.

'I'll fetch the King,' said Darius. 'The sooner he knows the eye has formed, the better.'

As Darius returned to the palace, Fossett stared down at the eye. In the dark mirror, he could see the two girls clearly. They were riding towards a large white campervan, and two people and two extremely excited dogs were waiting outside it to greet them. Fossett laughed as he witnessed the chaos of their welcome. People were hugging, dogs were leaping about all over the place, horses were stamping the ground and neighing loudly, and there was lots of kissing going on. Happy smiling faces abounded and were being covered with copious amounts of dog drool!

Fossett was also suddenly aware of one other thing. In an otherwise clear blue sky, small black clouds seemed to be amassing above them. The clouds appeared to be hovering high in the sky directly above the girls and their family. Once again, Fossett had a feeling that something evil and ominous was gathering, watching and waiting. A cold chill ran through his body, making him shiver.

'Is there a connection?' he asked himself. 'Are the girls in danger, and has anyone else spotted that cloud? There really is something very sinister about it.'

The King and Darius returned. The three fairies studied the mirror for some considerable time, talking quietly together. Fossett stayed where he was, watching them and remaining silent, waiting for an opportunity to speak.

'What do you make of it?' he finally asked when their conversation ended.

'Difficult to say with any certainty,' the King replied. 'But that black cloud above them worries me. Don't you think it rather odd, that it doesn't seem to move?' He continued, directing his comments more to Darius and Sebastian than to Fossett.

'We must call a meeting of the High Council immediately and set up a watch,' the King commanded. 'Darius, Sebastian, gather the Elders. We will meet within the hour in the Great Hall.'

'Can I help?' asked Fossett.

'Yes, Fossett…fetch Prince Kyle as quickly as you can. I want round-the-clock surveillance on the girls. Get him to organise it straightway. We gave our word to watch over them, and that is exactly what we will do. Quick, now,' the King ordered. 'No time to lose!'

Rachael had gone to feed the dogs, Michael was lighting the BBQ ready to cook tea, and the girls were working hard on grooming the horses and giving them their well-earned night feed.

'Dad looks worn out,' Dakota said, with tears in her eyes.

'Mum's the same,' Chaney added, 'and they both look thinner.'

'I expect they've been too worried to eat,' Dakota commented.

'Did we do the right thing, Dakota?' Chaney asked in an emotional voice, thick with guilt. She began to cry.

'Buggy, it's no use crying over spilled milk,' Dakota said, coming to her side and putting her arms around her affectionately. 'We were in a catch-22 situation.'

'What's a catch-22 situation?' Chaney asked, through her tears.

'It's a situation when you're in the wrong if you do something and equally in the wrong if you don't – a no-win situation, in other words. I think we made the right choice in helping Aislinn, even though we knew what torment we would be putting our parents through. We just need to make up for it now that we're back. We can start by making Mum and Dad realise, once more, just how much we do love them, and that they can trust us.'

'Do they think we don't love them?' Chaney said, crying even more.

Dakota was beginning to lose patience. 'For goodness' sake, Chaney, you were the one who was adamant we had to help Aislinn! Now we've got to live with the consequences of our actions. Grow up, will you, and help me start to make amends! You can begin by helping Mum with the dogs.'

'I'd rather help Dad with the BBQ,' Chaney replied with feeling.

'Right,' said Dakota. 'You go and help Dad, and I'll help Mum.'

Chapter Twenty-One
The Muffin Thief

Normality was restored. The family sat around a portable picnic table, enjoying the late-afternoon sunshine and the breath-taking scenery. Simba and Enzo were in their usual places either side of Chaney, only this time there were to be no titbits. Everybody cleared their plate.

'I'm sorry it's just mundane steak and chips,' said Michael as he served the meal. 'When we get back home, we'll go to the Cottesloe Beach restaurant and you can order your favourite dish. Rachael can have her lobster Thermidor, Chaney her fried chicken, and Dakota her red snapper.'

'Oh, don't worry about Tota's red snapper – she had that last night,' Chaney blurted out unthinkingly.

Michael and Rachael shot Chaney a look of absolute bewilderment.

'She means I dreamt I had it,' Dakota quickly added, trying to cover their tracks. 'By last night we had virtually run out of food, so we were daydreaming about our favourite dishes.'

Satisfied with the explanation, Michael continued. 'I found these in the freezer at home,' he said, bringing out two tubs of ice cream. One was bubble-gum flavour and the other raspberry ripple.

Chaney took one look at the bubble-gum ice cream, groaned and felt sick again.

'Oh, none for me, thank you,' she said, much to the disbelief of her parents. 'Have you got any grapes instead?'

'Is she ill?' Rachael asked Dakota, turning to look at her oldest daughter.

'No, just trying to turn over a new leaf,' Dakota replied, with a wide grin on her face.

'Well, I'm awfully glad to hear it,' Michael responded.

Michael, as a nature lover, had been waiting to show his daughters some of the unique flora and fauna of the area. As soon as the meal was over, he walked with them to the lakeside.

'Look,' he said, pointing to the unusual millstream palms which lined the shore. Scores of dragonflies darted about them. As they lingered, admiring their brightly coloured wings, a troop of kangaroos arrived to drink from the lake, and two flying foxes could be seen soaring between the branches of a line of trees on the far bank.

Chaney was particularly struck by the beauty of the dragonflies. There must have been a dozen or more different varieties, judging by the kaleidoscope of colours on display. Then it occurred to Chaney how similar the fairies' wings had been to the ones she was now watching. *That's it,* she thought to herself. *The fairies' wings were exactly like dragonfly wings.* She remembered their shape clearly and in her mind's eye visualised once again two pairs of strong transparent wings, ornately patterned with wonderful tracery across their length and breadth. She smiled happily to herself as she thought with fondness of her magical friends.

Satisfied they had seen enough, the family returned to the campervan. The girls gave the two dogs their final walk and swim of the day, and then checked on Star and Galaxy. Happy that the horses were content and had plenty of food and water, they re-joined their parents.

The family sat and talked long into the night. Inevitably, questions were asked as to why they had not returned at the allotted time. The girls could only say they had got lost. They had decided to say nothing about the fairies – after all, who would believe them? Worse still, their solemn vow to King Ariel would have been broken, and so they both stuck to the story like glue.

To Michael and Rachael, the days leading up to the endurance race the girls were to enter seemed to fly past. To Dakota and Chaney, the reverse was true; the days crawled by at a snail's pace. Every morning when Chaney awoke, she would put another line across her calendar, as one by one the days to the competition were ticked off. *How much longer is there to go?* was her first thought every morning and her last thought every night.

'Yes, at last!' Chaney said out loud as the day marked 'Packing' was duly ticked, quickly followed by the two days marked 'Travel'. Now after what had seemed an exceptionally long journey with only a very few stops to stretch their legs, they had arrived at the venue – a huge equestrian park, now bursting to its seams with expectant visitors. Anticipation was high, for tomorrow would see the start of the actual event. Chaney could hardly contain her pleasure. Finally, the long-awaited day had arrived, and she wrote 'Hooray!' on her calendar.

Dakota and Chaney were up early. The two girls had hardly slept a wink all night, so excited were they at the prospect of competing for the very first time in Australia's legendary 160-kilometre Endurance Horse Racing Championship. They tiptoed out of the camper trailer so as not to waken their parents and went to see if any of the race officials were about.

'We need the maps,' said Dakota, 'and then we can begin to look at the course and decide the best way to ride it. We need to plan our route carefully, and our success, believe me, will depend on thorough and meticulous planning.'

'Well, at least there's one thing we have in our favour,' replied Chaney with confidence. 'Star and Galaxy are the two best horses in the world.' Dakota smiled at her sister, and they walked on, hand in hand.

They made their way around the central arena, normally used for show-jumping events, but for this highly specialised competition, it had now been turned in to a spacious exercise area where not only could the horses and riders recover, but the vets could also carry out their required inspection of each horse after each leg of the race. There were a number of officials' tents pitched inside, but after the girls had given a brief investigative peek into each of them, it was clear that they were obviously empty.

'We're too early,' Dakota murmured, half to herself.

'Better go and give Star and Galaxy their breakfast then,' suggested Chaney, who was beginning to think breakfast might be a good idea for them also. 'We can come back later with Dad and get all the information we need then.'

Dakota concurred, and the two walked together to the stable block. The horses tucked into their breakfasts enthusiastically as if they too knew something special was about to happen, and from the excited nodding of their heads, it was clear that they were raring to go. Happy that the horses had been well fed and watered, the girls returned to the campervan just in time to savour the egg and bacon muffins that their mother had prepared.

'These are gorgeous,' said Chaney, as she inadvertently dropped her hand below the table. Enzo thought his luck was in and immediately grabbed the muffin in his mouth. It was swallowed in an instant. Chaney gasped in shock and horror.

'Is there any chance of another one, Mum? I really have an appetite this morning,' Chaney pleaded, with her fingers crossed.

'Oh, sorry,' her mother replied. 'That was the last of the bacon.'

Enzo recognised the expression on Chaney's face and beat a hasty retreat!

Just after 9 am, as they were exercising Star and Galaxy in the main arena, a klaxon sounded, and an announcement came over the loudspeaker system. All team managers and riders were invited to register in the main official's tent where details of the course, maps and other information would be issued. Once registered, the girls returned to the trailer to familiarise themselves with the course, and to locate where natural waterholes could be found in addition to the planned water stations the organisers had already marked on the map. The maps were spread out on the table, and all the family studied hard for several hours, until they were sure that they had chosen the best route available.

'Gosh – we start tonight at midnight!' Chaney read out loud. 'I'm going to rely on Star's eyes. He sees much better in the dark than I do.'

'There are over a hundred riders, I believe,' commented Dakota, 'and one of the officials told me that this year's course will really test both horses and riders to the limit. I think you're right, Buggy, about relying on the horses' better vision. Setting out at midnight is going to be pretty scary. We'll be running around on horses with a full head of steam and likely to be just as excited as we are. Galaxy definitely has better eyes in the dark than I do, and I would hate to lead us all safely for the first five kilometres and then have us all plunge down a wombat hole!'

'Well, anyway,' Chaney pointed out, 'this is a twenty-four-hour ride after all, so we've got to ride in the dark at some point, whether we like it or not!'

Looking at her watch, Dakota reminded Chaney that they needed to get both horses to their pre-ride vet check. The two horses passed with flying colours, and as the vets complimented the girls on the condition of their mounts, they also explained that after each leg, the horses had to come back to the arena and be vetted again.

Chapter Twenty-Two
Scorched by the Sun

It was just before midnight. Galaxy and Dakota and Star and Chaney were on the start line, with all the other horses and riders about them. Many of the horses were getting very fiery and worked up. There was such a hubbub of noise, Chaney worried she wouldn't hear the starting klaxon when it sounded. Then she heard Dakota's comforting voice.

'Remember the plan, Buggy. Just stick behind the lead group, relax and let Star follow. He knows where he is going; his feet will be on the ground, and he'll be running for it. They are both well-trained to stay behind the lead horse, so sit tight and let Star go on autopilot. Trust him.' As she spoke her final words, the klaxon sounded, and they were off.

Rachael and Michael and the two dogs were watching all the action from the side. The two dogs barked loudly as the horses galloped away. Michael had to hold onto to Enzo's lead very tightly. The young dog would have loved to join the field, and almost tore Michael's arm out of its socket as he jumped forward to follow Chaney and Dakota over the start line.

On this first leg, the arrows they had to follow were white. It was a fairly flat but winding route covering over 30 kilometres of bushland. Lack of experience meant that both horses were a little behind the lead group in the first five kilometres, but as the hours passed, they began to move further and further up the field. Some two hours later they sensed they were returning to the ride base, and as if their horses could smell home and food and water, they began to nose ahead of the field. Once in the lead, it became even more important to spot the markers. If they were to take a wrong turn now, the ride would be finished, and they would be lost.

'No worries,' shouted Dakota as the two girls rounded the final bend of that first leg and felt their horses accelerate towards the finish line.

Immediately, the horses were back in the vetting arena; they were given a thorough check over.

'Okay to go,' said the chief vet. 'Heart rate well inside the sixty limit, and no sign of any lameness.'

Chaney and Dakota could not believe their luck. They were the first team ready to set out on the second leg.

If the first leg had been flat, this leg was the opposite. The trail would take them right over the top of Mount Stromlo and down the other side, heading back home along a narrow causeway which ran parallel to a dried-up riverbank to the east of the park and the finish line. It was not an easy climb, and both Dakota and Chaney relied on their horses to pick their own route up the steep hillside. Once they reached the top, however, it was decided that Galaxy would lead the way down. He was just slightly more surefooted than Star, and it would be safer, therefore, for Chaney and Star to follow his lead. They did not choose a good line, however, and in several places as they descended, the gradient was incredibly steep – far more so than the girls would have wished for. Nevertheless, both horses kept their heads and their courage. After what was a painstakingly slow descent at times, they eventually reached the bottom and found themselves able to pick up the pace once more.

The sun was now high above them in a bright blue sky as they cantered on along the narrow causeway on the return trail, following the designated yellow arrows of the second leg. Dakota estimated they were about four kilometres away from the main arena. 'Nearly there,' she called to Chaney. 'Keep going!'

Suddenly Star, who was now leading, reared in the air, almost throwing Chaney to the ground. 'Whoa, boy, whoa!' Chaney cried, whilst regaining her balance. Dakota had reined Galaxy to a halt.

'What's the problem?' she called out to her sister.

'Snake – looks like a rather large death adder,' replied Chaney almost casually. 'It's lying right in the middle of the path and is obviously enjoying the sun as much as we are. We'll skirt around,' she said, pulling on Star's rein and leading him down off the causeway and around the obstruction. Once clear, they climbed back up onto the causeway path and resumed an easy canter home.

In less than an hour they were back in the main arena, but no longer in the lead. Several riders had returned ahead of them. 'We took a bad line on the descent,' Dakota explained to her parents, and between accounts of the last leg and plans for the next leg, the girls both drank heartily.

As soon as the horses had been vetted and cleared, they were off again on the third leg, and this time following red arrows. This was probably the trail they had looked forward to the most, for it would take them right through the centre of Stromlo Forest, and they both loved riding forest trails.

The trees would also offer some shelter from the heat of the sun, which by now was intense. The ride was breathtakingly beautiful; dappled shade, and golden rays of sunlight lighting their way along the forest path. All manner of trees surrounded them including the now much-loved jacaranda. As they rode beneath the familiar purple blossoms, they could not help but think of the Fairy Glen and all their new-found friends. They were so enamoured by their surroundings that they almost missed a critical set of red markers. Star, however, spotted the sudden change of direction in the trail and, ignoring Chaney's rein, correctly stayed on route. Chaney praised him when she realised how clever he had been.

The trees began to thin out, and they soon found themselves climbing up a track wide enough for them to ride side by side. They chatted as the long hours passed, until they reached the brow of a hill. The view was spectacular and looked out across a huge expanse of forest.

'Look there,' said Dakota, 'there's the waterfall and rock pool.'

Thanks to Star's sharp eyes, they had arrived at a point they had planned to reach. They turned both horses and sped towards the welcome supply of fresh water. The four of them drank thirstily. The water was crystal-clear and deliciously cold.

Having drank their fill, they remounted and returned to the route. The trail now returned them to the forest, but this time descending. Even underneath the canopy of leaves, the two girls were aware of the heat of the sun. As the hours passed, it seemed to get increasingly hotter, so much so that it was becoming uncomfortable to breathe.

A pitiless sun scorched the girls' backs and burnt bare necks red raw – a spiteful sun which continued to broil the land mercilessly. So intense was the heat that streams and waterholes had completely dried up. Worse still, the earth, now baked to a crisp, raised choking, suffocating dust swirls on the hot wind which continued to torment them.

'Dakota, this heat is unbearable!' Chaney called out to her sister, as she mopped her sweaty brow on the back of her sleeve.

'I know,' replied Dakota. 'I'm feeling it too, and so are the horses.'

The girls began to take even more care of their horses, often going without water themselves to make sure Galaxy and Star kept rehydrating from the little they had left in their water bottles. They were very sensible and because of the heat did not push the horses too fast. It proved a wise decision. They were soon out in the open scrubland once more, following the markers along a narrow dirt trail which led back to the equestrian park and the finish line. The road ahead of them seemed to shiver in the oppressive heat, making the task of picking out the best route even more difficult. Worse still, beads of sweat ran down their faces and dripped into their eyes which by now were swollen, sore and smarting painfully.

Neither girl spoke; it would have needed too much energy, and nor did they want to admit to each other how tired and hot they were feeling. As they became more and more dehydrated, they were concerned at how much their eyesight was being affected. So reduced was their vision that they were now having difficulty in seeing and following the red markers. Fortunately for them, Galaxy and Star with their excellent training were following the route with precision. The girls were even more shocked when they almost rode over a fallen rider lying in the middle of the trail. They dismounted and went to the aid of their fellow competitor. Chaney carefully held her water bottle for the rider to quench his thirst, whilst Dakota tended to the horse. It wasn't long before both horse and rider were much recovered.

'Your horse isn't gravely injured, but he's definitely gone lame. You won't be able to ride him, I'm afraid. Best if you stay here, I think. We'll leave you with some extra water and let your team know where you are when we get back,' Dakota advised the rider in as comforting a tone of voice as possible, noting only too clearly the look of disappointment on his face.

'Oh, I'm okay for water,' the young man replied. 'I think it's probably a loose shoe which has caused us the problem – that, and I have been pushing him hard.' He took the reins from Dakota and patted his own mount affectionately. 'We'll stay here,' he said, as he led his limping horse to the welcome shade of a nearby eucalyptus tree. 'You get on – we'll be fine.'

Remounting Galaxy and Star, the two sisters continued, anxious to get help as soon as they could. It was their first thought as they crossed the finish line. They quickly told officials where the fallen horse and rider were, and a search party was sent out immediately. Only then did they tend to their own needs. They desperately needed to rehydrate, and it was Galaxy and Star who received attention first. They took a little extra time to recover and were relieved to hear from their father that the horses had received the go-ahead, following the veterinary inspection, to continue. Some of the other horses had not.

'Field's down to about eighty now,' their father informed them. 'People are just not taking account of the demands put on a horse in these endurance events, even when the weather is favourable!'

'What on earth are you talking about, Dad? The weather's hardly favourable!' Chaney exclaimed in surprise. 'It was incredibly hot out there today. Wasn't it, Tota?'

'No, don't exaggerate, Buggy!' Dakota declared, disagreeing vehemently. As she spoke, she fired a warning glare across her younger sister's bows. Chaney needed to be alerted to the fact that if too much fuss was made about the conditions, their father would have no hesitation in pulling them out of the race altogether. 'It probably just felt ridiculously hot, possibly because it's the first time we've done this event – and I, for one, am definitely feeling the pressure.' Dakota felt a pang of guilt over lying to her father but knew she had no choice.

Michael nodded and added, 'The event would be called off if a heat wave or bad weather was forecast, and anyway your mother and I would certainly not let you carry on if it was. That would be far too dangerous.'

'We just need to stay calm and take it steady,' Dakota continued with conviction. 'Don't worry, Dad. We won't push the horses too hard, and we'll make sure we keep on taking in plenty of water.'

Chaney thought back to when she had pushed Star beyond his limits, back to the jump across the ravine. She patted Star's head, blinked away a tear, and then nodded her head in agreement.

As Dakota walked back to the waiting paddock to collect Galaxy for the next stage of the race, she was deep in thought. It seemed to her, once she and Chaney were out on the ride on their own, that the weather was beginning to alter. It was as if someone was turning the heating up on a thermostat and specifically targeting them. She also had the horrible feeling that they were being watched – a feeling which made her want to keep looking back over her shoulder. She tried to dismiss this unpleasant thought and push it to the back of her mind.

'I must be getting paranoid because of all this pressure,' she told herself. 'I simply have to concentrate and focus on the job in hand, and stop imagining things that don't exist...'

Chapter Twenty-Three
Storm Clouds Gather

They set off on the fourth leg, following blue markers. This leg was a combination of all the first three: an area of flat plain, a hillside ascent and a forest trail leading back to the ride arena. It was early morning, and although the sun was just rising in the sky, the air was already hot and dry. As they rode across the open bush, dust clouds rose in huge billowing drifts around them. The acrid grey dust got in their eyes and in their nose, making them blind for seconds on end or causing them to choke as they struggled for breath. But neither one of them complained. They journeyed on relentlessly, stopping only occasionally to water the horses. Slowly the terrain began to alter, and they found themselves climbing a steep hillside once more.

Both horses were sweating profusely, which was hardly surprising considering the increased physical demand being placed upon them as they struggled to make the steep climb. The girls slowed the pace, trying to minimise the intensity of effort required to reach the summit.

At last, they were at the top, but the view, although stupendous was also rather weird. Neither of the girls had ever seen a mirage before, but they recognised it for what it was. They looked down on a strange and eerie sight. The whole world seemed to be shimmering, wavering in a spiralling current of hot air rising into the heavens. The heat was unbearable.

'Come on,' ordered Dakota, 'we need to find some shade.'

'I thought you said I was imagining the heat,' Chaney said, somewhat puzzled.

'Well, to be honest, I had hoped we had imagined it. But this is real, all right,' she said, shading her eyes and looking up at an oddly coloured sky. A yellow haze seemed to hover above them. 'I feel as if someone has put a magnifying glass between us and the sun!'

After what seemed like hours, they reached the welcome shelter of the forest once more. They continued on the forest track until they passed an area of dense

132

thicket, and dismounting in the shadiest part they could find, they once again saw to Galaxy's and Star's needs before their own.

'We will have to be careful with this water,' warned Dakota, 'and in this heat, we ought to be watering the horses every hour, at least.'

'This has got to be much hotter than the forecast,' Chaney commented, wiping beads of perspiration from her brow. 'My clothes are soaked in sweat.'

Dakota nodded and added, 'I know Dad checked before we left what the weather was going to be. A maximum temperature of 30 degrees was the forecast. But you are right – this is way above that!'

She also noted with some concern that their water bottles were less than half-full! She was desperate for more to drink herself but steeled herself to the task and refrained from drinking any more. After the shortest of breaks, they continued on again.

The trees began to thin out, and before they knew it, the forest had been left behind. Although this leg was almost over, both the horses seemed edgy and unnerved.

'What is wrong with Star?' Chaney said in frustration. 'He really is champing at the bit. I'm having a nightmare in trying to slow his pace.'

'Well,' replied Dakota, 'I didn't want to alarm you, but Galaxy is acting just the same.'

'They must be able to sense something we can't,' said Chaney.

As she spoke, a sudden gust of wind blew a cloud of dust across their path. Chaney almost choked as she accidently inhaled some. The wind continued to build, and as it did so, the temperature began to drop dramatically. At first it was a welcome relief, but wearing clothing damp with sweat, the girls soon began to feel rather chilled.

Dakota suddenly called out loudly, 'Buggy, have you seen that sky? What is it with this weather?'

Chaney turned to look at the horizon. 'Yikes!' she cried back. 'There must be a storm coming. No wonder the horses are playing up.'

The sky above them was a hazy yellowish blue in colour, but on the horizon to the west of them, it was an ugly dark grey and getting blacker by the minute. Without realising it or even making a conscious effort, their pace had quickened. The horses were galloping with a real sense of urgency, but the sky above them appeared to be changing more rapidly than they could move. Suddenly there was a sound like thunder behind them, and the ground beneath them appeared to tremble. Before Chaney had the time or error of judgement to shout the word 'earthquake!' which was on her lips, the first giant hailstone fell less than one hundred feet from them. It was the size of a cricket ball.

'Chaney, we must find cover!' shouted Dakota at the top of her voice.

Chaney could hardly make out her words as the hailstorm ensued with incredible ferocity. It was like being in the middle of a battlefield, with hailstones hitting the ground like grenades all around them, shattering into millions of razor-sharp needles of ice.

Fifty yards to their left, Aislinn and Kyle were flying at top speed.

'The girls need some protection, Kyle, or else they'll be killed!'

'I know,' he shouted back anxiously.

Just then, Aislinn spotted a large boulder on the ground ahead of them. 'What about that rock?' she called out pointing to it with her wand. 'Can you use a magnifying spell?'

'Yes, good idea – well-spotted!' he replied loudly. He raised his wand high into the air and spoke once more in his ancient fairy tongue. Almost immediately, the boulder began to wobble and lurch from side to side. Then, suddenly, as the spell took effect, it magnified a hundred times in size. As it did so, its summit shot high into the air. In less than a second it had grown to the height of a double-decker bus, with its nose-like shape now dominating the landscape.

To the girls, it seemed as if pure unadulterated luck had saved them. Dakota suddenly spotted the rocky outcrop a little way off to their left. At its base was a large stone promontory, shaped like a giant Roman nose which jutted out towards the sky. It was just high and wide enough to offer protection from the storm. 'Follow me!' she yelled, racing towards its desperately needed shelter.

They reached it just in time and, pulling in as tightly as they could, drew themselves close against its inner rock face, whilst the ground just inches from their feet was blasted into total whiteness. The sound was deafening, with explosion following explosion. As they stood sheltering under the giant rock, it occurred to Chaney that it was like being aboard a battleship and at the mercy of sustained cannon fire. She imagined herself inside a Spanish galleon which was now alone, separated from the rest of its fleet, unprotected and under the merciless attack of the British navy. She felt outgunned, vulnerable and at risk. Her hands trembled as she held on tightly to Star's reins.

Several minutes passed before the storm had subsided, and they waited many minutes more before leaving the safety of their rock fortress. They watched the dark clouds move away, although the sky remained a weird, ominous yellow in colour. At last, only one black cloud hovered above them in an otherwise brightening sky, and the wind had died to nothing.

A little distance away the two fairies hovered in the air, side by side. 'They're safe for now,' said Kyle. 'Let's get back to the kingdom. My father expects the Shaman within the hour.'

'Do you really think the Shaman can help?' asked Aislinn, anxiously.

'The High Council believe so – that is why they await his advice,' replied Kyle. 'And I certainly believe he is capable of conjuring a spell more powerful than anything that you or I have seen. Even if Mother Nature does seem to have gone mad, he will find a way of pacifying her and of returning the world to peace and harmony once more.'

'I hope you're right,' continued Aislinn, in a worried tone of voice. 'I know this may sound silly, perhaps even neurotic, but I can't help wondering if Alba isn't somehow linked to all this freak weather. I often feel as if her evil eye is upon me…as though she's still watching and hating me with every fibre in her body!'

'Alba is dead, Aislinn. She blew herself to smithereens when she unleashed the Gemini spell,' responded Kyle.

'Are you sure?' queried Aislinn.

A voice in the back of Kyle's head told him he'd missed something – something crucial – but for the life of him, he couldn't think what it could be.

'You told me that the vanishing spell left no trace, no debris. But from your description of what happened that night, the air was full of black ash and smoke. It was so thick, it made you choke!' Aislinn reminded him.

Her words had a staggering effect on Kyle. He came to an abrupt halt in mid-air as if time had frozen; he remained suspended, hovering, unmoving and silent for several seconds. A sudden realisation had flashed across Kyle's mind.

'Come on,' he said to Aislinn in an unusually sombre tone. Grasping her hand tightly in his, he continued, 'I need to speak to my father and the Shaman – and the sooner, the better.'

We are still alive, Dakota thought to herself, *still alive, despite the best efforts of nature.* Finally, after taking a good, long look at the sky, she gave the all-clear.

'Okay, Buggy, safe to go, I think. Keep a firm hold of Star and stay close behind me.' They slowly moved away from their shelter and, as they did so, it was as if the ground was hissing at them out of spite and animosity. The hissing sound was so loud that Chaney half expected a gargantuan cobra to rear its head at any moment with its hood extended and fangs exposed, ready to strike them dead. She looked nervously around her, moving her gaze from side to side as – following her sister – she led Star back out into the bush.

The awful hissing noise seemed to follow their footsteps wherever they trod, and the unusual sound was clearly making the horses panic. Galaxy and Star were uncharacteristically jinking about, pulling at their reins and looking wild eyed and alarmed. The girls held a firm grip onto their bridles.

They watched the hailstones melt. The resulting water dissipated rapidly at their feet as if some underground, cavern-dwelling troll, desperate to quench his thirst, was sucking every drop deep into the bowels of the earth. The oppressive heat of the sun had also suddenly returned with a vengeance. Consequently, matching the amount of water disappearing into the ground, an equal amount was rising skyward as vapour. Huge spiralling columns of scalding hot steam were being drawn towards a gaping mouth which had formed in the black cloud directly above them.

We might have been killed! Dakota said to herself, shivering. *There are dark forces at work here,* she thought, but said nothing to her sister for fear of alarming her. 'Come on – we need to get back,' was all she did say.

Chapter Twenty-Four
A Table of Snakes

Gilpin was on watch duty over the eye. He had been nervously biting the fast-receding claws of his front paws for some time. As the hailstorm ensued, he held his breath. He knew Kyle and Aislinn were on their way to save the girls from danger, but would they arrive in time? The relief he felt as Kyle conjured the magnifying spell was indescribable.

'Thank goodness!' he said out loud, as the two sisters sought shelter beneath the overhanging rock.

'Whatever is it?' enquired Fossett, who had heard his friend cry out and had rushed to his side to see what the matter was.

'A dreadful hailstorm,' Gilpin replied. 'The girls could have been killed!'

The two animals looked down into the magic eye. They could see the storm was now subsiding and the girls, still safe, remained sensibly huddled for cover under their rock shelter. As they continued to watch, Gilpin's sharp eyes spotted something that Fossett, with his failing eyesight, did not. Vaporous columns of steam were rising skyward. The eye, changing its focus from Dakota and Chaney, reflected a shape drawn in the dark clouds above them. It was the shape of a mouth; black lips, wide open, forming a gaping hole into which the hot spirals of scalding steam were being sucked. Gilpin was struck by the shape of the lips. A feeling of déjà vu coursed through his consciousness. He had seen those lips before. *But no,* he thought to himself. *How can that be possible? She's supposed to be dead!*

'Fossett, can you take over the watch for a while?' he asked. 'I have to speak with the King urgently. I'll be back as soon as I can.'

'Of course, no worries, mate, and look after that nose of yours. We don't want any more accidents. It looks to me as if it's just beginning to heal!' Fossett replied obligingly.

Gilpin rushed to the palace as fast as his little legs would carry him. Two formidable-looking royal guards in their black and orange regimental uniforms barred the door to the Great Hall. They reminded Gilpin of two belligerent hornets standing watch over a nest about to be invaded by a rival swarm.

'I have to speak to the King on a matter of urgency,' Gilpin said firmly, addressing first one and then the other. The guards remained unmoved.

'The King cannot be disturbed,' said the taller of the two soldiers, staring down at Gilpin with a look of pure contempt.

'He is in a meeting with the High Council', said the shorter, pimple-faced guard, 'and will not want to be disturbed by a mouse.'

'I can assure you that what I have to say, the King will want to hear. I have vital information the High Council require. Be it on your heads if you do not let me pass. I know why the King has called his Elders together, and that the Shaman has been summoned too.'

Gilpin stood his ground, yet still the guards would not relent and resolutely refused to let him pass. The hard-faced hornets stared down at Gilpin who, determined not to be outdone, stared right back at them, trying to mimic their stone-faced expressions.

'I warn you; the King will be angry if I am not allowed to tell him what I know. I have been on the watch for several hours and have important news which the King requires.'

'Law and custom forbid your entry,' snarled the smaller soldier. 'Only those of high-born rank can enter the Great Hall.'

'But I have new intelligence for the Council's ears,' repeated Gilpin, continuing to press his case as hard as he could.

'You heard the man,' growled the other guard. 'Now git, hop it, shove off!'

Suddenly, a shadow fell upon the steps to the Hall. A tall thin silhouette loomed above them in the shape of a man, suddenly shielding Gilpin from the strong rays of the sun which had been on his back. Gilpin watched a spear tap three times on the stone steps and heard a voice speak in an ancient tongue. There was a groaning, rumbling sound, and a stunned Gilpin watched the steps on which he was standing expand by some measure. The great oak doors and the medieval building itself also magnified in size, and to Gilpin's amazement, the Shaman brushed past him and entered inside.

King Ariel was seated on his royal throne and talking to a number of his Ministers. The ancient oak doors to the Great Hall opened with a loud creak, causing him to look up. He smiled warmly as he saw the Shaman approaching the council table.

'My dear friend,' he said, 'you are most welcome.' Gesturing to the Shaman to take a seat, he waved his wand over one of the yellow cushioned seats placed on the western fringe of the table. The chair wobbled slightly and then grew. The Shaman smiled, nodded his approval at the King and sat down.

Like the medicine wheel gift Dakota had received from the Shaman, this table too was divided into four equal quadrants. Ten elders in red robes sat around the Eastern quadrant, ten in black robes sat for the South, and nine in yellow robes, plus the Shaman, sat representing the West. The white quadrant remained empty.

'We await my Elders from the North,' King Ariel announced to the already assembled committee members. 'And then we will begin.'

At that moment, Gilpin took his opportunity. The two guards had turned away from him to close the heavy oaken doors. There was a gap just wide enough for him to squeeze through. He shot forward and raced inside, crossing the stone-flagged floor at top speed. He had underestimated how slippery the floor was and found himself crashing into a chair leg. It was the chair on which the Shaman was sitting cross-legged. The Shaman leant over and picked up the – now slightly bruised – mouse and placed him gently on top of the table around which the Council were seated. Gilpin, with a large bump on his head and a nose which – due to its previous injury – had begun to bleed again, thanked him.

'Gilpin, what is the meaning of this interruption?' said King Ariel in a tone of voice which quickly conveyed to Gilpin his displeasure, followed by, 'Return to your posts!' barked at the two sheepish-looking guards who had poked their heads through the doorway.

'Sire, I have grave news. I think I know the root cause of all this freak weather and why Dakota and Chaney are in such danger,' Gilpin replied in earnest.

'And what is that?' said one of the Elders, with a slightly amused look on his face.

'Alba,' answered Gilpin. 'I am sure Alba is to blame.'

'Alba!' repeated the same Elder incredulously. 'Alba – Alba to blame. How ridiculous. Does the little mouse not know? Is he the only person in the kingdom not to have heard the news? Alba is dead!'

Gilpin ignored the Elder's sarcastic comment and, undeterred, explained what he had seen in the sky after the hailstorm – the gaping mouth and the black lips. These were lips which he remembered well and with good reason, having been on the receiving end of Alba's black magic on a number of occasions. When he had finished speaking, there was a stony silence. King Ariel looked slightly flummoxed, as if struggling to comprehend what Gilpin had said.

Another Elder stood to his feet, and looking at his distinguished colleagues, he said, 'The day I start taking the advice of a mouse is the day I will resign my position on the Council! A mere mouse, indeed, advising us! Whoever heard of such a thing?' His harsh guffaw resonated through the Great Hall.

King Ariel remained silent.

The Elder continued, 'Call the guards and have this creature shown out. We have important items to be discussed, decisions to make and work to be done. What we do not have is time to listen to nonsense and the ravings of a deranged mouse!'

As the Elder concluded his harsh words, something appeared to hit one of the high, narrow stained-glass windows above the doors to the hall. Seconds later Queen Charlotte flew in through the open window, upside-down and backwards. A zigzagging flight path eventually brought her to a hover in front of her husband, where she slowly righted herself into an upright position. Miraculously, her crown, which had been dangling dangerously from her wild and unkempt grey ringlets, plopped itself squarely back on top of her head. Rogue strands of hair magically wove around it, keeping it in place. King Ariel noted the crown's remarkable relocation on the Queen's head, and secretly congratulated himself on his clever spell.

'Hello, dear,' she said to her husband, as she adjusted her skirt in an attempt to regain her decorum. 'I hope I haven't disturbed you. Are you having a Council meeting?'

'Yes, any minute now, my love,' replied the King, feeling even more flummoxed.

Looking about her, Queen Charlotte soon spotted Gilpin. 'Hallo, Gilpin,' she said fondly. 'What are you doing here?'

'I came with what I thought was important information for the King,' he replied in a serious tone of voice, which belied his indignation at the way at least two of the Elders had treated him.

Whether it was being upside down for some minutes and therefore blood rushing to her head which had temporarily revived Queen Charlotte's full faculties, Gilpin was never quite sure. What he did know was that the ageing Queen now spoke on his behalf.

'Ah, yes,' she said. 'You'll never meet with a wiser or a more observant creature in the kingdom. Gilpin is renowned for his sharp eyes and his equally sharp mind.' She turned and faced the Council, and through her thick-rimmed glasses seemed to focus her myopic gaze on the two doubting Thomases in particular. 'Heed his words,' she said with conviction, 'or you will all be sorry.'

Flapping her good wing, she spun slowly around and spoke to Gilpin again. 'How are your parents?'

'Well, Majesty, very well,' he replied.

For the first time in a long time, King Ariel looked at his wife with an expression of admiration as well as love, very much as he had done throughout their courtship and the bulk of their married life. Her recent frailty and lapses of memory were forgotten. Every person in the Great Hall noted the Queen's control and clarity of diction. Also – for the first time in weeks – she hovered on a level, with her silver wings beating simultaneously. Most importantly, her faith and respect for Gilpin shone like a shooting star through the dark prejudice that had surrounded him.

'Husband,' she said, 'it is high time you made Gilpin a Knight of the Realm. Think, my dear, of his heroic exploits in the return of our dear Aislinn.' As she spoke, she noticed two of the Elders rudely whispering together, and that they were looking at Gilpin with expressions of contempt and mockery etched in their faces.

'We have been remiss in failing to acknowledge his brave deeds. This lowly mouse,' she continued, 'may not be of royal birth, but he has demonstrated extreme courage. How many commoners would have dared to come in person to the Great Hall to address you – our revered Ancients? Trusting in your wisdom, he has thrown caution to the wind and come to speak to our High Council of Elders, a Council which sits in haughty judgement over its citizens. Are you perhaps angry that this courageous mouse has demanded admittance to the Great Hall? The Great Hall', she repeated, 'where kings are crowned and the place from which the kingdom is governed. Are we forgetting that it was Gilpin who saved the life of the Heir to the Throne? Prince Kyle could so easily have perished. Do I need to remind you all that he would have been sucked beneath the quagmire, were it not for Gilpin's sharp eyes and quick thinking?'

Never had a truer word been spoken, for never had an ordinary citizen asked for, or been allowed, access to a meeting of the High Council. A proud Gilpin stood before them, and as he listened to his Queen, his love and devotion for her, which was already strong, increased tenfold.

Some of the Elders shifted uncomfortably in their chairs, many realising that they had indeed forgotten Gilpin's heroic efforts and the part he had played in saving Aislinn. Many too, had to admit to themselves that they had dismissed Gilpin's theory simply because he had behaved above his accepted station. Woodland creatures, after all, were not expected to advise the Ancients. King Ariel looked at the embarrassed faces of his High Council.

'The Queen has spoken with great wisdom,' he said, 'and we should heed her words.'

Chapter Twenty-Five
Return of the Yo-Yo
and Birth of a Hero

As when a dam gives way in some high valley of the hills and the water tumbles out of control through the breach, so the Queen began to lose her faculties and a rapid transformation took place in front of the entire council. Firstly, the left wing began to flap out of sync and the hiccupping yo-yo returned. Unable to hover on a level, the ageing queen struggled to remain airborne. Secondly, each time her feet touched the floor she would spring back up and launch herself at the King. All eyes followed her erratic movement, and the head of every council member and the Shaman bobbed up and down in perfect timing with the Queen. To anyone watching, they would have looked like a collection of nodding dashboard dogs. Finally, and much to everyone's relief, the King managed to catch hold of his wife and heads were still once more.

'Well, my dear, would you like me to accompany you to the palace?' the King asked in as composed a voice as he could muster and with his arm wrapped securely around her waist.

'Yes, but I did want to speak to Dilbert before I left,' she replied, adding to the King's concern for her welfare. The King was right to be anxious. It soon became apparent that not only could she now not fly, but her coherence too had vanished. She turned her head to speak to Gilpin.

'Well, my brave little mouse, and how are the decuplets? Your brothers and sisters must be twelve weeks old by now. I did enjoy the christening, Dilbert,' she continued, 'such lovely names. What were they now? Ah yes, I remember. Prancer, Dancer, Comet, Vixen, and Rudolph...'

The King interrupted her in mid-sentence, 'No, dear no. I think you're getting confused with Santa's reindeers...' Blushing in his embarrassment for his wife, he turned as red as Rudolph's legendary nose.

'I love Christmas', said the Queen, 'and all the jolly songs.' She began to sing *Rudolph the Red-Nosed Reindeer*, as the Council listened in shocked silence.

Only the Shaman seemed unconcerned. He remained sitting cross-legged, smiling and nodding in approval of the Queen and thinking to himself, *This is what life is about: singing and love and bravery.*

Just then, the doors of the Great Hall burst open, and a flustered-looking royal handmaiden rushed inside. Giselle, one of the Queen's most trusted servants, had come in search of her sovereign.

'Your Majesty,' she called out to the Queen, 'we've been looking for you everywhere. It's time for the Queen's afternoon nap, Sire,' she said to a grateful King, taking hold of Queen Charlotte's arm and gently leading her away.

'Lovely to see you, my dear,' said the King sadly.

In a valiant attempt to make a dignified exit, the Queen moved hesitatingly towards the great oak doors. Even supported by her loyal handmaiden, she looked a forlorn figure, a small pink shape moving slowly. All eyes watched them flutter past the historic tapestries which draped the walls of the hall. The Queen's tiny frame now moved across a backdrop of vivid colour – colour created by those magnificent drapes. Huge drapes in the shape of beautifully made tapestries which, like giant regal banners, depicted the story of the kingdom and of long ago. All who came to the Great Hall could not help but admire them. Encompassed in their design were stories of old, splendid tales of the many kings and queens who had ruled, from ancient times to King Ariel's reign.

For a brief, almost euphoric moment, the King had thought his wife restored to full health. But now with a heavy heart, he watched her yo-yoing up and down, clearly struggling to maintain control of her movement, even with the help of Giselle's guiding hand. The left wing was by now hardly beating at all, whilst the right wing was working overtime and flapping furiously in an effort to keep the Queen airborne. As a result, the ailing Queen's haphazard flight path made her look like a float on the end of a fishing line being tossed about on choppy water.

The King heaved a long sigh. How he missed his wife, her quick wit, her sense of humour and her once-profound female intuition. Deciding legal matters at court had been so much easier with Queen Charlotte by his side. In recent months she had enjoyed only rare moments of lucidity, and without his wife's support, King Ariel had found that sitting on the throne could be a lonely business.

As the Queen departed, ten distinguished-looking fairies wearing white robes arrived, closely followed by Kyle and Aislinn. Kyle kissed his mother briefly, and then she was gone. As the door closed behind her, a lively debate began once more in the Council Chamber, whilst the Elders from the North took their seats. Despite her relapse, the Queen's words echoed in the ears of those members of the Council who had heard her speak. What the Queen had started, Prince Kyle, Aislinn and the Shaman were about to finish.

The King rose from his throne, and taking the royal sceptre from his Chief Minister, he called the Council to order. The sceptre made of gold had a magnificent blue diamond at its head. The King placed his right hand around the diamond and once again spoke in the ancient tongue. The dazzling blue crystal began to glow, casting an azure hue throughout the Great Hall. To Gilpin's even greater wonder, suddenly every object and every person seemed to shimmer, vanish and then reappear in a uniform size.

Gilpin found himself staring into the eyes of the Shaman, which were now on a level with his own. For a moment he felt as if the Shaman was reading his mind, and then other thoughts took over his consciousness.

Firstly, he could scarcely believe that he was sitting on his own chair. His back legs were long enough to reach the floor, and his front paws were folded together on top of the table. He noted, with considerable satisfaction, that he was holding his paws in the exact manner of the Fairy Elders. They too had their hands folded and had placed them neatly on top of the ancient council table.

Secondly, and perhaps even more thrillingly, was that for the first time in his life Gilpin felt enormous. He could no longer be described as a little mouse, but more of a giant rodent. It was a grand feeling.

I look as important as them…never mind this lowly birth nonsense. What's even more gratifying is that with this growth in stature, I appear more like a bear than a mouse, he thought to himself, trying to suppress a smile. *Now they'll listen to me!*

So it was that the meeting of the High Council began. With the Elders of the North now present, the King asked Gilpin to relate his theory once more. Only too willing to address the Council again, Gilpin rose to his feet. He knew Alba was behind the attacks on Chaney and Dakota and that she would stop at nothing to succeed. He needed to convince the honourable assembly gathered around him that the pestilence spell had somehow backfired, and that far from eliminating Alba, she still existed.

When he spoke, the sound of his own voice shocked even him. Gone was the high-pitched squeak, and in its place, he heard a low, deep vocal tone coming out of his mouth. Large lungs and an equally enlarged diaphragm produced an altogether different sound, and a rich baritone voice echoed through the Great Hall. Gilpin chose his words carefully and spoke with great dignity and passion. His powerful, bear-like address made them all sit up and listen. As he finished his speech, he stared directly at two Elders and noted a brief look of fear flash across their faces. Gilpin knew he had done all in his power to convince the Council of Alba's existence. 'I rest my case,' he said, and resumed his seat. His argument received further support, not only from Prince Kyle but from Aislinn also. The Shaman too fully acknowledged and accepted Gilpin's theory.

When Kyle and Aislinn had finished their address to the Council, the Shaman rose slowly from his chair and climbed up onto the table. He began to dance around the table, chanting, singing and turning, pointing his spear first at one Elder and then another. When he reached the King's chair he stopped, and in a loud voice, speaking in the ancient tongue, this is what he said:

'The dreamtime is come again. Alba is a sky-being and exists in the spirit of the cloud. Her energy, her evil as a bunyip remains, and it is getting stronger, even outside the kingdom. The spell she unleashed and from which she survived has given her great power, a terrible power even over the forces of nature, and the wind has become her special ally. She has tricked the wind into believing she is a Sky God. We must show her deceit and make her ally her enemy.'

Grave faces around the table listened in silence. The Shaman started to chant once again and danced back to the very centre of the table, where he sat down cross-legged. He placed his spear flat on the table in front of him, and immediately, the snake carvings with which it was decorated seem to come to life. They slithered out from the wood, dozens of them, and began to slide a twisting, winding pathway toward the King. Inch by inch they slid towards him, moving slowly, smoothly and sinuously, gliding silently across the polished surface. A yard from the King, at the head of that ancient council table, the snakes stopped. They began to hiss loudly, raising their rattles high in the air.

Although Kyle trusted the Shaman implicitly, his heart was beating, and he feared for his father's safety. The snakes looked and sounded as if they were about to strike. King Ariel sat motionless, with an expression of calm but close interest on his face.

Gilpin watched the serpents displaying their warning rattle and shivered as he listened to the loud and frightening sound. The rattling echoed off the high walls and reverberated around the Council Chamber. Then to Gilpin's amazement, the snakes began to wrap around each other, forming a giant coil which began to spiral around and around. The coil started to move from quadrant to quadrant until, in front of his eyes, it no longer appeared to be a column of twisting, writhing snakes, but a miniature whirlwind. Suddenly, it lifted off the table altogether and soared high up into the great vaulted ceiling, whirling around and around above the heads of the assembly gathered below. All eyes followed its movement – until suddenly, there was a blinding flash of light.

It was gone, and the Shaman was no longer sitting on the table but standing behind the King, his carved spear in his hand. Once more he spoke in his ancient tongue.

'Gilpin speaks true. We must destroy the evil sky-being. Now let us work our magic together.'

All the Elders, most especially the King, nodded in agreement. At last, the brave mouse received the recognition and respect he was due. It was a 'Eureka!' moment, and a lowly Gilpin found himself cheered and applauded by his betters. As the clapping continued, the Shaman pointed his spear at the two doubting Thomases, and before they knew what was happening, they found themselves lifting Gilpin up onto their shoulders. A slightly stunned and embarrassed mouse was carried around the Great Hall on a lap of honour, though much to the annoyance of two disgruntled hornets. The royal guards had deserted their posts to see what all the fuss was about and were not best pleased that the intruder was now in receipt of such rapturous applause.

As the commotion finally died down, it was back to business. The High Council returned to their places around the table, and talks began in earnest as to how Alba could be defeated and destroyed. Discussions went on long into the night.

Chapter Twenty-Six
Tough Decisions

The relief as they entered the ride arena was indescribable. Even before they had dismounted, the two sisters could feel a sudden and inexplicable drop in temperature. Simultaneously, Dakota and Chaney looked up to see a clear, cloudless blue sky adorned with a now benign sun high above them. They immediately felt safe again and ran eagerly into the welcoming arms of Michael and Rachael and to the extra-gooey drool of two ecstatic dogs waiting to greet them.

When the happy reunion was over and the horses had been fully tended to, they made their way back to the campsite. Dakota instinctively checked the thermometer in the campervan. It was reading a perfectly normal 29 degrees! She was mystified. The judges and officials were remarking on the ideal weather conditions, and according to the girl's parents, there was no talk of calling the event off.

It seemed that the excessive heat they had experienced, both before and after the unaccountable sudden drop in temperature, and the incredibly frightening hailstorm had been unique to them. None of the other riders had any complaints at all, and certainly not about the weather. The officials listened to Dakota's account of the freak hailstorm, but as is human nature, they were inclined to make light of it. More worrying for Dakota and Chaney was the total ignorance everyone displayed in terms of how hot they were finding conditions. Why was it that they were the only riders in the field to be experiencing these freak weather events?

Once again, grave doubts began to enter Dakota's mind. *We must have done something wrong,* she thought to herself. *It's as if the fates have turned against us, as if we've become suddenly jinxed. Have we perhaps ridden unawares into sacred Aboriginal ground and angered the spirits of their ancestors?* There was no doubting that something was out to get them. It was as if an incensed Mother

Nature was throwing everything she had in her arsenal at them. *We've upset somebody,* she thought, *but who…and why?*

More importantly, they had a critical decision to make. Should they carry on in the race, especially as the final leg was the longest of all, at over 50 kilometres? Dakota was worried. She was also in the throes of a dilemma. Should she tell her parents exactly what had been happening on the ride? If she did, it was likely they would insist on them withdrawing from the endurance race altogether.

Dakota went back to the campervan to fetch the medicine wheel the Shaman had given her. As she grasped it, she immediately felt comforted. She held it momentarily close to her breast and then pressed it to her lips. She closed her eyes and could see the magical Aboriginal Shaman standing beside her. He was smiling and nodding his approval. Opening her eyes once more, Dakota tied the wheel around her neck, and as she did so, her whole body seemed to relax. A warm glow flowed through her, and she felt strangely energised, protected and secure.

'This stays with me from now on. Wearing it is like getting a hug from Dad,' she said to herself. 'I wish I could tell him about the danger we are in or at least ask the Shaman for help…we definitely need all the help we can get.'

She turned to leave the van and return to the start line. It was then that she saw Simba. He had followed her back and was standing in the doorway. Dakota tried to push past him, but the old dog refused to move. He was barking and whining intermittently and clearly wanted his beloved mistress to stay put.

'Simba, I have to go,' Dakota insisted, 'otherwise I'm going to miss the start of the last leg.'

The dog had other ideas, and grabbing the tail of her riding jacket in his jaws, he began pulling her back from the door.

'Simba, will you stop it! We're not in the sea now,' Dakota ordered.

Just at that moment, Chaney burst in through the door. 'Dakota, what on earth is keeping you? We're going to miss the start at this rate!'

'It's Simba,' Dakota replied. 'He obviously knows something is wrong and doesn't want us to ride.'

Chaney looked at her sister's worried expression. 'We're in another catch-22 situation, aren't we?' she said.

Dakota nodded.

'If we tell Mum and Dad about the freak weather conditions that have affected us in this race, they'll pull us out straightaway. But if we don't tell, it will be like betraying their trust all over again. I'm right, aren't I?' Chaney said in a grim voice to her sister.

'Buggy, I think you're finally growing up,' Dakota replied fondly. 'This time I'm going to let you make the decision.'

Dakota went silent and waited for Chaney to make the call. Chaney thought for a moment and then knelt at Simba's side. She took the old dog's head in her hands and looked him straight in the eye.

'Simba, we have to finish this race. You must let us go. It would be cowardly to pull out now.' She kissed his wet nose. 'You do understand, don't you?'

'He understands, and I absolutely agree,' Dakota said. 'Let's go!'

The old dog reluctantly allowed them to pass, and the two girls ran back to their horses and the start line. Simba, with his head and tail well and truly down, followed slowly behind, whining miserably as he did so. As Dakota mounted Galaxy, the medicine wheel she had tied around her neck seemed to tighten.

She felt as if it were trying to pull her off her horse. Could it be that, like Simba, the wheel did not want her to ride? The necklace began to feel extremely uncomfortable. *It's like wearing a shirt with a collar two sizes too small,* she thought to herself. Momentarily, she let go of Galaxy's reins, hastily undid the leather thong on which the medicine wheel was suspended, and quickly tied the necklace around her left wrist instead. Instantly, she felt as if her left arm was being pulled backwards, and Galaxy, sensitive to his mistress's rein as always, took two steps backwards and wheeled to his left. Dakota corrected his position straightaway and brought him back alongside Star on the start line.

Although Chaney had made the decision to continue, she had said nothing to Dakota about how she was feeling. Her whole body was tired and aching even before the final leg was due to begin. They had already spent over fifteen hours in the saddle and every muscle was painful to move; her entire body felt stiff and incredibly sore.

'Back to white markers, Chaney,' Dakota shouted, as they left the comfort of the arena. Their parents were standing to the side of the start line for the last time. Rachael had hold of Enzo on his lead, and he was jumping about excitedly, like a spring lamb in a meadow. His ears were pricked, and his tail was wagging furiously. Michael had Simba's lead. The old dog was whining quietly; his ears were down and his tail between his legs. Unlike his younger counterpart, he made no movement at all.

The starter sounded the horn, and the final leg began. All the horses and riders set off to loud cheering and whistling from the many spectators who had gathered to see them off. At first the field stayed well-grouped, but little by little the two Spanish riders seemed to be galloping into an early lead.

'Let them go,' Chaney heard Dakota shout. 'There's a long way to go yet. Stick to the plan: sure and steady.'

Chapter Twenty-Seven
Lightning Strikes

The two girls rode on in silence with just the sound of hooves beating the ground rhythmically and steadily in their ears. Once more, Star and Galaxy were allowed a long rein, enabling the horses to follow their own course. The two horses galloped side by side, united in their endeavour and in the struggle to overcome the oppressive heat which seemed to increase with every passing mile. It was a heat which sapped every ounce of strength and energy. The girls surveyed the landscape ahead. The trail they were following was a straight red dirt road, dusty and rock-hard. It snaked before them seemingly endlessly and appeared to reach the far horizon and beyond.

It was Chaney who first noticed the change in the sky this time. It had been a bright blue as their journey had started, but after only an hour or two out she had watched the dark yellow clouds gather above them. Those clouds were now becoming ominously black, and light was fading fast, although it was still well before sundown.

They had left the plains and were heading due east towards the mountain range when they saw the first flash of lightning. A darkening sky was suddenly illuminated, and even before the first strike had vanished, a second and then a third strike were clearly visible. Chaney counted to fifty before the clap of thunder resounded in the air, making her shudder with fear and dread. She had always hated thunderstorms even as a small child. However, they pressed on with their journey, moving on to higher and higher ground with every passing minute.

By the time they were ascending the lower slopes of Mount Stromlo, the lightning was getting nearer. The storm had appeared to move away from them at first but had now clearly changed direction and was heading their way. Worse still, the smell of smoke was in the air. By the time they had reached the summit an hour or two later, a thick column of smoke was clearly visible, and a red glow stretched across the horizon. They began to descend on the other side, clinging to a narrow track in single file and with Dakota and Galaxy leading the way. As they did so, they were suddenly aware of great palls of black smoke ahead of them. The palls of black smoke completely blotted out their vision, and Dakota lost sight of the path.

Just then and with little, if any, warning, they were enveloped in an inky black cloud. Dakota was temporarily blinded and found herself choking on the foul-tasting, acrid dust which now surrounded them. She panicked and urged Galaxy forward, desperate to get out from under the thick, suffocating smoke which had totally obscured her vision.

At exactly that moment the medicine wheel made its presence felt again, as Dakota's left wrist was yanked back sharply. Galaxy stopped dead in his tracks. An unexpected and welcome gust of wind swept across their path, swiftly clearing the air of the awful black smoke that had engulfed them. To her horror, Dakota saw immediately that Galaxy had stopped at the edge of a steep cliff. One step further and all four of them would have perished. There was a sheer drop of at least fifty feet. Dakota shivered as she realised that had they stumbled over the edge, not one of them would have survived.

Once again, the Shaman's necklace seemed to pull at her wrist, and Galaxy wheeled gently to his left and began following a narrow track which traversed back and forth diagonally across the steep descent, taking them safely down. They reached the lower slopes, and as the ground levelled out, both riders put on a spurt. Dakota and Chaney hurried Galaxy and Star along the clearly marked trail, desperate to get back to safety, but the storm stopped them in their tracks. Lightning crashed overhead and hit the ground just yards from where they were.

'Get off Star, quick!' Dakota screamed as she herself dismounted. Gesturing for her sister to follow, she led them down into a small hollow at the side of the track. They made the horses lie flat on the ground, and the two girls crouched beside them talking very quietly, trying to calm them and desperate to keep them from bolting. The horses were sweating profusely, and both looked petrified and wild-eyed.

Glancing up, Chaney could see a huge black cloud hovering above them once again. As she looked, it seemed to her that a face had appeared at its centre. It was an evil face, hostile, angry and full of hate.

Crash! Another strike hit the ground, but this time even closer. Chaney had not even begun to count before a deafening thunder filled the air. The sound had scarcely died away when the girls suddenly felt their hair stand on end. They could hear a buzzing noise from the edge of the hollow in which they were sheltering, and the rocks themselves seemed to be glowing blue in the night light.

'Move, now!' cried a familiar voice as Prince Kyle, sword in hand, landed at their feet. 'Quick!' he shouted, urging Star, Galaxy, Chaney and Dakota to their feet.

They were lucky to escape, for within seconds there was another blinding flash as a huge bolt of lightning struck again, directly hitting Kyle's outstretched sword. Kyle was thrown backwards as if he had been punched in the stomach by a giant invisible fist, and as he hit the ground, another blinding flash of light rebounded back off his sword and up into the heavens. There was a loud, almost deafening rumble of thunder as the lightning flash re-entered the black clouds from whence it had come, and myriads of crackling sparks of electricity filled the air. The rocks above the hollow which had been glowing blue were instantly blown to smithereens.

As Chaney mounted Star once more, she strained her eyes in the darkness, anxiously seeking out Kyle's shape. *Please let him be alright!* she thought to herself. She nudged Star forwards to the edge of the hollow.

Prince Kyle lay motionless on the floor but with his now-glowing sword still firmly in his hand. Chaney could see that he was dressed from head to foot in a fine filigree silver chain mail. Instantly, Chaney was reminded of the medieval knights of old, of Camelot and King Arthur. She felt as if she was a damsel in distress and Kyle was her saviour – her knight in shining armour. Dakota drew Galaxy to her sister's side, and both girls watched with relief as the fairy prince recovered consciousness and stood to his feet.

'It's Alba,' he said struggling to catch his breath. 'She has been responsible for this awful freak weather, and you are in grave danger. No time to explain now. You need to make a run for it,' Kyle urged. 'Please mount up. The sooner you get going, the better.'

Alba! Of course, ...she's been the dark force at work, manipulating the weather for her own wicked and vindictive ends, Dakota thought to herself as she remounted Galaxy. *We helped to save Aislinn's life – and now she wants to take ours!*

They were off, once again following the white markers that would lead them home. Both girls knew that they were in the middle of a bush fire. Glimpses of crimson could be seen in the scrub all around them. They galloped on along the trail which passed directly through a small copse of eucalyptus trees. Their horses had only just cleared the trees when the fire struck. There was an explosion of searing heat, and licks of flame leapt forty feet into the air, bending and shifting and cracking. The heat was a solid wave, and it was moving their way faster than ever.

Steadfast determination not to be defeated, and courage not to be overcome, kept them going. The two horses and their riders bravely galloped on, and the merciless flames followed, engulfing all in their path. The air was full of heavy suffocating smoke, and the heat was blistering. Temporarily blinded by the heat and smoke, they reined their horses to a halt, rubbing their aching eyeballs, desperately seeking the white markers they needed to show them their path of escape. The horror of the situation was made worse by the dreadful uncertainty as to how their family was faring, not to mention all the other riders and horses in the event. The smoke cleared in a sudden gust of wind, and the white markers pointing the way were visible once more.

On and on they raced. The forest lay ahead, and as they looked towards it, their hearts sank. On its western border, huge pine trees were already flaring like giant torches, giving off strips of blazing material. The wind was increasing, and this fiery debris was being tossed and hurled over enormous distances. Wherever it landed, new fires would spring into life. More and more trees would become engulfed in flames, and then they too would send their cruel messengers to make fresh fiery conquests.

'It will mean riding further,' shouted Dakota to her sister, 'but our only hope is to skirt the forest.' Unknown to Chaney, Dakota had put her faith in the Shaman and was allowing the medicine wheel to guide her.

They rode in an easterly direction until at last the landscape began to look familiar. To their relief, they found themselves following a trail from the first leg of the race, which they recognised immediately.

'This trail will still take us back', Chaney called out loudly, 'but across the bush plains.'

'The plains will be like a tinderbox – the ground's so dry!' Dakota called out in a worried, anxious tone.

'I don't think we have a choice, do we?' Chaney replied.

Dakota nodded in agreement, and looking behind once more, she could see other riders making the same decision. The fire would travel much too fast through the forest, and both girls knew that there would be no escape if Alba had anything to do with it. The wind was picking up, and worryingly, it was behind them. Would they be able to outrun the fire with the wind now assisting in its progress?

Just then, as if their situation wasn't desperate enough, Alba vented her rage and hatred of the two sisters like never before. A spiteful, vengeful face formed in the dark clouds directly above them. Narrow, viper-like eyes, resembling two black slits and as cold as ice, glared down with evil intent. A cruel mouth twisted into a smile, as if to say, *Now at last I have you. It is time for you to learn that no one crosses Alba and gets away with it!*

The girls looked up at the same moment and instantly recognised the wicked face hovering high above in the inky black sky. Fear hit them like an electric shock, and blind panic quickly followed. In both their minds an awful realisation dawned: alone and unprotected as they were, how could they possibly escape Alba's wrath?

'Chaney, ride for your life!' Dakota shouted. 'Our only chance is to outrun her!'

Star had won many flat races in the past, but the speed at which he and Galaxy covered the ground at that moment would have had to be seen to be believed. As the horses put their heart and soul into making good their escape, the sound of hooves pounding the ground with such high velocity was like that of rapid machine-gun fire.

But Alba was not going to be beaten. The black lips spat out, and the girls felt a sudden blast of hot air hit their faces. Then they heard the deafening sound as fire bolt after fire bolt rained down upon them. Where each fire bolt hit the ground, the brush and long grass became an instant inferno. The girls had no choice but to rein the horses in. They were surrounded by a circle of flame. Eyes wide with terror watched the flames reaching forty feet into the air and bursting forwards. Searing red and yellow plumes of intense heat torched the ground, crackling and rushing towards them. The horses were whinnying noisily, rearing and wheeling, crying out to their mistresses to give them direction.

Dakota could feel the medicine wheel pulling her on, but the fire was too frightening. She couldn't think, couldn't act. She felt helpless, powerless to save them from their situation. There was nothing she could do to prevent them from being burned alive.

Then Chaney saw him. The pirate from the ravine was in the midst of the flames. He brandished his cutlass, cutting through the fire first this way and then that. Sweeping wide-armed parries seemed to slice through the inferno, cutting

156

a path just wide enough for the horses to pass through. Chaney screamed out to Dakota as loud as she could, 'Dakota, follow me!' and she spurred Star into action.

In a massive leap of faith, Chaney rode straight towards the path the pirate had created, and as if by magic, both horse and rider rode safely through the conflagration. Dakota followed close behind, staying right on Star's tail. At last, the circle of flames had been left behind, and open grassland stretched out before them. They had escaped a fiery death by the narrowest of margins – only seconds later, and the flames would have closed in.

As Chaney watched the white Andalusian moving away from the inferno, she thought she caught sight of the pirate again. The wicked captain seemed to be standing just feet from where they had made their exit from the circle of fire. In front of her eyes, the figure began to alter until, once more, it was the Shaman who was watching her escape. Chaney could see his tall, gaunt outline and his painted Aboriginal body clearly visible, standing bravely in front of a solid wall of red-hot flames. He was smiling at her, and the expression on his face was one she recognised. She had seen that same look on her father's face many times: a mixture of pride, admiration and love.

Dakota had evidently not been privy to Chaney's visions – either of the swashbuckling pirate cutting a swathe through the flames with his mighty cutlass, or of the Shaman standing fearlessly before a sheet of fire.

When the Shaman spoke, he spoke only to Chaney.

'You have faced your greatest fear, Chaney. I am proud of you. Have faith and place your trust in those who love you.' He spoke in the ancient tongue and somehow Chaney understood him.

It was a defining moment for the dark-haired girl with the rebellious nature. She flashed a smile back at the Shaman which would have lit the darkest room and melted the hardest heart. Chaney would never be the same again. In that instant, she made up her mind to trust others and to be trustworthy herself, to have faith in the people who loved her, and more importantly, to be faithful to them.

I can change, she thought to herself. *I can be a person people can rely on, and in future I'll always try to face my fears with courage.*

Chapter Twenty-Eight
A Cockeyed Bob

In Australia they call it a cockeyed bob. In England, the most common word is tornado; but by any name, tornadoes are fierce swirling windstorms that may be deadly and awesomely destructive. As if being in a life-threatening situation already was not enough, the girls could clearly see the tornado heading towards them. A huge spiralling column of black cloud and dust was hurtling across the scrubland behind them. Even with the bush fire getting ever nearer, they knew they would have to find shelter. They rode on, desperately straining their eyes for the sight of anything that might protect them from the swirling wind. As they looked back, they could see the updraft tearing bushes, shrubs and grasses out of the ground and sucking the debris skywards. The tornado was acting like some giant sticking plaster ripping the vegetation away and leaving nothing behind.

On and on they raced, but there was no sign of shelter – only desolation as far as the eye could see, with mile upon mile of wilderness lying before them. A few desert shrubs and eucalyptus trees punctuated the landscape here and there, and of course, there were the now-familiar white markers. They stuck to their course, their eyes seeking ahead for the next gate to pass through. It was not easy to follow the trail on a clear day, but with smoke all around them, the white markers seemed almost hidden at times amongst the long grasses.

Chaney could not believe her sister's navigational skills. She seemed to know instinctively where every marker lay, and as a result, Chaney gladly resigned herself to letting Star follow Galaxy's lead. *Blue eyes must have an advantage over brown,* she thought to herself.

Dakota could see the tornado gaining on them. She wanted to check Galaxy's direction in an effort to avoid the twisting funnel of wind which appeared, for all intents and purposes, to be following them and, worse still, catching up fast! But the medicine wheel kept pulling her on, accurately picking up the trail and hitting every marker spot on.

There was nothing for it but to keep going, and suddenly they were in the thick of it. All around them trees, shrubs, plants, every blade of grass, was being torn from underfoot. The tornado engulfed them, and they were lost in a deafening sound.

Flying debris was all around, and yet still they were galloping on. In all the chaos, suddenly Chaney felt something brush against the side of her face.

'Whoops – a little too close!' she heard Prince Kyle call out at that very moment. 'Keep going,' he continued. 'All will be well, and soon Alba will be no more. Just keep going.'

At the same moment, Dakota thought she could hear Aislinn's voice above the hullabaloo of sound which surrounded her. 'Do not stop, Dakota. We will do all in our power to protect you – just keep going!'

Then the voices were gone, and the cannonade of the tornado engulfed them once more. Both girls pressed their horses on mercilessly, following the advice they had been given. Minutes later they became aware of the sound of hooves beating the ground, and suddenly the tornado had passed and was ahead of them. They watched it twisting and snaking, moving further and further away, and as they watched, it seemed to them that it, too, was following the markers!

Chaney cast a look behind, and to her amazement, she could see all the other riders were safe, but hot on their heels. She gestured to Dakota to look back and shouted gleefully, 'I think the race is still on!'

'Forget the race,' Dakota shouted back. 'That will surely have been abandoned. Let's just get back as fast as we can and in one piece!'

They were now riding a trail at least a kilometre wide but void of any vegetation. A barren track stretched out in front of them and was leading them home. As they rode on, they watched the tornado stripping the trail clear, until all at once they were on the brow of a hill looking down at the Equestrian Park with all its outbuildings, its car parks, camp sites and the main arena. The girls galloped on as they watched in fear and trepidation as the tornado seemed to circle around the entire park. To their astonishment, they could still see people walking about, tents still upright and horses happily tethered in the arena – straight after the tornado had passed right through! Everything seemed completely unharmed!

'How can that be?' Chaney asked.

'I don't know,' replied Dakota, 'but I'm glad they've survived.'

Then as quickly as it had come, the tornado seemed to vanish. The lower part of its cone seemed to turn inwards and upwards and disappeared into the top half. For a moment there was no movement at all; and then came the explosion.

The girls had never witnessed anything quite like it before. A huge gust of wind hit them as the top half of the tornado's cone exploded in a massive blast which seemed then to separate and split into a million bright lights. The lights hovered high above the ground for a brief second and then in a single giant stream seemed to enter a swirling, but now slowly dissolving, black cloud which had been suspended above them. Before they had had time to take on board what had just happened, they became aware of the sound of hooves coming up behind them. Sneaking a quick glance back, Dakota recognised the two Spanish International riders catching up fast.

'Let's go, Chaney! The race might well have been cancelled, but I'd still like to prove a point by getting back first,' she roared, and spurred Galaxy into action.

Star followed their lead, and soon the two horses were galloping flat out, heading side by side towards the final gate and what ought to have been a clear victory. Excitement surged through them as they raced down the home straight towards the arena. They could see the finish line coming ever closer and closer. All their fear and anxiety melted away, replaced by an almost overwhelming sense of pride and jubilation.

Every single rider safely crossed the finish line that day, and all with their own stories as to how they had escaped the fire and miraculously ridden through a tornado! When the two girls tried to describe what it felt like to be chased by a whirlwind, it had been its awful sound which had terrified them the most. Dakota described it as hearing a thousand wolves howling and driven mad through starvation. Chaney, however, had been most affected by the fire. She remembered the intense heat and the horrible crackling noise of the flames as they engulfed the trees and vegetation all around them.

The girls' parents explained that the tornado had created a natural firebreak, and as a result, the riders were able to get back safely. Even more amazing was the fact that the tornado had encircled the entire main venue. The bush fire's progress had been stopped as a result, and fire crews were out in force making the whole area safe once more.

Chapter Twenty-Nine
Miracles Happen!

It was late evening and the whole family were gathered around the dinner table. Michael had baked a delicious giant pepperoni pizza, and this time Chaney was keeping her hands well above the table. Enzo was complaining quietly.

'Well, girls,' asked their father as he served Chaney her third slice, 'what will you remember most about this week, and do you think you've learnt anything?'

Dakota responded immediately. 'I'm going to follow my heart a bit more readily from now on. If this experience has taught me one thing, it is that sometimes events happen which have no rhyme or reason! But, if you have a good heart and follow your conscience, you'll never go far wrong.'

'I'm just the opposite!' It was Chaney's turn to speak now, and she spoke with a sudden maturity which was well above her young age. 'I'm going to listen to my head instead of my heart for a change and try to be more logical. I've got to stop being so impulsive and do a lot more thinking before I act. Above all, from now on, I'm determined to be sensible and reliable.'

Hearing these wise words, Michael and Rachael exchanged yet another one of their raised-eyebrow looks. Chaney saw the look and registered its meaning.

'Well, I'm going to try, anyway,' she continued with a grin on her face, 'and whilst we are talking about this whole experience, can I also say that I am even more proud of Galaxy and Star – and, of course, my big sister.'

As she spoke, Chaney reached out to take her sister's hand across the table. In the blink of an eye, the whole family had joined hands and were smiling warmly and happily at each other. As they did so, the tails of two Newfoundland dogs were also wagging with great gusto.

'I've got a special family,' said their father, even more proudly.

'Woof, woof, woof!' barked Simba and Enzo in unison.

'Yes, and two wonderful dogs,' agreed Michael.

Years later, Dakota and Chaney would tell their grandchildren all about their adventures.

'We felt uplifted, somehow, to have survived all that Mother Nature threw in our path. She was so benevolent at times and yet so malevolent at others. As we get older,' they would explain, 'we realise that our experiences affect us in a much more profound way than we understood at the time. It changed us both for the better and brought us even closer together. We had a wonderful adventure and the gift of fabulous memories which have lasted a lifetime.'

Later that night, when they were tucked up in bed, Chaney whispered very quietly to her sister, 'Dakota, do you realise Prince Kyle saved our lives? In fact, the fairies must have helped us today, several times over!'

'I think you are right,' agreed Dakota, 'and I believe the Shaman must have helped too. I just hope their spells were powerful enough to put an end to Alba once and for all.'

'They were,' said another familiar voice. 'Kyle and Aislinn sent me to tell you', continued a happy Fossett, who had suddenly appeared on their windowsill, 'that you don't need to worry about her ever again. This time she really is gone for good!'

'Woof, woof!' Simba's large head appeared at the window, right behind Fossett.

Fossett had the fright of his life, fell off the windowsill and landed with a loud bump on the floor. The girls immediately leapt out of bed and gave the old albino wallaby the hug of his life.

'Woof, woof, woof!' Simba barked again, only this time even louder.

'Buggy, let him in, for goodness's sake – before he wakes everyone up!' Dakota ordered.

An anxious Newfoundland was soon sniffing and licking their surprise visitor with enthusiasm, covering him in dog drool.

Fossett went on to explain how the fairies had come to realise that Alba had not been destroyed when her wicked spell on Aislinn had backfired. Indeed, far from it, she had gained in power. No one knew for certain what had gone wrong, but Alba had clearly made mistakes in the way the spell had been conjured. There had certainly been errors in the way it had been targeted, too, which explained why the sphere had delivered a small amount of its poison to Aislinn.

'Small, maybe,' said Dakota, 'but potent enough to kill her, nevertheless.'

'Quite so,' replied Fossett, who then continued his account of Alba. Although her physical body had been destroyed, her spirit, her soul had survived the spell; and as a result, Alba had been able to exist as an unformed but malevolent entity. Unleashing it incorrectly in the way she had, had somehow increased her powers. As a result, she had become even more dangerous.

'She was in that horrid black cloud,' said Chaney.

'Exactly,' replied Fossett, 'and had such magical power that she was able to control the weather and the atmosphere. It took the Elders, even with the help of the Shaman, some time to come up with a spell powerful enough to obliterate her totally – hence the tornado. Fairies try not to use extremes of nature in their spells unless they must. Can frighten the humans, you know,' Fossett explained, sounding more like Prince Kyle every moment. 'Now,' he said, 'before I go, I have one other task to carry out. You are both invited to Kyle and Aislinn's wedding on Christmas Eve.'

'Hooray!' the two girls cried out happily.

'Oh, and I almost forget,' Fossett continued. 'Aislinn sent this potion for Simba. You need to mix it with a bit of water.'

'What's it for?' asked Dakota.

'Aislinn called it her "Double A" spell,' Fossett replied.

'Oh no, please tell me it's not another Gemini spell!' Chaney asked, with some considerable concern.

'No, no, no!' Fossett assured them emphatically. 'It does have a dual purpose, though. But the two purposes are entirely planned. As we've been watching you in the magic eye, Aislinn spotted that this poor old boy', he explained, patting the dog's head with his own front paw, 'not only suffers from arthritis but also gets bullied at times by your other dog. The potion will sort his arthritis out and improve his alpha male status.'

'What do you mean – alpha male status?' Chaney enquired.

'Quite simply, which dog is leader of the pack,' Fossett explained. 'Simba is the older dog, so by rights we feel he ought to rank above Enzo. Aboriginal and Fairy culture are similar, you know. In our world, the Ancients – as we call them – are always treated with the greatest deference. We cherish their wisdom and experience. Aboriginal society does the same.'

Chaney fetched Simba's water bowl. Dakota poured the potion into a small amount of water, and they watched the old dog drink every drop with relish.

'I'm surprised Aislinn hasn't thought of making a potion for Queen Charlotte. If anyone needs a tonic, I'm sure she does,' remarked Dakota as tactfully as possible.

'Oh, but she has,' replied Fossett. 'Indeed, Aislinn prepared a special potion for her just yesterday. As a result, you wouldn't believe the change in our beloved Queen – if you were to see her now. Why, she even had her first aeronautical acrobatic lesson this morning! There were one or two narrow misses, of course – but the King made her wear a crash helmet, so she was quite safe really.'

'That sounds exciting,' said Chaney, trying not to laugh as she visualised a crash helmet big enough to contain all that hair.

'Speaking of the King,' said Fossett, in a voice filled with emotion, 'I haven't seen him so happy in years – not since the Queen has been ill, anyway. He's so grateful to Aislinn, and no wonder. She is so clever with her potions. Kyle was funny yesterday. He actually said to me, "It's embarrassing: my parents are like a couple of newlyweds, kissing and cuddling all the time!"'

'Well, it just goes to show that Aislinn was definitely worth saving,' Chaney remarked, with obvious pride.

'She certainly is a remarkable fairy,' agreed Dakota. 'Thanks for making me see sense, Buggy.'

'You're welcome, Tota,' was the reply.

'Before I return to the kingdom, there's something I've wanted to ask you for some time,' Fossett continued.

'What's that?' Chaney enquired, immediately curious.

'The nicknames you use for each other. Where do they come from?' Fossett asked.

Dakota laughed as she explained. 'Well, when Buggy was little, she couldn't say my full name properly, and she always called me Tota instead. After a while, it's kind of stuck. And then,' she continued – trying to control her laughter sufficiently enough to be able to talk – 'when Buggy started to walk, she became a bit of a handful. You know the saying…the terrible twos. As a toddler, she was always having temper tantrums or getting up to mischief. She loved hiding keys in waste bins or burying jewellery in the garden. Mum has never ever found her engagement ring!'

Fossett looked slightly shocked, and Chaney felt her cheeks burning with shame.

Dakota continued. 'When Buggy was about three years old, she went through a stage where she delighted in stuffing roll upon roll of toilet paper down the toilet. Oh, and the thing for which she is best remembered, of course, is the habit she developed of putting dirty, muddy handprints all over the clean washing on the line. She insisted on doing that nearly every day, regardless of the punishments she got. Reprimands, no matter how severe, were ignored…just like water off a duck's back. Mum and Dad used to say she was a right little beggar and as hard as nails. "Little beggar" got shortened to "Buggy" over time.'

'I see,' said Fossett, by this time also laughing himself. 'I'll be able to tell Gilpin that when I get back. Well, Tota, well, Buggy,' he concluded, 'you two need to get some sleep!' And with that, he hopped back out through the window and was gone.

'Are you sure the expression was little beggar?' asked Chaney looking doubtfully at her big sister.

'Close enough,' was Tota's reply, as she laid her head on her pillow and fell fast asleep.

Dakota and Chaney awoke to a lot of noise and commotion the next morning. As they rubbed the sleep from their eyes and stepped out of the campervan into the warm morning sunlight, they could see their parents returning hand in hand from walking the dogs.

'You two have really missed out this morning,' Michael said, laughing. 'We've had one heck of a walk with the dogs! Well, I say walk, but most of the time we've had to jog to keep up with them. It's as if Simba has had a new lease of life – and would you believe he beat Enzo to every stick your mother and I have thrown for them this morning!'

'It's absolutely true,' Rachael said, grinning widely. 'Looking at him now, you'd hardly think Simba was the age he is or suffering from acute arthritis.'

The two girls stared at the old dog with interest. He looked bright-eyed and bushy-tailed and seemed the epitome of health and vigour as he pranced about them on the grass.

It was then they noticed that people were out in force, talking and discussing a unique phenomenon which had occurred overnight. They were all gazing in wonder at the path the tornado had cut, which during the hours of darkness had miraculously transformed from the barren track void of all vegetation it had been, into a feast of flora. A winding ribbon of sky-blue flowers lay before them and seemed to stretch as far as the eye could see.

'And do you know how long it is?' someone said. 'I heard it was exactly 17 kilometres long and almost a kilometre wide in some places, they reckon!'

'The floor of the sky,' said Chaney. She and Dakota put their arms around each other and began to tread the soft blue carpet which wound its way around the arena, leading to the stable block and then back out into the bush. The two sisters looked out across the fabulous landscape and, together, drank in the sheer beauty of the scene. As their eyes followed the wide path of dazzling blue flowers to the far horizon, the girls were filled with a sense of wonderment and fulfilment.

'What an adventure we've had!' exclaimed Chaney.

'True, absolutely true – but it's back to reality for us now, and we have horses to feed,' Dakota said contentedly.

'While you do that, Mum and I will clear these dishes away and start packing,' said Michael.

As he spoke, he noticed Enzo drop a large marrow bone at Simba's feet. The old dog lay down and began chewing contently on this unprecedented gift with saliva dripping copiously from his jaw. Michael was astonished, and even more so as he watched the young dog push Simba's water bowl along the ground until it was right under the old dog's nose.

'Did you see what Enzo's just done, Rachael? It's nothing short of a miracle!'

Hidden in the branches of a boab tree situated on the hillside just above them, the Shaman sat watching the two dogs with interest. He nodded his head in approval and smiled. 'That's better. Always respect your elders, young pup,' he murmured to himself in his ancient tongue.

At the same time, King Ariel had finally gotten around to repairing Gilpin's nose. 'Shall we get you fixed, then?' he said to the small brown mouse.

'At last!' Gilpin replied. 'I thought you'd never ask.'

'No time like the present,' King Ariel continued, 'while everyone else in the kingdom sleeps on and recovers from their heroic, magnificent exploits of yesterday.'

'Did I tell you about my lovely hug from the girls yesterday, Gilpin?' Fossett enquired. 'And did I mention the dog drool? It's worse than we thought when we were watching them in the eye, you know. Simba covered me in it!'

'You've told me everything several times over,' Gilpin replied, rather nasally.

Fossett looked on cheerfully as Gilpin's nose twitched, quivered and returned to normal. 'That's better, my old mate. Now you'll look your best for the award ceremony when the King bestows you with your "Knight of the Realm" badge.'

'Quite so, Fossett, quite so,' agreed the King, 'and richly deserved.'

Seconds later, the happy trio heard a loud whirring sound, and a shape suddenly appeared in the air above them. The shape whistled around the King, circling him at top speed. Gilpin used his sharp eyes to make out what it was, but it was moving so fast that all he could see was a blur of yellow and pink.

The spinning body came to an abrupt stop. It was Queen Charlotte. It took Fossett a moment or two to recognise her. No longer in need of her thick-rimmed glasses, her beautiful blue eyes sparkled with merriment, and her long golden tresses, pinned up in a neat French plait, shone in the warm afternoon sunshine.

Taking hold of her husband's hand, she said, 'I've come to get you. The royal tailors have arrived, and the father of the groom is required. We need to have you measured for your wedding robes. That done, we can have our afternoon nap.'

'Afternoon nap?' queried the King, sounding slightly puzzled.

The Queen giggled and then winked at him, first with the left eye and then with the right. The King still looked puzzled, and Queen Charlotte flew up to him, whispering something in his ear.

The King started to laugh. 'Oh yes,' he said, 'I do need a rest. An afternoon nap is an excellent idea.' He turned to Gilpin and Fossett and, with a twinkle in his eye, bade them both farewells. The royal couple flew off, hand in hand, towards the palace.

Chapter Thirty
Flying Lesson Fiasco

It was Christmas Eve, and another glorious summer's day had dawned. The girls woke early, and the annual 'Blue Moon' event took place as normal. Two trays of cooked breakfast were delivered to stunned parents. Michael raised a faint smile, and Rachael managed to feign pleasure. The clock – reading 5 am – looked on in amused silence, as trembling hands tried to lift scalding hot cups of tea to half-comatose mouths and tired eyes attempted to remain open. Four fried eggs, slipping and sliding on a layer of bacon fat, did their best to escape onto clean bedlinen; and itchy, scratchy toast crumbs successfully dropped with every mouthful into waiting, hungry pyjama tops.

For Dakota and Chaney, the next four hours were spent with the horses, and their usual daily chores carried out with even more vigour and attention to duty. The horses received a welcome hose-down, accompanied, of course, by the traditional water fight, before being finally left in the paddock with plenty of forage and fresh water for the long hot day ahead. The summer lean-to had by now been erected to afford welcome shade over the water trough, under which Star and Galaxy could shelter during the hottest part of the day. Satisfied their horses would want for nothing, the girls returned to the house. Loud barking could be heard from the garage.

'Grab your bags, you two,' Michael instructed. 'Everything else is in the car ready to go, including a couple of overly excited dogs.'

'Yes, we can hear,' commented Chaney, grinning.

Minutes later, the car set off.

'I hope South Beach isn't as crowded as last year,' remarked Rachael. 'If you remember, there was hardly enough space to set up the BBQ!'

'Oh yes, I remember,' Michael replied. 'And, Buggy, for goodness's sake, this year wait till I say the chicken is cooked before you help yourself. We don't want a repeat of last year with you and your mother up half the night!'

'Too true,' agreed Chaney, 'I certainly couldn't afford for that to happen again – especially on this Christmas Eve of all nights! Can you imagine anything worse, Dakota? My being ill would spoil everything.'

Dakota elbowed Chaney and cleared her throat. Chaney clapped her hand to her mouth and glanced anxiously at her mother. Rachael was gazing out of the car window and had clearly not picked up on the phrases 'especially this Christmas Eve' or 'spoil everything'. Had she done so, awkward questions would inevitably have been asked. Chaney listened instead to the silence and breathed a sigh of relief.

'I thought for a minute you were about to give the game away,' Dakota said, as the two dogs towed the girls back to shore. They had been out swimming for some time, and with the BBQ now ready to serve, Michael had sent the dogs on their errand of retrieval.

'I nearly did,' replied Chaney. 'I'm so excited about being a bridesmaid! I wonder how our dresses will look?'

'Superb, I should think,' Dakota answered with confidence. 'Aislinn expressly told me that her handmaiden, Giselle, has made a wonderful job of them, and since it is she who is going to come for us tonight, I'm sure she can make any last-minute alterations should they be needed.'

'I do hope so. I want to be the prettiest bridesmaid ever,' Chaney continued happily.

'Argh!' screamed Dakota as a huge wave broke over her head. The force of the water was so great it caused her to lose hold of Enzo's tail, and Chaney watched with uncontrollable laughter as her sister was rolled over and over by the wave whilst being swept unceremoniously up onto the beach. When Dakota finally managed to stand up, her bikini bottoms were around her ankles and full of sand. She dived back into the water to cover her embarrassment.

Chaney, who by now had her arms around the old dog's neck, could not stop laughing and was convinced by the movement of Simba's chest that he too had the giggles. Enzo, of course, thought Dakota was merely playing, and lunged back into the water after her. He seemed to think the bikini bottoms were his new plaything, and so it was some time before Dakota was able to leave the protection of the sea. The BBQ began without her.

'Don't worry, I'll eat yours for you,' shouted Chaney, struggling to control her laughter as Enzo raced off down the beach for the umpteenth time with Dakota's bikini bottoms between his teeth.

The remainder of the day was spent munching delicious food, playing ball games on the beach or bodysurfing in the sea. A cooling offshore breeze had arisen, and the breakers now coming in on the tide were just the right size for some exciting surfing.

They returned to Kookaburra Heights in time for a late supper. Michael and Rachael had expected the usual reluctance to go to bed from the girls, but this year, clearly tired by a day of swimming, snorkelling and surfing, the girls had asked to go to bed almost as soon as they were home.

'We're both going to sleep in my room tonight,' Dakota explained as they disappeared upstairs together, waving an unprecedented 'goodnight' to their parents. Michael and Rachael looked at each other in disbelief.

'Long may sisterly love continue,' commented Rachael.

'Yes, indeed, and one less bedroom to tiptoe into with a Christmas stocking,' Michael agreed, smiling.

It was 10 pm and the pre-arranged time that Giselle ought to arrive to collect the girls. Dakota and Chaney were sitting in their pyjamas on the edge of the bed, staring at the open window. Suddenly the silence was broken by a chorus of noisy kookaburras calling out into the night air. It seemed to Chaney they were announcing, 'Here she comes, here she comes…'

The birds were right, for just at that moment Giselle landed on the windowsill. In her left hand, she carried her wand, and draped over her right arm was a package containing the two bridesmaids' dresses. The girls shot forward excitedly to greet her.

'Glad to see you're ready and waiting,' Giselle said warmly. 'Now let's get started. Firstly, a little bit of magic. Do not be afraid of anything I do. Most of this is Shaman magic, and you know how much he adores you, so no need to worry. I need you to get under the bedcovers and lie down as if you were both asleep.'

The girls did as they were bid and then listened with hearts pounding to Giselle's magic words. Holding her wand aloft, she spoke softly into the night air:

'The Dreamtime is come to be.

Its magic power has set you free,

Rise up, I say, and fly with me.'

Dakota and Chaney climbed out of bed and walked towards Giselle. When they looked back, they could see themselves still lying in bed, as if fast asleep.

171

They looked at each other in amazement and instinctively reached out to touch one another to see if they were real.

'Ouch!' said Dakota, as Chaney's probing finger jabbed a little too hard into her shoulder.

'Now, for my last little bit of magic,' Giselle went on. 'Close your eyes and stand perfectly still until I tell you otherwise,' she commanded.

Dakota closed her eyes, and Chaney squeezed hers tightly shut.

Giselle waved her wand above the girl's heads, saying:

'Although of human frame and mind,
Tonight you'll be of fairy kind.'

'Can we open our eyes now?' asked Chaney, after a moment or two of silence.

'Yes, please do – we need to get you dressed and over to the kingdom,' replied Giselle.

When the girls opened their eyes, they could hardly believe the transformation which had taken place. They had shrunk in size to be the same stature as Giselle. They stood, too flabbergasted to speak, looking in awe and wonder at their now-diminutive figures. It was then that they felt an odd tickling sensation between their shoulder blades, and suddenly two pairs of fully formed wings sprouted on their backs! Both girls lost their balance and almost toppled over, but Giselle soared down from the windowsill and caught them just in time.

'Now,' she said, 'I think I had better give you a lesson in flying.'

Making sure they had regained their balance and could stand upright of their own accord, she began her instruction.

'Wings are no different to arms and legs,' she explained. 'When you want to move your arm, you send a message to your brain and your brain reciprocates by sending a message for your arm to move. And, hey presto, your arm moves – exactly as you wanted.'

'My arm must be the exception to the rule then,' interrupted Chaney. 'When Dakota's at her bossiest, I often feel I want to slap her – except I don't, of course.'

'You did at Rhoda's birthday party last year!' exclaimed Dakota.

'Perhaps my brain was working properly for once,' suggested Chaney, looking at Giselle rather sheepishly.

'I think it's more the case that if you had a brain, you'd be dangerous,' goaded Dakota.

Before Chaney could reply, Giselle interjected quickly, 'Girls, girls – we have no time for silly bickering.'

'You sound like our mother,' Chaney said, laughing.

Giselle ignored the remark and reiterated, 'I think we need to get back to our flying lesson. In hardly any time at all, we will be at a wedding ceremony, and you will be acting as the chief bridesmaids! Do I really need to remind you?'

'Sorry.'

'Sorry.'

The replies came in such quick succession that they sounded like an echo.

'I'm going to fly onto the bed and then I want you to follow my example – Dakota, first. Now listen carefully. I simply think to myself what it is I'm going to do, and my wings respond accordingly.' Giselle flew smoothly onto the bed. 'Okay, Dakota…now it's your turn.'

Dakota began to flap her arms. Nothing happened.

'Think wings, not arms,' Giselle encouraged. 'You're a fairy now and your wings are just as much a part of you as your legs and arms. Close your eyes if it helps. Relax the rest of your body and think wings – only wings.'

Dakota closed her eyes. When she opened them, she was hovering just inches below the ceiling light. She screamed aloud and plummeted down onto the bed, landing head-first on the pillow. Giselle helped her up. Sitting, resting her chin on her hands and her elbows on her knees, Dakota gazed down at her annoying sister. Chaney was snorting with side-splitting laughter.

'Okay, clever clogs, let's see if you can do any better,' suggested an indignant Dakota as she stood up alongside Giselle.

When Chaney finally stopped laughing, her facial expression changed from jocularity to serious concentration. The wings began to beat, slowly at first, causing Chaney's feet to leave the floor. Desperate to gain height, Chaney's wings flapped much faster, until suddenly, her body swerved wildly to the right. Chaney instinctively put her arms out to save herself. The wings stopped beating, and she dropped back onto the floor, red-faced and embarrassed.

Giselle spoke out in her defence. 'You did well, Chaney. The take-off was good – now, concentrate on direction. Focus all your efforts on flying to the bed and come and join us. Try again.'

Chaney focused her gaze on her smiling, now rather smug, sister. She folded her arms in front of her, leant forward, screwed up her eyes and held her breath, forcing her mind to think, *Wings, fly me up!*

Before Giselle could even contemplate helping, Chaney hit the ceiling like a stone fired from a catapult and crashed back down on top of Dakota. Dakota, however, was ready and had her arms outstretched to catch her. 'There you go, little sister,' she said, as she helped Chaney regain her feet.

Chaney's flushed and bruised face was a clear indication of her shame. *The ignominy of it,* she thought to herself, *to think that Dakota did better than me!*

Dakota pointed upwards. 'I'll leave you to explain the dent in the ceiling to Mum!' she commented, adding further insult to injury.

Chaney gritted her teeth and said nothing.

'Now back down to me, if you please,' requested Giselle from the floor, 'and slowly, if you want to attend the wedding in one piece!'

The improvement over the next quarter of an hour was incredible. The girls gained enormously in skill and confidence. Giselle was happy.

'We're ready,' she subsequently announced. 'Great work! You can both fly beautifully. Well done. Time to try your dresses on, I think.'

Tiny pyjamas were stowed in a box of paper tissues on top of a bedside cabinet, and the most gorgeous, handmade ivory chiffon bridesmaids' dresses were duly donned. The dresses, with a strapless empire bodice neckline and a short A-line skirt, fitted perfectly. Giselle helped tie ebony sashes – the final touch to each dress – around their waists, and they were ready to go.

'One last thing, however…stand still please, Chaney, whilst my wand gets rid of the black eye and split lip. And promise me – no more crashing into ceilings or racing around like a March hare gone mad!' Giselle requested, smiling affectionately at her young charge.

'I promise,' Chaney replied. 'I won't let you down. Aislinn and Kyle mean everything to me.'

Simba woke up. He had been lying under Michael's feet, more than happy to be used as a footrest for most of the evening. Lifting his head, he barked loudly. Michael, who had also been asleep, gradually opened his eyes. Simba barked again and stood up. Moving to Michael's side, he grasped his master's shirt sleeve in his jaw and attempted to pull him out of his chair.

'What is it, boy? What's the matter?' Michael reluctantly stood up and followed Simba out of the room. They headed along the hallway and up the stairs, finally stopping outside Dakota's bedroom. Simba pushed his nose against the door, whining softly.

'Shush,' Michael warned, 'we don't want to wake the girls up, do we?'

Simba whined again.

'Okay, if you insist – I'll just check on them.' Michael opened the door at the very moment that three pairs of wings disappeared through the open window.

Simba barked again and made to enter the room. Michael stopped him in his tracks.

'No, Simba, no! Stay! I'll check on the girls. Stay!' he commanded.

His head peered around the door. Clearly visible in the moonlight were the frames of his two daughters, sleeping peacefully under the bedclothes. Closing the door as quietly as possible, he steered an anxious dog back to the lounge.

'Whatever it is you're worrying about, stop it.' Michael had always believed that animals knew things, sensed things that humans could not. He patted

Simba's head and reassured him. 'Dakota and Chaney are fine,' he said, returning to his chair. 'Now come and be my footstool again.'

Simba, however, declined the invitation and walked across to the large panoramic window which overlooked the back garden instead. His eyes looked up into a sky in which three tiny specks of light whizzed like small shooting stars towards the fairy kingdom.

Chapter Thirty-One
The Big Day

Aislinn's delight in greeting the girls on their arrival at the royal palace was clear for all to see. She was ecstatic in her compliments about their dresses and how beautiful they looked. Her chamber was a hive of activity – royal handmaiden after royal handmaiden helping the bridal party to get ready. There were to be eight bridesmaids in total and four little pageboys. Dakota and Chaney had the honour of being the chief bridesmaids and would carry Aislinn's train as she made her way up the aisle. All the bridesmaids were to wear identical dresses of ivory chiffon with a contrasting ebony sash and ivory silk slippers. The pageboys were dressed in matching ivory jackets worn over ebony leggings, and to complete the ensemble, shiny, patent black leather shoes would adorn tiny fairy feet.

Dressed in a tunic and mantle of white satin embroidered in gold and edged with velvet and ermine, Aislinn was a vision of loveliness and elegance. As the sisters practised carrying her Monarch train, it seemed to shimmer in the candlelight. Reflecting the glimmering flames, hundreds of diamonds had been hand-stitched into the delicate material cascading from a tapered waistline. Aislinn's slender waist was encircled by an ebony belt made of the finest silk and richly worked with gold thread and encrusted with jewels. On her head, she was to wear a garland of white flowers over loose-flowing hair: beautiful, silky, golden and hanging to her waist.

'The garland of white is a symbol of virtue,' Giselle explained.

There was a loud knock on the door. Giselle left the girls to answer it. She returned moments later, looking flushed and excited. 'They are ready for us, and our transportation is arrived and waiting,' she said, looking at Aislinn with eyes already filling with happy tears. 'The Captain of the Royal Guard is here to escort us to the West Gate.'

The party made their way across the wide palace courtyard with its neat gardens and gurgling fountains. Proud statues beckoned them on, as they passed below the spikes of the now-raised portcullis and stepped onto the lowered wooden drawbridge, until the carriages came into view. Dakota and Chaney could scarcely believe their eyes. They had expected to see Cinderella-like horse-drawn carriages, but these were not carriages at all.

Instead, eyes wide with astonishment focused on beautifully decorated wooden gondolas. They could not help but admire the ornately carved, wide open boats festooned with the same white flowers used to make Aislinn's garland. Each boat glided effortlessly across the water, guided and harnessed as they were to a team of six pink flamingos.

'Wow,' exclaimed Chaney. 'I've never seen such incredible birds.' She watched, fascinated, as the tall, elegant birds towed the boats to the bank. Proud heads displaying two yellow eyes and a keel-shaped, cream-coloured bill with a distinct black tip were supported on long, curved necks in the shape of an S. She noted their thin, spindly legs, seemingly much longer than the length of the birds' bodies, as they waded silently through the shallow water. What struck her most was how high the birds held their heads and how perfectly still they kept them.

Indeed, the flamingos reminded Chaney of ballerinas trying to improve their posture and having to practise walking with a book balanced precariously on their heads. 'They look very regal,' she said to Giselle.

'And so they should, especially since they actually belong to the King,' replied Giselle. 'Nowadays, they can only be found here in the kingdom. In all other parts of Australia, the flamingo, beautiful though it is, is sadly extinct.'

As they descended, steep steps cut into the rock face which led down to the water. A wonderful fragrance filled the air, and a spectacular landscape came into view. Fields of green and white stretched away into the distance, and below them lay a veritable mosaic, a rich tapestry of emerald green and the purest, most pristine shade of white. Great swathes of highly perfumed white blossom rose from a bed of soft, lush grass. A multitude of flower heads with their white petals lying like snowflakes almost covered the entire riverbank.

'Has it been snowing?' Chaney asked, in all innocence.

Giselle began to laugh.

'I can see what Chaney means,' echoed Dakota. 'What is all that white stuff?'

'The white you can see everywhere are the petals of a very special flower. It's called the Christmas orchid – and doesn't it smell gorgeous?' said Giselle, laughing.

'The fragrance is wonderful,' replied Dakota.

'Well, this particular orchid is unique to our fairy world,' explained Giselle, 'and flowers but one day of the year. Every Christmas Eve it bursts into flower in its thousands and fills the kingdom with heavenly scent and colour.'

'How fantastic is that?' remarked Chaney. 'So, you always have a white Christmas!'

'I've never thought of it like that,' replied Giselle, smiling, 'but yes – I suppose we do!'

'Yes,' agreed Chaney, 'and the boats almost look as if they've been left outside on a winter's night, and gently falling snow has gradually covered them in drifts of white. How beautiful. No wonder Kyle and Aislinn chose Christmas Eve for their wedding day.'

Royal courtiers helped the party to board the boats which were moored securely to the gently sloping grass banks. Plump gold cushions lined the seats on which the bridal entourage would sit. They took their places, helping Aislinn to board first and assisting her with her bouquet and train. Then once the entire party were safely seated, the convoy was off, gliding silently along a narrow brook of crystal-clear water which meandered its lazy way to the very perimeter of the Glen.

Chaney trailed her fingers in the slow-moving, softly flowing azure water. A gentle current channelled the pretty boats downstream, and a silver moon, reflected in the water, graced their journey with light. There could not have been a more romantic setting, and no bride could have looked happier. The joyful expression on Aislinn's face, and indeed every member of the bridal party, said it all. Radiant smiles abounded as they sailed the short distance to their destination.

In the quiet, Chaney was sure everyone could hear her heart beating. She wondered if Dakota was feeling as nervous but didn't like to ask. *Nervous, but happy too,* she thought to herself. She listened contentedly to the sound of lapping water in her ears, the rustling of the trees lining the banks and the odd twitter of a bird calling to them from an overhanging branch.

The gondolas arrived at the Glen, and the wedding party disembarked. Magical jacaranda trees welcomed them with open arms, and once again their blackened, twisted branches had changed to form delicate spires which soared into the air, slender and fragile. Glorious rods of gold pointing to the firmament adorned with glowing purple blossoms illuminated the whole of the Fairy Glen, turning it into a giant cathedral. Thousands of candles floated high in the air above the assembled fairy gathering, bathing the expectant congregation in a flickering, twinkling light. Every member of the kingdom was present to celebrate the long-awaited royal wedding.

There was one difference, however. A huge Christmas tree, like the eighth great wonder of the world, loomed high, high over anything else in the Glen – towering above the jacaranda trees. It had been erected to one side of the Glen and was fabulously decorated with sparkling, miniature dangling glass ornaments of every colour. At the end of each branch, candle holders containing brightly lit candles enhanced its beauty still further, creating a strange and almost ethereal glow.

As the bridal party entered the Glen, a fanfare sounded, and then the wonderful golden harps the girls had heard all those months before at their first fairy banquet began to play. A strange, haunting melody accompanied Aislinn, her bridesmaids and pageboys as they walked down the aisle. Slowly and regally, they made their way towards the high altar, a high altar decorated with still more white flowers, where Kyle was waiting in nervous anticipation.

Dakota and Chaney did an excellent job. The Monarch train was carried to perfection and held throughout the long, slow procession to the high altar at its full width and length. It was a spectacular sight. Gasp after gasp could be heard as Aislinn passed by the congregation, for never had there been a more beautiful bride to behold. The train, especially its dazzling diamonds reflecting the candlelight, showed Aislinn in her full glory. From the moment Aislinn appeared in the Glen, Kyle could not take his eyes off her.

Chaney thought Kyle, too, looked magnificent. He was dressed in brilliantly coloured robes made of satin, velvet and brocade. On his head, he wore a golden crown encrusted with sapphires, rubies and emeralds, and lining its brim was a narrow band of the whitest ermine.

The ceremony was altogether beautiful. Kyle and Aislinn made their vows. The words spoken were of the ancient tongue, but the love and the devotion of the young couple, one for the other, left no doubt in the sisters' minds as to what was being said.

After they had finished speaking, the Shaman stepped forward and presented the couple with the gift of two beautifully marked eagle feathers tied together, symbolising their now-unbreakable union. Gilpin was next and proffered two pairs of handwoven moccasins, wishing them eternal happiness as they walked through life together. Fossett presented gold wedding rings, two perfect circles with no beginning and no ending. Gently and lovingly the rings were given, each to the other, and a pledge made that the rings would stand for eternity as a token of their never-ending love.

Finally, King Ariel approached them, and taking both their right hands, he placed them on top of an old leather case he was carrying. The case had very ornate gold lettering on it, but from where they were sitting neither Chaney nor Dakota could quite make out the words.

'The case contains the Royal Scrolls. They are hundreds of years old and truly priceless. Kyle and Aislinn will swear allegiance to the kingdom and to uphold its customs,' Giselle explained. 'The fact that his father has given him the treasured Scrolls will mean a great deal to Kyle.'

The girls watched Kyle embrace his father, and then another fanfare sounded. The entire gathering stood to their feet, and a wonderful rousing anthem was sung by all. As the music and singing stopped, Kyle kissed his bride. A huge cheer went up, and the happy couple waved and smiled at the assembled crowd.

Dakota and Chaney watched admiringly as once again the banqueting tables and chairs arrived out of nowhere, and the wedding feast began. Sitting on the top table with Kyle, Aislinn and the King and Queen, they felt incredibly honoured. Queen Charlotte had insisted on sitting next to Chaney and on tasting every dish Chaney conjured up. She watched the plates of food arrive with interest and tried each one with relish. Chaney found it all very amusing, particularly the Queen's craving for bubble-gum ice cream.

Time seemed to pass so quickly that before they knew it, the banquet was over, and all the fairies were finding partners for the dance. Chaney and Dakota were sitting to one side and waiting excitedly to watch the magnificent flying display they had witnessed once before. But it was not to be. Two young male fairies approached, arm in arm with Kyle.

'May I introduce my friends to you?' Kyle asked politely.

'Of course,' they replied.

'This is Darius,' he said, as a tall, dark-haired fairy bowed low, 'and this is Sebastian.' An equally tall but golden-haired fairy also bowed courteously to the two, somewhat embarrassed, girls.

'Would you care to dance?' Darius asked Chaney.

Chaney looked into the biggest, darkest eyes framed by the most enormous, long eyelashes she had ever seen. The whitest teeth in the handsomest of faces beamed a smile, and Chaney felt her heart stop. She struggled to speak.

'Are you worrying about flying? I promise I will not let go of your hand. Come...you are too beautiful to sit out like the proverbial wallflower,' Darius concluded, gently taking hold of Chaney's hand and helping her to her feet.

'W-wing, w-wing,' she stammered. 'I just need to think wing!'

They took their place right next to Aislinn and Kyle.

'Well,' said Sebastian, 'you're not going to be outdone by your sister, are you?'

Dakota looked into blue eyes as vivid as her own and instantly recognised her gallant suitor. 'It was you, wasn't it? You were the fairy who spoke to me after saving Chaney and I from the dingoes.'

'I was only too happy to be of help,' he replied. 'What you did for Aislinn, and Kyle is beyond words. We – all of us, can never thank you enough.'

'We only did what we thought right,' she answered, 'and to be honest, neither of us considered the danger. We were foolhardy rather than brave.'

'No, Dakota, I disagree. What you did was an act of great bravery as well as great kindness, a spontaneous gesture of goodwill which defines your character. You will always respond in the same way. If your help is needed, you will give it, whether the request is from someone or something – your fellow humans, the animal kingdom or the kingdom of nature.'

'Sebastian, I am a simple girl; your thoughts are far too profound for me to understand,' Dakota responded, smiling into wondrous eyes the colour of a summer sky.

'Then let me say this,' he concluded, 'you will make me the happiest of fairies if you will join me in the next dance.'

Dakota smiled a brilliant smile and gladly accepted the proffered hand. So it was that they too joined Kyle and Aislinn as the aerial throng made ready for the music to begin again.

As with Giselle before, flying progress was astronomic. Dakota mastered all the key moves as dance followed dance, keeping time and place with care. Sebastian was a wonderful teacher, and Dakota felt easy and comfortable in his company. It was almost as if she had known him for years. They danced almost every dance, only stopping now and again for a glass of berry juice. The conversation flowed between them, and Sebastian's quick wit and wicked sense of humour had Dakota laughing time and time again. Sebastian too was very enamoured of Dakota and loving every moment spent with her.

Chaney was in her element. She was dancing with the best-looking fairy in the entire Kingdom and thought him very dashing. They whirled around at top speed, trying every move, even the most complex ones. Darius congratulated her many times and encouraged her bravery. There was one slight problem in that Chaney would at times get ahead of the group and find herself out of position in formation. On one occasion, when she should have ended up partnering King Ariel, she found herself taking Queen Charlotte's hand by mistake.

Queen Charlotte squealed with delight and, enjoying the diversion, grabbed Chaney's hands and whisked her high into the air. They soared above the other dancers, spinning and turning at breath-taking speed. Chaney began to feel so dizzy, she thought might lose consciousness altogether! To her relief, Queen Charlotte came to an abrupt stop. Roaring with laughter, the Queen pulled Chaney to her. 'Oh, what fun we are having! Are you ready for a bit more excitement?'

Chaney thought she had no option but to nod her head in agreement.

'Well, then, take hold of my wand and don't let go of it, or me, until we stop,' she said, passing her wand to Chaney and then gripping her right hand firmly. She stretched out her free arm, raising a clenched tight fist high above her head. The arm reminded Chaney of an inverted exclamation mark. Was the Queen about to make some sort of a statement, she wondered? Had she been wearing a leotard and cape, Chaney thought she would certainly have looked more like Superwoman than a fairy queen.

'Tally-ho!' shouted the queen, as she launched forward and began to dive towards the Glen floor. Chaney found herself flying at the speed of a skyrocket. As the ground hurtled towards her, the wind pulled at her face and tore at her eyes. She could feel her cheeks billowing in and out uncontrollably as her mouth filled with air. On and on the Queen pulled her, like a desperate mother towing her child, racing to catch the last bus.

The wand had obviously been primed and emitted an endless stream of bright, cascading, silver sparks – sparks which left a dazzling, glittering vapour trail behind them. Chaney could hear the whoosh and crackle as the wand did its job and provided the audience below with a glorious, impromptu firework display.

The daredevil duo hurtled down towards the watching dancers below. Several ducked as Queen Charlotte swooped back and forth across the assembled pairs who were waiting patiently for the dancing to begin again. Then with pinpoint accuracy and at break-neck speed, the Queen pulled her young charge back to the summit of the giant Christmas tree. Once at the top again, Superwoman and her sidekick paused briefly for a moment.

'Well, a most successful dry run, I would say, which by the look of it has achieved its purpose. So my dear – if you are ready – now we've got everyone's attention, let's give them the main event. Hold on tight!' cautioned the Queen as she hauled Chaney into her second nerve-wracking, high-speed descent.

They circled the tree from top to bottom, zooming in between close branches as if they were threading a length of cotton into the eye of a needle. As they descended past each tier of branches, the candles were extinguished. Then once at the bottom, they soared back up to the top, candles bursting again into flame as they whizzed past, every tier exploding into a different colour. Reaching the top once more, Queen Charlotte stopped and waved down to an astonished Kyle and Aislinn.

'For you, my dears,' she called out. 'Just to add to the night's magic.'

For a moment, there was silence. Then Kyle started to laugh. Soon everyone was laughing and clapping at the Queen's and Chaney's antics. King Ariel stepped forward to reclaim his wife.

'Come, my love,' he said affectionately. 'I think we've had enough excitement for one Christmas Eve. Let us leave Kyle and Aislinn to lead the dance. After all, this is their wedding night…not ours.'

'Quite right, dear husband, quite right,' agreed Queen Charlotte, taking back her wand from a trembling Chaney. 'Darius, come and collect your delightful partner. I do apologise for stealing her away.'

Darius took Chaney's shaking hand and escorted her to the refreshment area. Chaney drank the sweet berry juice he offered her, and with his encouragement slowly regained her composure and nerve. Once recovered and refreshed, they returned to the dance, and Chaney proved herself to be the perfect partner. She was thrilled to see that the dark eyes were gazing at her with a definite look of admiration. Darius's expression was not hard to read, and he scarcely ever took his eyes off her.

Chapter Thirty-Two
Return of the Sprouts

It was over all too soon and time for home. Sebastian and Darius were to accompany the girls on the return journey, and as they flew, they discussed the events of the day. There was much to talk about. It was early dawn as tiny feet landed once more on the windowsill of Dakota's bedroom.

They said their fond farewells. Darius kissed Chaney's hand and thanked her for a wonderful evening. 'I'm sure we'll meet again one day. In fact, I will see that we do...' was his parting comment.

Sebastian kissed Dakota on the cheek. 'When you are next out competing on Galaxy, make sure you look for me. I'll be in the crowd somewhere, watching and wishing you well,' he said.

'I will,' she replied, 'and thank you for making this night so special. I'm going to miss you.'

The girls watched sadly as the two fairies flew away.

'Goodnight, my darling Darius,' whispered Chaney into the early morning light.

'Darling Darius!' echoed Dakota in a surprised tone of voice. 'For goodness's sake, Chaney, slow down. You've only just met him!'

'I know, I know,' replied Chaney. 'But he is perfect for me. His looks and personality are exactly to my taste. I simply adore dark-haired men, just like Dad, but mysterious and vigorous at the same time – and so exciting to be with! Oh, and those eyes! Did you see those eyes? Every time I looked into them, I thought I should drown!'

'Not really. I was too busy admiring Sebastian's wonderful blue eyes. They were bluer than mine, you know, and unbelievably vivid. I don't think I'll ever be able to forget how they sparkled with vitality and enthusiasm. And he was, oh, so kind.' Dakota sighed and, taking hold of her sister's hand, they flew together back down onto the bed to join their giant and still-sleeping frames.

'Dad's been in already,' commented Chaney, pointing to the two Christmas stockings secured on the bedposts at the bottom of Dakota's bed.

The tired girls landed on soft pillows. For a while, neither of them slept. One kept seeing a vision of the handsomest dark eyes and a broad, white, beaming smile; the other, an image of eyes the colour of a summer sky, full of life, and a face which lit up with friendly creases.

When they woke, they were no longer tiny shapes on a pillow but back to their normal size and tucked up in bed. It was Chaney who spotted the dragonfly necklaces first. Where she had been sleeping on the pillow when they had first arrived home lay a small, silver necklace, a delicate filigree chain on which a dragonfly pendant was suspended. Dakota's was identical.

'How lovely!' exclaimed Dakota. 'And what a wonderful souvenir of the day.'

'Let's wear them to breakfast,' suggested Chaney.

It was an odd Christmas Day. Appetites seemed to have vanished and presents remained unopened until late afternoon. Conversation during the morning was rather stilted and disjointed. Michael and Rachael gave up trying to play the usual games of Charades, Monopoly and Cluedo. The girls showed no interest in eating or playing and seemed to prefer sitting quietly in a chair, gazing out at the horizon. It was as if they were lost in their own world of daydreams – a world no one else could enter. Even the horses and dogs took a previously unheard-of back seat – although in fairness to the girls, normal service was resumed well before dinner, and all the animals received their special Christmas treats. Throughout the morning long sighs could be heard. Dragonfly necklaces continued to be held tenderly in fingertips and pressed even more tenderly to pouting lips.

In the stable block, two contented horses whinnied softly to each other across the low wooden barrier separating their cool and clean stalls. The contents of delicious Christmas nosebags had been swiftly consumed and fully appreciated. The girls had prepared a special treat for them consisting of oats, corn, beans, peanuts and large, diced chunks of apple and carrot. The now-empty nosebags had been rehung, grooming tack stowed, saddles polished and glistening coats of jet black and pure white brushed to perfection. An Arabian and an Andalusian stallion literally shone with health, their bodies gleaming in the late afternoon light.

As Dakota closed the latch on the stable door, the dining room gong sounded.

'Great!' said Chaney. 'Christmas dinner must be ready, and I'm starving!'

Appetites recovered, they raced back to the house and took their places at the table. Chaney looked down in dismay at her starter. Six large tiger prawns lay dead on a bed of limp rocket.

No worries, she thought. Enzo's heavy head was already resting on her knee, and an open mouth dripping saliva was waiting to be fed.

Chaney's face lit up, however, as Rachael brought a large bowl of hot, freshly baked crusty bread to the table, accompanied by a deep dish of balsamic vinegar and oil – her favourite dip. Ambidextrous skills made sure that bread, dip, prawns and rocket quickly disappeared and at least two sets of lips licked in happy synchronisation.

Starter over, Michael carved the turkey whilst Rachael brought individual plates of freshly cooked vegetables to the table. Chaney's plate had slightly smaller portions on it than the rest of the family, as was normal procedure – unless chips were being served, in which case, she was always served the lion's share. Once again, she looked down in dismay. Six large Brussels sprouts, like the heads of decapitated goblins, peered up at her from her plate. Butter oozed over the unwelcome shiny green leaves, slowly congealing at the side of her plate.

Enzo remained at the table whilst turkey, stuffing balls, chipolatas, carrots, potato and broccoli were duly eaten. He left in disgust as Chaney finished the last stuffing ball herself. The rest of the family had finished eating as six green sprouts began to be pushed around the plate, circling and circling like plucked vultures. Only Simba, loyally and steadfastly stayed at Chaney's side – he knew his duty!

Michael left the table to fetch a bottle of his favourite dessert wine – a white Sauternes. Rachael and Dakota began clearing plates to the dishwasher.

'Come on, Buggy,' said her mother. 'I'm not serving pudding until we've all cleared our plates.'

All backs were turned as the racks in the dishwasher were duly loaded.

Chaney sprang into action, and six sprouts were loaded into Simba's mouth like bullets into the barrel of a gun. The sprouts were gobbled down quickly and swallowed in one. Chaney was impressed. Aislinn's tonic was still having remarkable effects on Simba. *Even Enzo couldn't have cleared my plate any faster,* she thought to herself.

Pudding was served, and after dinner the whole family curled up in chairs in the lounge to watch television. Suddenly the programme they were watching was interrupted by a series of instantly recognisable sounds. Had anyone been watching Simba instead, tell-tale body language would at least have given a warning. He raised his tail, and shortly afterwards, his bottom fired a volley of loud trumpet blasts as he unloaded his full arsenal into the atmosphere.

In seconds, it was as if all oxygen in the room had been extinguished. It was replaced by a foul, evil-smelling gas, filling the air around them with a thick, pungent, hideous odour making it impossible to breathe. Bodies shot from chairs to the nearest evacuation point, with heads hanging out of rapidly opened windows – who cares about mosquitoes, anyway? Feet were tripping over themselves to get through doors, as lungs near to bursting were desperate to breathe again. The vile smell remained for some time, lurking in every nook and cranny, and refused to be ousted, no matter how much aerosol was sprayed. Even Enzo stayed with his nose pressed up against the doorstop and with his front paws covering his face. Only Simba, the perpetrator, seemed immune.

Soon afterwards, Chaney volunteered to take the dogs for their evening walk.

'You are a good girl,' said her mother.

'Stay upwind of Simba,' Michael advised, with a smile and a wink.

Back in the kingdom, too, Christmas Day was finally ending. It had been a wonderful wedding, and after a night and day of celebration, tired but happy, Gilpin and Fossett lay back in the long grass of the now-deserted Glen. The scent of tulip and lily wafted across their sensitive noses as a gentle breeze stirred through the pretty flowerbed near to which they were lying. The majestic crowns of tall black tulips and their ebony petals were dancing and swaying inside a ring of stargazer lilies – lilies proffering to every busy bee in the kingdom deliciously heavy, long orange stamens encrusted with pollen, crying out to be visited and projecting boldly out from the centre of every flower head. The lilies were a spectacular sight, providing an array of magnificent flower heads made up of equally long curling petals the colour of ivory. The outer edges of each petal were splashed here and there with a hint of the softest pink and the surrounding air was filled with their heady perfume.

'I spy with my little eye, an endless and beautiful blue sky,' said Gilpin. 'What's more there's not a cloud in sight.'

'What a perfect day!' replied Fossett, 'and don't you just love happy endings? If I didn't feel quite so exhausted, I could easily burst into song.'

'Oh, please don't,' begged Gilpin. 'I know everyone else says your singing inevitably makes them nod off, but in my case, the reverse is true.'

Fossett didn't answer; he was already fast asleep and dreaming that he was about to step on stage at the Sydney Opera House, ironically, to sing *Nessun Dorma*, his all-time favourite aria.

Gilpin gazed down affectionately at Fossett's peaceful, smiling face. He could tell he was dreaming from the rapid eye movement he could see beneath the unusual, but familiar, bright pink lids. 'That's the ticket,' he whispered under his breath. 'We're all in need of a good night's kip. Sweet dreams, my wise old cobber.' And with that he lay back in the long grass and was fast asleep himself in seconds.

END